A tongue lolled against sharp teeth. An ear cocked toward the scents. Two humans, male and female.

Paws moved, and the distance between them vanished. The male looked up, and the terror on his face was delicious enough to swallow. Then fangs cut through sweet skin, through sinew and muscle, as easily as water, and the blood pulsing with warmth flowed down the gullet, and there would be no pause until all of it was drunk.

A howl began to rise; it soared and sang above the stars, the cold stars.

"It's only a dream," Matt was whispering, rocking Jael back and forth. "Just a dream."

ALSO BY THIS AUTHOR

Vectors

NIGHT CRIES

Terry Krueger

A DELL BOOK

Published by
Dell Publishing Co., Inc.
1 Dag Hammarskjold Plaza
New York, New York 10017

Dell ® TM 681510, Dell Publishing Co., Inc.

ISBN: 0-440-16362-5

Printed in the United States of America
First printing—June 1985

NIGHT CRIES

PROLOGUE

Glencoe, Illinois—May 27, 1972

As Jael Clarke rode home from graduation, exchanging stories with her sister, Julie, she suddenly shook her head, swallowed a giggle, and wondered why she wasn't as happy as she was supposed to be. She broke off the conversation and looked over her father's shoulder as he turned at the gatehouse. The maples, birches, and elms were so tightly packed along the driveway that they reflected the headlights like a tunnel. When the car left the forest, the tennis courts, bright enough for play in the moonlight, appeared to the left; to the right lay the main estate grounds. They drove around the loop in front of the mansion and parked under the huge oak.

"If you have any problems," their mother said, "you have phone numbers where we can be reached."

"Don't be too disappointed if there aren't any problems," Julie said.

Their father turned around. "You two have been after an unchaperoned party for years. Don't blow it."

Julie and Jael leaned into the front seat to kiss their parents, then opened the doors and climbed out. As the car pulled away Jael watched the taillights disappear behind the mansion, then reappear and grow smaller and smaller until they vanished in the woods. She leaned against a huge white column while Julie unlocked the front door, then walked into the anteroom and turned on the lights. The lower level had been transformed while they were at graduation: a shower of red, blue, and yellow ribbons dangled from the chandelier; a congratulatory banner was strung across the balcony; a flock of helium-filled balloons wandered across the ceiling.

Julie smiled and shook her head. "A mind-boggling but lovable idea," she said. "I remember basically the same decorations at birthday party number eight. Should we clean them up before people start arriving?"

"How long do we have?" Jael asked.

Julie glanced at her watch. "Two hours or so." She Frisbeed her graduation cap across the foyer and onto a love seat. "Rick's coming early. How about Todd?"

"He has family obligations until ten," Jael said. She pulled on a string and watched the balloon bounce. "Let's pretend that they're *our* idea. People will think they're camp."

Julie nodded her head in agreement, and they ran up the winding staircase, then down the long hallway to Jael's room. While Jael carefully removed her cap, gown, and graduation dress, Julie shed hers in a heap. *We may look the same,* Jael thought, *but there* are *differences.* She finished folding her clothes, then watched Julie preen and pirouette in front of the mirror. It was like looking at herself: long, long legs, red hair down to the middle of her back, and huge green eyes. Cute, everyone said, never pretty or beautiful, always *cute.*

Jael walked to the dresser and lifted one of the eighteen stuffed giraffes from its display case. They were gifts from her parents and Julie, one for each birthday. In the closet was a new collection, one she'd made on her own: beer and wine bottles. Her parents, being parents, avoided asking their significance. Jael wandered back across the room, stopped at the piano and played a few discordant notes, then, after another few steps, plopped down on the bed. She had outgrown the lacy bedspread, but, like the giraffes, it was hard to leave behind.

She lay on her back and stared up at the canopy—more lace, more velvet, more ruffles. How could something so familiar become so very depressing? She stroked the giraffe, left it on the bed, walked to the window, and stared out into the night. The estate, beautiful in the daylight, was eerie in the dark. Maybe it was her mood, maybe the occasion, but the cloud shadows and the moonlight transformed the paths into writhing serpents, the gardens into cemetery plots, the Japanese pond into a pool of tar.

She shivered and turned toward Julie. "Ever get the feeling you don't have things under control anymore?"

"Now and then," Julie said softly. "Now and then." Jael moved over and Julie walked to the window and shared the view. They touched hands and closed their eyes and concentrated until the thousands of invisible threads that bound them together settled into place. It took a moment, but they soon exchanged something between thought and feeling, something more vivid and intimate than either. In that instant Julie's strength flowed into Jael and eased her uncertainty. Once, in sophomore biology, as the teacher drew diagrams on the board and explained how a fertilized egg split to become identical twins, someone shouted that Mrs. Clarke's egg *never* split. It didn't seem funny to the twins because it was close to the truth. When Julie and Jael shared consciousness, they could become as close as they had been before the split. *Nothing* else could be that intense.

"We'd better get dressed," Julie finally said, breaking away. "Rick will be here any minute."

"Can't he wait?"

"Somehow that doesn't sound like him," Julie said. She turned toward Jael, put her hands on her hips, tilted her head, and started to nod. "You're worried about college."

Jael shrugged.

"Look, we'll be roommates at Juilliard; we're not even that here. We'll still have each other. And our music. The only difference will be some new faces." Julie paused. "God, I hope there'll be some new faces."

"I like most of the old ones," Jael said.

"But think of the freedom."

"We already have freedom."

"Imagine not having to chew clove gum after a keg party," Julie said. "Not having to sneak out to the gazebo to smoke."

Jael started to smile. "Not having Mom wait up for us at three A.M. every Saturday. . . ."

"Or watching Dad interrogate every guy we bring home," Julie said. "*That*'s freedom." She flopped down on the bed and picked up the giraffe. She held it gently as though judging its weight, then tossed it to Jael. "Didn't I give you that? Fourth grade?"

Jael inspected it. "Sixth."

A mischievous smile spread from the corners of Julie's eyes to her mouth. "Which was the year you spent trying to get what's-his-name to notice you were alive."

"Scott Allen?" Jael smiled, then made a sour face. "Hardly."

"Memory lapse," Julie said. "I distinctly remember standing in the snow outside the gym with my teeth chattering, waiting for him to descend from heaven so my sis could—"

"Paul McCartney, seventh grade" was all Jael had to say, and Julie was hiding her face and blushing to the roots of her hair. "Paul McCartney T-shirts. A picture of Paul McCartney on your bedstand so his face could be the last thing you saw before you went to sleep."

"True!" Julie said.

Jael leaned forward and whispered the killer in Julie's ear. "Making me listen to 'Yesterday' forty-three times in one afternoon."

Julie laughed and buried her head under a pillow. Suddenly they were both laughing and hugging each other, and leaving for college wasn't so scary anymore. But they needed more.

They walked across the room to the piano. Jael waited for Julie to sit, as she always did when they performed, then sat on the bench next to her. Julie began the bass line of Mozart's "Sonata in C for Piano Duet," and Jael eased in with the melodic line, and the parts started to weave through each other, to merge and mingle, and their minds operated in a practiced way, an abstract way that transformed the squiggles on the paper to notes, the notes to counterpoint and harmony, and they began to share and it wasn't like playing the piano, no, it was like being the piano, more like being the sounds themselves, because the thoughts and feelings flowed as freely between Julie and Jael as the music, and there was no wondering, no guessing who should play first while the other should pause, because they *knew,* knew because they were different facets of the same being, united and pulsing with energy. There was no awareness of the fingers on the keyboard or the notes themselves, just the energy of the sounds, the energy of the thoughts that had composed the music, energy . . .

A bell rang.

The communion stopped and the room took shape again. Jael heard Julie say something about the party and felt the air stir as

Julie went to answer the phone. Jael sat in a strange stupor, watching a world partly composed of concrete objects, the piano, the posters on the wall, the yellow and brown decor, and partly a world of energy where things glowed and breathed, a world that seemed more real than the bench on which she sat.

Jael heard mumbling, then a click as her sister hung up the receiver. Julie nodded toward the phone. "Rick," she said. "Relatives dropped by. If I don't rescue him, he'll be stuck there half the night."

Julie ran to Jael's chest of drawers, changed into jeans and a tie-dyed blouse, then slipped on some sandals. Jael stood and walked up to her. "I might be a little while," Julie said.

Jael hugged her. "Give him a kiss for me," she said.

Julie ran from the room. Jael heard her footsteps in the hall, then a pause, then a door slamming. A garage door opened, and Julie's Mustang started with a roar. Jael glanced from the window just as the car's headlights looped around the oak and sped up the driveway.

Jael shook her head once, then twice, to clear the grogginess the music and the moment had caused. Then she dressed and walked from the second floor down into the foyer and onto the thick shag of the dining room. Bowls of crackers, pretzels, and chips rested on the table with a note that the dips and drinks were in the fridge. She walked through a curtain of ribbons into the kitchen. A punch bowl filled a shelf of the refrigerator: wedges of lemon, lime, and pineapple floated in the punch like the wreckage of a fleet. Jael dipped her finger into the punch and lifted it to her lips. No alcohol. Maybe her father had left the bar unlocked. Not likely, but worth a try.

Jael walked from the kitchen past the rec room and library, past the recital room. Her knees buckled and she felt as though she were trying to stand on a moving toboggan; there was the hollow-in-the-gut feeling that her body was going one way, her legs the other, and then she was on her back looking up at the ceiling. She put her hand to her mouth. Saliva covered her chin.

Jael rubbed her fingers across her face, then back over her forehead to her scalp. She tried to shake the dizziness from her head, but it wouldn't leave. Then a pain shot through her as if something were trying to claw its way outward from her chest. She had heard that heart attacks began this way—she was too young—but the pain in her chest kept growing and growing, and her own name started to echo through her mind. Julie's presence was there, inside her, all around her, screaming mindlessly.

Jael started to crawl toward the garage. Her movements were more instinctual than conscious, more as though something were pulling her down the hall, past the parlors and bedrooms. The shag carpet scratched and burned and the concrete garage steps and floor were searingly cold. She crawled to her Mustang's door, opened it, and climbed inside. The keys were in the ignition. The engine roared and she reached into the glove compartment for the button to raise the garage door. The pain in her chest kept tugging, tugging her toward the steering wheel. She backed out, shifted into first, then weaved around the driveway and into the woods. She didn't pull the knob for the headlights until she reached Sheridan Road. The gatehouse across the road exploded in white.

She pulled out and managed to shift from first gear to second, then to third, and the mailboxes streaked past, the outlines of houses dissolved into a blur, and the white dashes of the center stripe became solid yellow. She reached the series of twists, declines, and rises known as the ravines. The air there was heavy and cold, like the draft from a catacomb. *Let it be a mistake!* Jael thought. *Let it all be a dream!*

She eased up on the gas pedal and coasted through the first two curves, then leaned into the third as she accelerated. The back of the car slipped sideways, moved toward the front, and Jael turned into the slide. The car straightened and moved up the far crest.

Julie was nearby. Her presence, everything that made her Julie, pounded and throbbed. She was there, nearby, not at Rick's but in the forested ravines.

Jael slammed on the brakes, ground gears until she depressed the clutch, and backed the Mustang wildly down the slope. The sense grew stronger, a power like two halves of a magnet invisibly reaching out for one another. The brakes screeched again, and Jael pulled the contents of the glove compartment onto the floor:

maps, Kleenex, cigarettes, a screwdriver, but no flashlight. The pain kept throbbing, throbbing, and soon she was outside of the car, leaning against the fender. Behind her, on the road, a puddle of oil glared red in the running lights; tire marks slid over the shoulder and into the ravine.

Jael took two steps; the waves of pain returned. She doubled over and fell to her knees, then rolled onto her side. *Concentrate on breathing,* she thought. It helped. A little.

She crawled past a torn guardrail down into the ravine. The rotting leaves at the bottom were soft and wet, and their stench filled Jael's nose. When she looked up, Julie's Mustang lay on its side with a back tire spinning round and round as slowly as a Ferris wheel in a nightmare. Jael stumbled to the car. Blood, colorless in the web of moonlight and shadow, oozed from a split in Julie's scalp, etching a net as it followed the lines of her forehead and pooled in her eyes.

She moved.

In all Jael's fantasies, Julie had been the one to do the saving. But now? What if Julie shouldn't be moved at all? What if she had a punctured lung or a broken back? As soon as Jael saw smoke rising from beneath the hood, she yanked on the door until it opened with a scrape. Jael tugged on Julie's arm, but the front of the car was crumpled against a tree, and the steering wheel pinned Julie to the seat. What to do? What to do? Simple. Just push the lever on the floor, just slide it back, the seat would move, and Julie would be free. Jael reached down.

The car exploded.

Jael was thrown backward, rolled, and stopped against a tree. She lay on her back and the moon shined through a mass of swirling leaves and the stars looked more like an artist's conception of what the galaxy should look like than the real thing. An orange-red glow lighted the underside of the leaves.

The car was a tray of flames.

Jael tried to crawl toward it, tried to get Julie, but the heat was literally a wall, and something burned through her wrist, and Jael screamed and fell forward, and there was a smell as vague as the days when she and Julie ironed each other's hair and didn't move the iron fast enough—then the worst smell in the world: broiling

13

meat. Waves of sensations swept over Jael: sinking into deep water, pressure crushing in from all sides. Facial muscles twitched. Hearing stopped. Then her body twisted and jerked and each breath was fire and blistered her lungs and the skin blackened and curled back on her fingers, and there wasn't any cool or warm anymore, just hot, hot, and Jael willed her eyes to open, but no, they wouldn't, and she couldn't black out, and the hair sizzled and fell from her head, and she tried to brush parched lips with her fingertips, but there were no lips, just bone, and then Jael looked up and saw that the fire, the car, were thirty feet away, and that the flames weren't burning her at all. No. It was worse. Much worse.

She was sharing Julie's death.

Seeing what Julie lacked the eyes to see, feeling what Julie was beyond feeling. Then the lights started. Green lights. Red lights. Yellow. Swirling lights. Blinking lights. Lights that were too bright to comprehend but impossible to escape. Then the noises. Loud hummings and cracklings. A pounding deep enough to shake the earth through her body. A screech like the wind whistling forever. Then there were images, gusts of memory, scenes that had roots in the past, in the very core of her beliefs, but blended into an order that was random, out of control: Julie squashing worms after a rain; sun slashing off the lake; a mountain of bodies writhing like maggots on meat. Images streamed past in a torrent, a dam-burst of thought that rolled on and on and built into a towering wave . . . and crashed into Jael. One final image: a twitching hand thrust through a windshield—an ID bracelet melted into the flesh.

There was another explosion, then a feeling of separating into atoms, each infinitesimal unit somehow connected to the others, then a surge of light and a freedom that pulled her further and further away, and a tunnel of light appeared and someone called Julie's name . . .

. . . and it was gone, all of it.

The communion.

The feeling of belonging.

Julie.

Jael lay under the tree, shivering in the heat of the fire, vomiting and choking on the smells. She wasn't whole anymore. The strings that joined her to Julie had been snipped and she was alone. And as Jael crawled away from the burning car, up the gully toward the road, she saw, behind the headlights of stopped cars and the silhouettes of gawking people, a future as lonely as the glare of the single flashlight that bounced down in the darkness toward her.

PART ONE

PART ONE

ONE

Chicago, Illinois—January 12, 1981

Jael straightened her skirt, took a deep breath, and entered the classroom punctually, exactly sixty seconds late. There was a time that she would have thought it was impossible to be both late and punctual, but two years of university teaching taught her otherwise. The one-minute delay allowed her students to exchange the names and addresses, the ball scores and who's-dating-whoms, that were so important to undergraduate life. While the first minute belonged to the students, there was an unspoken agreement: When Dr. Clarke arrived, the class began.

Pronto.

She placed her books on the podium and looked around the classroom more for effect than to note faces. Water stains and sun-bleaching had turned the walls yellow. The room's sole radiator clanked and sputtered; it was cold enough for ice to form around the window frames, and she shivered through her blazer and vest. The building was a Romanesque brownstone built in the 1880's, the room a leftover assigned to junior faculty. Jael walked to the blackboard (the fact that it was black betrayed its age), took the chalk holder from her pocket, and printed in large block letters:

SEMINAR IN ESCHATOLOGICAL LITERATURE
THE ANCIENT ARTS OF DEATH AND DYING

She turned back to the class and asked her first question, "What's it like to die?"

The students laughed uneasily.

"I'm serious," Jael said, then paused a moment to let the tension build. "The Tibetan Book of the Dead. The Egyptian Book of the Dead. The Immrama, the Celtic voyages into the after-death world. The Aztec *Tonalpohualli.* Why would anyone sign up for a course with such a reading list?"

There was a long silence before Jael continued. "This course can't provide proof of life after death. It *can* show you the beliefs of the ancient magic cultures, and it's amazing how similar those beliefs are." She turned to the blackboard and wrote the names of the texts. The students were so quiet that the radiator's clanking sounded like a gong.

Jael turned around. It was time to start her students thinking. "This room was assigned by computer," she said. "Randomly assigned. It is affectionately known to the students as 'the meat locker' and to the faculty as 'the house of the dead.' " She paused to indicate that the next statement was a question and to pay attention. "What's the meaning of the term *synchronicity,* and how does it apply to the relationship between the course's title and the room's nickname?"

Five hands shot up, an incredible number for so difficult a question. It was going to be a challenging group, the kind she liked best. Jael nodded toward a student with a quasi-punk hair-cut and designer versions of 1940's clothing.

"Mr. . . . ?" Jael asked.

"Benjamin Carver," he said, turning on the type of smile that she hadn't seen since her last Coke date as an undergrad. "Is it all right to call you Jael?"

Jael stared at him until he looked past her to the blackboard. "Until you've earned it, I remain Dr. Clarke. Now, Mr. Carver, synchronicity?"

"A meaningful coincidence between psychic and external events," he said. When his eyes returned to Jael's face, they were unsure.

Jael nodded to let him know that he was doing just fine, that he had a chance to impress her and that wasn't easy, then said, "That's only half an answer. Apply it to the specifics."

"You decide to teach a course on after-death literature. You turn the class description in to a computer. It assigns you a class-room know as 'the house of the dead.' That's a meaningful coin-cidence."

"And that's an excellent answer," Jael said. She smiled at him as a reward and watched him blush.

The semester's first conquest.

She'd had her share of conquests since she started teaching. Her undergraduate seminar on eschatology wasn't as prestigious as Saul Bellow's gatherings with aspiring writers, Mircea Eliade's legendary classes on comparative religion, or anything Chris Shaw taught, but she was gaining quite a following. Most of the students in class had been on a waiting list for a semester.

"Everyone expected to be excused early today," Jael said. "Wrong. I expect you came prepared to take notes."

There were mandatory groans from the students.

"You will read an average of one text per week," Jael said, "and I don't mean scan like you would a Gothic romance or science fiction novel, but *read* to intelligently discuss the material." She took a handful of mimeographed papers from her briefcase and distributed them. "These include a reading schedule and background information on our first text, the Tibetan Book of the Dead."

Jael waited for the rustling of papers to stop, waited until the students had finished removing the pens and notebooks from their packs, before she continued. "To the Tibetan Buddhist, reincarnation is a fact," she said. "The Book of the Dead contains instructions which are chanted over the corpse so that the bodiless soul will understand the sights and sounds it encounters as it journeys toward rebirth. We'll get to the book's psychological and philosophical implications next meeting; first let's take a look at the country and its history."

She walked to the blackboard, reached up, grasped the wooden frame on the map of Tibet, and pulled down. She no longer assumed her students understood that Tibet's enormous mountains had kept the people isolated and the religion unique: Nothing could be assumed from a public school education anymore. The map unrolled in a flash of primary colors. Jael started to turn back to the class when she saw something white where there should only have been blue: a heart-shaped piece of paper. Although she noticed typing, she only focused on the four words that were written in red ink, *Dear Jael* and *Love, Chris.*

They told her enough.

She wouldn't disrupt the momentum of the first day's lecture, not even to read a love note. The atmosphere of the entire semester was established on the first day, and *nothing* could be allowed to disturb it. Jael kept her body between the map and the students, carefully unfastened the Scotch tape, edged back to the podium, and placed the note on the class list. She was already having a hard time concentrating! Temper, temper, she thought. Chris was only trying to be cute. He was a natural; he scarcely planned classes, never doubted his ability. No matter how often they talked about it, he would never understand how hard Jael had to work at teaching.

Jael cleared her throat to gain attention, then began the first day's lecture as she always did: She explained the effect of Bon, the pre-Buddhist religion, on the Book of the Dead. Soon she moved to Tibet's conversion to Buddhism, and halfway through the section on early Chinese influence she heard whispering. Time to react. She increased her pace, started firing questions, raised her voice. The students caught her excitement, and she wheedled, challenged, and badgered them through the British invasion. By the end of the first hour the air sparked with energy. A potentially boring section was over, and not an eyelid had closed, not a head had drooped. It was time to move into the period of the Chinese takeover, but as Jael reached to the podium for a picture of the Dalai Lama, she noticed Chris's note. Her curiosity returned and her mind wandered; that could be fatal on the first day. She stopped the lecture and held up a copy of the handout, "Tibet: 1950–55." "You have ten minutes to read this," she said. "I expect everyone to contribute when we continue."

Jael stared at the class until all the students started to read, then she picked up the note. It said:

Dear Jael:

I would have loved to see how you managed to read this without letting the kiddies see, but the logistics of the room just didn't allow it.

Do I have news for you!

Too bad this note isn't the place to tell it. The Pub is. Do promise that you won't get too curious. I'd hate to be responsible for disrupting your class.

Love,
Chris

P.S. It won't kill them to be excused early just this once. It is amazingly good news, after all.

Jael stuffed the note into her vest pocket, leaned against the blackboard, and chewed on her lip. Then she went back to her notes. Chris Shaw or not, he was going to have to wait until her lecture was over.

Jael pushed the heavy red door, stepped inside, and leaned against the bar until her eyes adjusted to the light. The lounge was exactly what she expected from a tavern called The Pub. It was dark and dismal, stank of sour beer, and lacked imagination in everything from the red lights above the booths to the black velvet painting above the bar. Of course, these were the reasons Chris liked it. His sense of irony, if not his taste, was more developed than hers. When the shadows became outlines, then hardened into people, Jael walked to the booth by the jukebox. She crunched peanut shells with each step she took. Chris smiled when he saw her, and his incredibly blue eyes seemed to twinkle even in the dim light. He stood, then bent down to kiss her, but Jael held up her hand.

"Being red-haired and *cute*"—she spat the word out like profanity—"is like being named Muffy or Mimi. Whatever respect I get from my students, I have to earn."

"But—"

"I'm not through being angry yet," she said, placing a hand over his mouth. "With your blond hair and your bass voice and your six feet three, you'll never know what earning respect is like."

Chris gently moved her hand from his mouth. " *'Yo escucho entre el disparo de los besos,'* " he said melodiously. " 'I am listening between the explosion of the kisses.' " He almost sang the words. He tilted his head and the cords of muscle stood out on

23

his neck. A vein throbbed, an action so delicate and vulnerable that its contrast to Chris's entire being made Jael smile.

"Is that from a poem by Vallejo?" she asked.

"Pablo Neruda," Chris said. Then he smiled his impish smile, the one that belonged on a truant grade schooler instead of the chair of the department. "It's from 'Sexual Water.' "

Jael rose up on her tiptoes and kissed him on the cheek. An intentionally sisterly kiss. "It's useless to try and discuss anything with you," she said.

"To argue with me, you mean," Chris said. He ran his fingers through his perfectly trimmed beard. There was a trace of distinguished gray at his sideburns—not that he needed it.

Jael sat on the bench. "At least you could say you were sorry for disrupting my class."

"But I'm not," Chris said. He sat and rested his arms on the narrow table. "I'm incapable of disrupting your class. You're the best young teacher in the department."

Jael smiled and shook her head. "Why is it that even when I lose an argument with you, you make it sound like it's a draw?"

"Diplomacy, my love," he said. Chris reached into the large leather briefcase that sat on the bench next to him and removed some envelopes. "Now the news: exhibits A, B, and C." As soon as Jael reached for the letters Chris pulled them away. "Not so fast."

Jael hooked a strand of hair with her little finger and placed it behind her ear. "At least tell me who they're from."

"Admirers," Chris said. Jael leaned over the table and tried to grab the letters, but Chris hid them behind his back, then slipped them into his briefcase. He removed a bottle of Hennessy X.O. cognac and two brandy snifters. "Care to join me?"

"I'd prefer the letters," she said.

A student walked past their booth, stopped at the jukebox, and slipped in a coin; after some static a country singer blared from the speaker above Jael's head. She rolled her eyes at the music, and Chris shook his head. Then he leaned toward her and said, "The Ford Foundation, the National Geographic Society, and the National Endowment for the Humanities agreed that the grant proposals submitted by professors Shaw and Clarke were among the most interesting they'd seen in years."

"We're going to Tibet," Jael said. Just the thought of it made her gasp.

"I wish you said 'Chris' with the same reverence," he said, taking her hand and kissing it.

Jael drummed her fingers on the table in excitement. "I can't believe it!"

"Believe. We had three things going for us. One, we will be the first western academics in thirty years to visit Tibetan monasteries. Two, the grant proposals were thoroughly researched and brilliantly written." Chris poured cognac into the snifters and held one out to her. After she took it they clicked glasses. "To a month on the Roof of the World," he said.

They sipped.

"You didn't mention the third reason," Jael said.

"My pull, of course," Chris said.

"To your pull," Jael said, laughing. She took a deeper drink. The cognac was warm and smooth and made the announcement almost believable. "Let's leave tomorrow!" she shouted.

Chris laughed. "My friends in the Chinese Embassy said the visas will be ready whenever we need them." He paused and drained the last of his cognac in a gulp. "Don't forget classes. And I have lectures to give in London in June and Leipzig in July . . . and we should stop in D.C. to give our thanks to the folks who are making this possible."

Jael held her breath and closed her eyes. Time for the big question. She felt her voice start to quiver. "What did they say about the chapters from *The* One *Cult* I included?"

"They found them interesting," Chris said.

Jael paused and studied his expression: discomfort. "What about the money I requested to purchase artifacts?"

"There's plenty of money for everything," Chris said, looking toward the door. "They were more than generous."

They were *his* friends, *his* lectures, *his* pull. "I'm beginning to get the impression we're talking about your proposal instead of our proposals," she said. "My part of the grant was rejected?"

"Everyone who read your chapters said you were a fine writer with original ideas."

"That's not an answer," Jael said.

"You're right," Chris said, nodding. He exhaled loudly. "This is the reality of the grant world: No matter how good a teacher you are, no matter how original your intellect is, until you get that first book published, you're just another applicant with some theories." He sat back against the bench and cleared his throat, a sure sign he was about to assume the role of father figure. "If you expect justice, even a pat on the head, then you'd better switch professions."

"Will you please cut the shit and give me specifics?" Jael said.

"You present more proof and fewer theories, and they'll reconsider your application next year."

"Thank you," Jael said. She stared at the table and shook her head back and forth. "So I end up tagging along on your money and political connections?"

"Why ask?"

"It all boils down to whose briefcase the letters are in."

Chris leaned over, removed the letters, and handed them to her. "Chin up," he said. "They all compliment your work."

She placed them in her briefcase without opening them. "I'd rather read them when I'm alone." She glanced around the room without really seeing anything.

"Look," Chris said, "there's not an associate professor in the country who would have received the kind of money you asked for. Not one." He put his hand under her chin, then drew a fingertip along the curve of her jaw. "Let's not pout. There's an old Chinese saying, the gist of which is: 'It's better to be well connected than talented.' You have the incredible good fortune to be both."

As soon as Jael set her brandy snifter down on the table, Chris offered to refill it. *Why not?* she thought. About halfway through the new drink, she started to lose her taste for both cognac and The Pub. She shook her head and tried to organize her feelings into thoughts. Maybe things weren't so bad after all. At least the foundations knew her name . . . and the trip to Tibet provided the chance to find her proof. Chris picked up his snifter and drained it. With his J. Press shirt and Harris Tweed jacket, he was the perfect young professor on his way up—not that he had far to go. He always went after power instead of women; he was a good enough anthropologist to know that one meant the other.

Chris took her hand and stroked her fingers one at a time. He twisted the emerald ring on her right hand as she always did when she was nervous. "Look at it this way," he said. "If you ever find support for this 'master religion' thesis of yours, I'll be the one asking you for letters of recommendation."

Jael leaned over the table, touched his cheek, and kissed him on the tip of the nose. "Sure," she said. She leaned back against the bench and exhaled in a whistle. "Sorry about being a bitch. I probably should be thanking you."

"I'm waiting."

Jael took his cheeks in her hands, just stared at him for a moment and smiled, then kissed him deeply and smelled the chalk dust on his beard—chalk dust and the juice from the orange he must have peeled with his teeth for lunch. "I have an idea," she said. "Let's celebrate. Dinner. My treat."

"This *is* a special occasion," he said.

She decided on the Blackhawk and walked to the bar to phone for reservations. The receiver was still at her ear as Chris stood, picked up her briefcase, and brought it toward her. Even when she'd first seen him when she was a graduate student in his seminar on pre-dynastic Egypt, Jael had wanted to touch him to feel if he was as lean as he looked. He hadn't disappointed her. She placed the phone back on the bar, and he took her arm, walked her to the door, opened it for her, then followed her into the gray Chicago winter. A bus roared past and sprayed slush; a police car stopped, turned on its blue flashers, and sped away. A huge snowflake caught on Jael's eyelash and blurred her vision until she brushed it off. And as Chris ran along the salt-stained sidewalk, trying to hail a cab, Jael thought of how he had backed her appointment to the faculty, of how he had taken her on the expeditions that led to her first articles, and of how nice it was to walk

into a crowded room with Chris on her arm and watch the heads
turn. And she couldn't decide whether she really loved him or
was merely accustomed to walking in his steps like a dog that had
been taught to heel.

TWO

Wilmette, Illinois—May 31, 1981

The waves rolling in from Lake Michigan scattered seaweed and snails, gravel and dead fish, all along the shoreline. Birds circled and soared, then veered toward the beach. Whenever a gull found food, its cry would attract others, and the squawking and fighting would begin. They reminded Matt Griffin of a day in court, particularly the divorce cases, when everyone pecked and gouged for the scraps. He stopped walking and wondered why his mind kept drifting to divorce litigation. He hadn't handled a divorce case in years. It was a thought he didn't want to pursue, so he stared out at the lake and watched waves curl toward shore.

"Look out, Dylan," Matt shouted.

His son was playing tag with the surf, chasing the foamy water as it retreated toward the lake, then running back up the beach before the next wave broke. He was too slow this time; the water was knee-deep as it surged past him. "The fish are nibbling me!" he squealed.

"Careful," Matt shouted. Of course Matt knew that Dylan was only joking, that the fish were grains of sand rolling over his toes, but the boy jumped as though piranhas were eating him. He was a cute kid. He deserved a tickling.

Matt continued down the beach. Behind him, around the point of land, was the harbor and boat docks, and a quarter mile beyond, the dome of the Baha'i Temple; to his left the thin fringe of elms by the parking lot; straight ahead were condominiums, private beaches, and open sand to the horizon. Dylan squatted and picked something out of the glistening water.

"This an emerald?" he asked, handing a green, translucent object to Matt.

"Are we in a pirate cove or on Gillson Park Beach?"

"Oh, *Dad!*" Dylan squealed, rolling his eyes.

Sometimes it was hard to keep track of how fast Dylan was growing. The year before, he was interested only in pirates and outer space; now, as a first grader, he wanted "the facts," whatever they were. The object in Matt's hand was familiar enough; he'd found plenty just like it when he was a kid. "It's part of an old Seven-Up bottle," he said, handing it back. "A little worn by the waves and time, I guess."

Dylan wasn't paying attention. Instead he looked toward the parking lot. "Mom ever gonna get here?" he asked.

Yeah, Mom. "There are small-craft warnings out. Once she hears we can't go sailing, she'll probably go to the office and try to get caught up on some work," Matt lied.

"She's never on time anymore."

"I know, Dylan." Matt ruffled his son's fine brown hair and looked into his eyes: Bekki's eyes. Then he pointed Dylan up the beach and patted him on the butt. And the boy was gone, sprinting over the sand and rock. It took him five seconds to cover the same distance that took Matt thirty. "Stay close!" Matt shouted as the boy swerved toward the water.

Bekki's reason for being late had nothing to do with the wind or work. She had had a lover, a new lover, for two months now. Normally it wouldn't have mattered. Not too much, anyway. Twelve years of marriage to the same person was a long time, certainly enough to allow for an occasional infidelity. They'd both had them.

Bekki had been raised in Chicago's northern suburbs—in affluence; Matt, in rural Wisconsin. Their standards had been different. During the time they'd been together, she'd taught him a suburban urbanity—paradoxical, maybe, but that's what it was. Their affairs were never mentioned as long as there was no guile, no silly attempts at camouflage. Affairs were more like hobbies than crimes, like sailing or horseback riding, something that, while demanding a certain amount of time, never flowed into the marriage.

Never before, anyway.

Whomever Bekki was seeing, it had gone beyond the recreational stage. No excuses were possible today. It was a holiday, for God's sake; more than that—a family ritual: the first day the sailboat was out of dry dock. There was a time he would have made an angry, loud, very public scene. Messy, Bekki would have called it.

His scene-making days began to dwindle when he and Bekki met as undergraduates; they vanished altogether when he married her and entered the upper class.

He sighed and plopped down on the sand so he could simultaneously keep an eye on Dylan and the row of bikinied sunbathers who basted on towels near the park. A wave tickled Matt, lifted his testicles, suspended them in icy water, then gently returned them to the sand. A blond woman rolled over and her bikini top fell off. *Thank God for cold water,* Matt thought.

A huge wave crashed into his back and tumbled him onto his stomach. Sand bounced off his neck and ears: It *did* feel like fish nibbling. He did a push-up as the wave slid under him. Someone was giggling. He looked up and saw Dylan standing less than ten feet away, making no attempt to hide his amusement.

"You didn't warn me, stinkpot!" Matt growled. He stood slowly, unfolding, playing the Creature from the Black Lagoon, then reached out for the boy.

And the race began.

If he runs for the rocks, Matt thought, *he's lost me.* But Dylan wasn't interested in strategy, he was interested in being caught. Matt grabbed him, deposited him on a shoulder, and headed into the waves. He held on to Dylan and bent lower and lower, and Dylan screamed just before a wave broke over them. Matt stood, shook the water from his eyes, relaxed his grip on the boy slightly, and started to sink again. Dylan squealed and squirmed.

"Do I have to swim out there and save both of you?" a voice called. Bekki's voice. She must have checked for them at the dock, then walked across the park to the beach.

"Help, Mom!" Dylan shouted.

"Save me from this monster!" Matt said.

Bekki waded out to them, lifted Dylan from Matt's arms, and carried him back toward the beach. Waves lapped at the back of Matt's legs. Bekki took the towel that was draped over her shoulder, and when she shifted Dylan's weight and tried to dry him, he

31

wiggled free and ran up the beach. She leaned over and kissed Matt's cheek. "Sorry I'm so late," she said. "The wind made it pretty obvious we wouldn't be sailing today." Then she nodded toward the row of sunbathers and smiled. "Of course, you had no problem entertaining yourself."

Matt bit his lip.

Bekki took his hand, and they started to stroll after Dylan. *Gutless,* Matt thought, *I am gutless, gutless.* It had to be the life-style; he'd never felt like this while he'd lived on the farm. He pried up a rock with his toe and turned it over. It was coated only with sand. If this were northern Wisconsin, each rock would teem with insect larvae, which could be impaled on a number-ten hook and used to lure monster trout from beneath logjams. When he was Dylan's age, he could already handle a fly rod, do chores, weed the garden. . . . "When I mowed our ditch," Matt said, "the smell of fresh-cut mint would blend with lilacs from the hedge."

Bekki grinned and said, "Where did *that* come from?"

"Sorry," Matt said. "I've been drifting in and out all afternoon." He wanted her to ask why. If she only asked why, it would provide him an opening line, a chance to talk about their marriage. No way. Not even a nibble.

Instead she said, "You should take a long weekend. Your court schedule can't be so busy you can't fit in a long weekend. Maybe take your dad fishing?"

"Would you come?"

"I haven't sketched the floor plans for the Woodleys' new game room," she said. Her mouth lifted nervously at the corner. "I have wallpaper and fabric to order, not to mention finding new carpenters."

"All right!" Matt said too loudly, too sharply. Then he held up his hands, lowered his voice, and said more quietly, "All right." He threw his head back, took deep gulps of air, and tried to let the cool breeze from the lake lower his temper. He looked back at Bekki. "Maybe some fresh air would help Dylan sleep."

"If he gets any more than he had today, he'll burst."

"Forget I mentioned it."

Bekki walked slightly ahead of him. How full of contradictions she was. Fashion-model thin, but her high cheekbones made her face seem full. Her short hair would have looked butch on many women, but it made Bekki's eyes appear doelike, terribly vulnerable. Her legs were probably her greatest asset and an equally great puzzle: They were as long and feminine as legs could be, but the way she stood, her feet apart, her hips thrust slightly forward, made her appear sexually aggressive in a masculine way. And if there was one thing Bekki wasn't, it was masculine. Matt caught up to her and kissed her on the back of the neck. There was no taste of sweat, none of sour perfume, just soap. Recently used soap. When Bekki pulled away from him, Matt noticed a scratch that started at her inner thigh and disappeared under the elastic of her swimming suit. She paused, turned, and walked back toward him. Matt picked up several flat stones and threw them into the lake one at a time. They sliced into waves before they could skip. He bent over and searched for more stones.

"Is there something wrong, Matt?" Bekki asked.

Matt threw a stone, three skips this time.

"Matthew?"

"You showered before you came," Matt said. He leaned toward her and gently, very gently, brushed his fingertips along her inner thigh. "And you really should tell him to keep his fingernails trimmed."

"Let's not," Bekki said. "Not here. Please."

"Let's," Matt said. "This liberal cuckold nonsense is starting to wear thin."

Two gulls landed within ten feet of them and started to pick at dead fish. Bekki tried to scare them away with a stick, but as soon as she turned to Matt, they returned. "I'm sorry," she finally said.

"If this were the farm," Matt said, "I'd quite simply kick the shit out of him."

"Up there you wouldn't have had affairs of your own."

Matt picked up another rock and threw it so hard it hurt his shoulder. "Jesus, Bek, it's not the scratch. It's the shower. It's putting the family second. It's making excuses. If you're trying to hide him, you feel guilty. If you feel guilty, it means that you love him and I've as good as lost you."

33

Dylan came running toward them, scattering gulls, leaping over clumps of seaweed, holding his collecting bag in one hand and his probing stick in the other. "Careful!" Bekki shouted. "You'll lose an eye!"

Dylan backed away from her. "You didn't have to yell," he said.

Bekki took Dylan's hand and pulled him toward her. She kissed the tip of his nose, then his hair. "Sorry," she said.

"Your hand's shaking."

"Your father and I are having a discussion," Bekki said.

"A fight," Matt said.

"Don't fight," Dylan said, blinking and frowning. "You never let *me* fight."

"Don't worry, Cap'n," Matt said. "We just want to be alone for five mintues."

"Please don't fight."

"We won't," Bekki said. "Just give us a few more minutes and we'll buy you a Dairy Queen on the way home."

Dylan nodded without enthusiasm. He probably realized it was the best offer he was going to get. He walked to a spot fifty feet from them, easy listening range, and used his stick to draw in the sand.

And suddenly it was Bekki who seemed helpless. She started to talk, then stopped, then drew lines in the sand with her toe. It was a vulnerable, terribly attractive gesture. "He's a friend, Matt." She looked up and shrugged. "I guess the older I get, the less I keep track of the time."

"A pretty feeble excuse," Matt said. "Pathetic is what it is. In fact, it sounds like you don't care enough to concoct a decent lie." He let his arms droop to his sides, then shrugged. "Let's move away," he said. "If we don't leave this rat race behind, we'll be done within the year."

Bekki started to shake her head.

"What about Dylan?" Matt continued. "They caught some punk pushing downers in the playground. . . ."

"No, Matt—"

"I hadn't heard of drugs when I was six," Matt continued. He rested his hands on his hips and stared at her. "There are boundary disputes in Wisconsin. Inheritance squabbles. And it's not as though we need the money."

"They'd have to put me in a straitjacket after my first quilting bee," Bekki said. She just kept shaking her head, standing there with her arms crossed, the wind blowing her hair and goosebumps rising on her arms and legs. "I still love you," she said. Then she paused, but not for long enough. "But I love him too."

"So now what?"

She shook her head slowly, calmly, as she always did when she had to make a difficult decision. "I'll stop seeing him," she finally said.

"Now?"

"Soon. Let me talk to him first."

"Cut it cleanly or it will go on and on and soon there won't be anything either of us can do." Matt laid an arm on her shoulder and rubbed the back of her neck. "Call him when we get back; I'll stay in the room if you want."

She stepped back and said, "You're joking."

"Do I know him?"

"No," Bekki said. Then she looked up, shrugged, and added, "What difference would it make?"

"When I fantasize ripping out his throat, I want the head to have a face."

"I'll stop," Bekki said. "I promise." She hugged Matt and rose on her tiptoes so she could kiss him on the lips, but there were tears in her eyes, and that didn't forebode anything good. They stayed that way for a few moments, until Bekki's calves grew tired or she grew tired of the pose. She released Matt's neck and spun away. "Where's Dylan?" she asked.

Matt turned and frantically searched the waterline for a bobbing head of brown hair. He had run two steps toward the lake when Bekki shouted and pointed to a spot up the beach. Dylan. He was a hundred or so feet away. He was still drawing in the sand, drawing so intently that he hadn't noticed his parents' argument was over. He didn't look up as Bekki and Matt weaved through the piles of seaweed and carefully tottered through the gravel. Matt bent over the boy. "That's the strangest dog I've ever seen," Matt said.

"It's not a dog," Dylan said. His voice was flat, distant.

"Whatever it is, I like it," Bekki said.

"He doesn't like you," Dylan said.

Good for him, Matt thought. He bent to study the drawing's detail. It was amazing for a child, but was it bizarre. It was a canine of sorts, a wolf perhaps, but with an anteater's snout; tall, square mule's ears; and the large, padded feet of a cheetah. "What is it?" Matt asked.

Dylan glanced up with an expression that, if Matt hadn't known the boy's age, he would have thought was a sneer. "It is what it is," Dylan snapped.

Matt held up his hand and jokingly said, "Back off. One fight's enough for the day."

Dylan added some lines to the creature's neck, an embellishment to the tail, then stood up and blinked. And smiled. It was as though something had passed from him. "Let's let the wind blow it away," he said.

"I really am impressed," Bekki said. "Want some lessons?"

"I want a Dairy Queen," Dylan said.

"Ditto," Matt said.

Dylan reached out and took a hand from each of his parents. It was evident he had decided that his parents had misbehaved long enough, and it was time for a more rational mind to be making the decisions. Then Dylan nodded, gave each hand a tug, and led his parents up the beach, through the park, and to the car.

THREE

Wilmette, Illinois—July 7, 1981

Jael awoke when she felt Chris move, a quiver in the waterbed. Light glowed around the closed curtains, slid down the wall, and pooled on the rug. It was the first time in a month she'd awakened to sunlight instead of the terror of the nightmare. Maybe having Chris sleep over helped after all. She watched him in the gray light; a spot of saliva stained the pillow by his mouth. He snorted and mumbled something, and Jael noticed how sour his breath was. With a face all soft and puffy from sleep, he looked just like *any* thirty-eight-year-old man.

Enough of this silliness, she thought. *Imagine what he thinks when he wakes up first.*

She glanced at the clock—eight-fifteen. By that time tomorrow they'd be on their way to Tibet. Jael rolled onto her back, took one, two, three deep breaths, and eased herself up. She tiptoed naked from the bedroom, partially closed the door, took three steps into the sunken living room, then walked to the huge window that opened onto the balcony. She pulled the cord and the drapes slid. Slowly the room filled with light. She stopped just before the glare reached her eyes, then, after another deep breath, yanked the cord.

Beyond the window, Lake Michigan stretched as far as she could see. On a clear night the lights from Benton Harbor forty miles across the water were visible. Although the haze from Chicago had already started to gather, Jael could see far enough into the lake to realize that this was the only place in the Midwest she could live: the city for culture, the suburbs for escape, and blue water every morning from thirteen stories up. During the weeks she had had the nightmare, she had watched the sun rise blood-red, fire red, on the lake every morning. Mongolian tribes believed that the colors were caused by warring dragons; it was the perfect image for four-thirty A.M., when every sensation had the elemental beauty and horror of dreams.

Jael started for the kitchen, then stopped at the Steinway and touched the keys. She hadn't played seriously since Julie had died. The magic just wasn't there. Of course, the same could be said for everything else. She played C-G-C to accentuate the sunlight.

"Strauss," Chris shouted from the bedroom. *"Also Sprach Zarathustra."* His head emerged from a crack in the doorway.

"It wasn't meant to be a quiz," Jael said.

"Don't I get a prize?"

Jael rolled her eyes. "You get to help me feed the animals." Chris frowned and his head disappeared. "And bring my bathrobe!" she shouted. In seconds he walked from the bedroom wearing one bathrobe, carrying another. As he approached her he untied his waistband, opened the front of his robe, and pulled her against him. He held her bathrobe out of reach with one hand while he stroked her thigh and bottom with the other. "Chris," Jael said, slapping his hand away, "we have breakfast at my folks' at ten."

"Sorry," he said without the slightest conviction. As she put on the bathrobe Chris cupped his hand behind her head and massaged the muscles where her spinal cord met her skull. "How'd you sleep last night?" he asked.

"The best in weeks."

"No nightmares?"

"No dreams of any kind."

"If we made the sleeping arrangements permanent," he said, bending to kiss her neck, "the bad dreams might stop and—"

She didn't let him finish the sentence. "We've been through this enough," she said. "I need the privacy. So do you. If we lived together, we'd take each other for granted."

"I had something more respectable in mind."

"I know," she said. She touched a fingertip to his lips so he wouldn't say any more. There was more than privacy at stake. Chris would professionally, emotionally, smother whomever he married. And Jael felt she was just learning how to breathe. "The fish food is in the cabinet under the aquariums. Follow the instructions I left for the maintenance man."

She walked into the kitchen, took two apples, a pear, a peach, sliced them into wedges, and returned to the living room. When she removed the black cloth from the floor-to-ceiling cage, Osiris, her cockatoo, lifted his crested head and ruffled his pink-and-white feathers. He squawked, flapped his wings, and jumped to a higher perch. All twenty-plus inches of him.

Jael fed him until she ran out of fruit, then reached into the cage and ran her fingers along the edge of his crest. First he nuzzled her with his beak, then moved so her hand stroked the entire length of his back and his tail. He squawked. Jael glanced up at the clock above the refrigerator: eight-thirty. "You shower while I finish with the menagerie," she shouted.

Chris walked into the kitchen and draped his arms over her shoulders. "Here's a better idea," he said. "I'll go straight to the airport. That way *you* can explain to your parents why *I* keep dragging you all around the world."

"This is one trip I would have made without you."

"I know that. You know that. Now, will *they* believe it?"

Jael smiled and cocked her head. "They like you better than most of the men I've brought home."

Chris kissed the top of her head. "What about their daughter?"

"She likes you better than any of them," Jael said.

Chris moved a hand up her neck and stroked her hair. "Enough to let me soap her back?"

The bathroom had a shower stall across from the bathtub. Jael let Chris adjust the water—his nipples weren't as sensitive to the cold water as hers—and didn't enter the spray until steam formed on the glass. The hot water loosened her muscles; she inhaled the steam. She turned around and let the water massage the back of her head, cascade over her shoulders, across her breasts, and down the flat of her stomach to her legs.

Chris adjusted the nozzle until the spray was a mist. "Turn around," he said. She faced the wall and felt first the sponge, then his hand soaping her shoulders and then the small of her back. He pulled her away from the water and tightly against him. The hair on his chest stuck to her soapy back. He reached around her and soaped first her stomach, then, in slow, slippery circles, one breast, then the other, then her thighs in long, firm strokes, and she turned to him and pulled him away from the spray so their bodies would stay slippery and slide, not rub, and they kissed and caressed, and they moved against each other rhythmically, and soon he lifted her, and she locked one leg behind his thigh and let him move so she wouldn't lose her balance, and it wasn't so bad being tall after all, and the more he moved, the more she wanted to move, so he lifted her, cradled her in his hands, and she locked her legs around the small of his back, and he leaned against the wall, and then she did the moving, which was best for both of them, ran her fingers over his knotted muscles, and he grabbed her harder, and his movements became more natural, more urgent, and she had complete control so she copied his rhythm, moved faster and faster, and made him finish first, but not by much. They stayed locked together, kissing and stroking, nuzzling each other's wet hair, until the sensations eased.

Chris backed into the spray and jumped and squirmed. Jael wasn't as sensitive, so she resudsed, then washed off the soap, and was standing on the floor mat before Chris turned off the shower. When she handed him the towel, he gave her a kiss on the forehead and said, "Good morning."

Jael followed the driveway's loop and parked under the oak as her father walked through the front door and onto the portico. He wore a faded polo shirt and baggy cotton pants. When Jael ran up the stairs and hugged him, he lifted her off the ground and spun her around. "We didn't expect you to be on time," he said, kissing her. "Your mother's still practicing." He nodded toward the second floor. Thin notes from a harpsicord filtered down, a Vivaldi adagio played with a light hand and mathematical precision. "Why don't you join her?"

"She'd see how rusty I am," Jael said.

Chris walked up and exchanged greetings, then Jael placed one arm around her father, the other around Chris, and led them toward the side of the house. The pathways that wound through the gardens and ponds were covered with red-brown gravel. The air smelled of roses and the heavy stench of fish, seaweed, and water from Lake Michigan. Jael's father turned to Chris, cleared his throat, and said, "You certainly choose unusual vacation spots to take my daughter. The jungles of Central America. The Sahara. Now Tibet."

"This trip is as much mine as Chris's," Jael said. "I would have gone eventually even without the grants."

"Then it's you I should turn over my knee." Her father turned toward the sun and squinted. He looked like a Roman senator with his wavy white hair, his angular chin and nose, and the practiced arrogance when he narrowed his eyes. "If I ask you a straightforward question," he said to Jael, "you won't get angry with me."

"Probably," Jael said, "but that's not going to stop you."

He didn't even smile as he nodded. "How much of this trip has to do with Julie?"

"You want it straight?"

"Naturally."

"A lot," Jael said. She paused for an instant. "She's why I study after-death literature instead of music."

She tried to walk away, but her father wouldn't let go of her hand. He turned to Chris and asked, "I suppose you approve of this?"

"As long as she keeps her opinions on parapsychology away from her data, it's none of my business. She makes her own decisions," Chris said. "Besides, I'm not sure how much I believe this telepathy talk."

"Believe it," Jael's father said. He turned to Jael. His face was wind-dried and his green eyes angry and concerned. "Why start this all over again?"

"Call it an obligation," she said. "On the night Julie died, I went further into the otherworld, if there is such a thing, than any westerner ever has. The sights and sounds described in the Tibetan Book of the Dead are incredibly close to what I experienced. I want to know more. Wouldn't you?"

"Thank God it's not my decision to make," he said, leading her to the gazebo. Thirty feet beneath the bluff, the lake surged over the beach and left flecks of foam on the sand. The gazebo's latticework gleamed in the sun, and its steps were slippery, glazed with lake spray.

"I expect to be spoiled," Jael said as her father held the door open for her.

He nodded toward two large serving carts. "Eggs Benedict," he said. "Crepes for dessert."

"You often have dessert for breakfast?" Chris asked.

"One final indulgence for my daughter's sweet tooth," her father said. "A shortcoming you must be familiar with." He pulled a wicker chair from the table and slid it under Jael as she sat down. She leaned back, stared at the round skylight in the ceiling, and savored the fragrance of baby's breath and iris from the table bouquet. *How many times,* she thought, *did Julie and I sneak out here, intending to smoke cigarettes, only to lie on our backs, smell the gardens, and stare at the sky instead?*

The music stopped. Soon a glint of sunlight reflected from the sliding patio door as her mother stepped outside. At first she walked slowly, but when she looked up and saw people in the gazebo, her pace increased. She hurried up the stairs and embraced Jael.

"Why didn't you tell me you arrived?" she asked. She stepped back and her green silk dress rippled in the breeze.

"I wanted to hear you play. It was exquisite."

Her mother shook her head and turned to Chris. "She inherited the silver tongue from her father."

"Chowtime," her father said. He raised his eyebrows and smiled playfully. He lit two alcohol burners—one for the eggs, one for the sauce—then plugged in the toaster for the muffins. Jael's mother poured coffee and straightened the bouquet. Within minutes they were eating.

Her mother leaned across the table and patted Jael's hand. "How have you been?"

"Except for an occasional nightmare, fine," Jael said. When her mother gave her a questioning glance, Jael said, "Don't worry, after my first hike at ten thousand feet, I'll sleep like a baby."

Her father finished a bite and asked, "How long will it take to get to your first monastery?"

"It's nonstop from O'Hare to Seattle," Chris said. "Then an hour layover. Then straight to Tokyo. There's a commercial flight to Peking, but only military flights to Gonggar."

"Gonggar?"

"Tibet's only airport. Then it's another sixty miles by car to Lhasa, the capital, then a week by pony or yak to Bod Ombu."

Jael's mother shook her head. Her hair was blue-white and her features sharp and brittle. "Why Tibet?" she asked.

"I need to establish contacts for a long-term study," Chris said. "How the switch to communism affected the average Tibetan's life span, productivity, things like that. Without data from the monasteries, I'd have to rely on what the Chinese provide."

Her mother turned to Jael. "What about you?"

"I have two reasons," Jael said. "One professional and one personal."

"*Professional* must refer to that book we keep hearing about," her father said.

"It's called *The One Cult.*" Jael paused and rubbed the back of her neck. "My problem's that it's not a book yet, just ten chapters of amazing data."

"On what?"

Where to start? Jael thought. *Where to start?* She tapped her fingers on the table and looked out toward the lake. "Parallelisms in ancient cultures."

"English, please," her father said.

"Sorry. The Egyptians, Celts, Babylonians, and Aztecs, just to name a few, all had similar gods, built sophisticated astronomical observatories, maintained hereditary priesthoods, believed in transmigration of the soul . . . The resemblances just keep going on and on." Jael poured a fresh cup of coffee, blew on it, and took a sip. "The most convincing proof is the after-death texts, but they're a bit obscure."

"Don't patronize us," her mother said. "We've read your articles."

Jael brushed a strand of hair from her face and tucked it behind her ear, then rested her elbows on the table. "Despite the fact these cultures developed on different continents, thousands

43

of years apart, their after-death tracts all read like translations of the same road map."

Her mother tilted her head and looked askance at Jael—her usual expression of disbelief. "The title of your book implies that you don't think the similarities are coincidental."

"Exactly," Jael said. "What if five, six thousand years ago a dominant culture spread. It would have brought its religion to whatever regions it conquered. Over a period of time the *One* culture would fade, but traces of its religion would survive in ceremonies and texts."

"How did it spread across the ocean?" her father asked. "Where did it start? Atlantis? Outer space?"

"I'll leave that kind of science to the *National Enquirer,*" Jael said, smiling. "I have to prove it existed before I can speculate on its origin."

Her mother started to shake her head. She rested her spoon on the side of her plate, leaned back, and said, "Let's backtrack. Your strongest proof is these texts?"

Jael nodded.

"If these texts all have 'maps' that are like your experience at Julie's death . . . ?" Her mother paused. "Are you suggesting that this *One* religion had a ceremony, something that allowed their priests to pass into another dimension?"

"Mother," Jael said in a sugary tone, "a scientist would never draw such a farfetched conclusion."

"But she could write her book so her readers couldn't help making it," Chris interrupted.

"No kibitzing," Jael said. She leaned forward and rested her chin on her hands. "This much I *know:* These cultures had no fear of death. None. Celts, Aztecs, and Babylonians would sing hymns of praise as they patiently waited to be sacrificed. Egyptians were so sure of an afterlife, they could legally repay their debts in the next world."

"They clearly weren't capitalists," her father said.

Jael's mother seemed less amused. She pushed her glasses up to the bridge of her nose and leaned back. "And you're going to find answers to all your questions in Tibet."

"I don't know," Jael said. "I do know that the monasteries

have mystical tracts no westerner has ever read, ceremonies with roots in prehistory." Jael stared at her mother and held her gaze, something that was never easy to do. "You've heard stories of Tibetan monks who could levitate? These monasteries have monks, hermit saints, who've meditated in caves for thirty years. Their forerunners compiled the Book of the Dead. Imagine what these men have learned from thirty years of complete silence and darkness."

"I'm not sure I want to," her mother said, wrinkling her nose. She leaned back and folded her arms. "It's no wonder you have nightmares."

"Don't start on that."

"At least we deserve to know what these dreams are about," her father said.

"It would bore you."

"Try us."

Jael shook her head. A breeze blew in from the lake and rippled leaves on the elms; their shadows scattered across the floor like minnows. She sighed and looked up. "There are not night-*mares,*" she said. "There is only one. It arrives just before dawn, and when it does I'm through sleeping for the night."

"Does it involve a crash?"

"No leading the witness," Jael said. She took a bite of the eggs Benedict. Even the muffin was cold. She had to wash it down with a sip of coffee. "As it starts I'm in my living room, playing a bizarre atonal piece on the piano. The sheet music is in hieroglyphs. Suddenly there's a flash on the balcony so brilliant, I can see a silhouette through the drapes."

"What is it?"

"I know what it is during the dream, but as soon as I awake it's gone," Jael said. "The truly macabre thing is that despite the fact I've seen every horror movie ever made, and I know whatever's out there is deadly beyond imagination, I'm drawn to it."

She poured some more coffee, added sugar and cream, and stirred it. The ripples were soft and heavy. "Anyway," Jael continued, "now I know how the women in the old Dracula movies used to feel when they walked open-armed to Bela Lugosi. And it isn't sexual as in a physical itch; no, it's more subtle than that.

More powerful. It's like a spiritual itch, if that makes any sense. It's like all my questions about the things I'll never know will be answered in one spasm of knowledge." She took a long sip of coffee. "Pardon the expression, Mother, but it's like an orgasm of the soul."

"Then the nightmare ends?"

"No. There's a roaring so loud it hurts my ears . . . yet, somehow it's still seductive. Then I start to change. The closer I get to the balcony, the crueler, more cynical I am. People become things, like cattle or sheep, things to be used. I step to the window and slide it open and the sky is filled with planets and strange constellations and I take another step. . . ." Jael shook her head, trying to clear the dream image.

"Then what?" her father asked.

"Then I wake up."

Her mother frowned.

"If you're thinking there's anything to do with Julie, Mother, you're wrong. The thing's got red hair, but yellow eyes and fangs. . . ." In that instant of description she glimpsed the creature, and it took her breath away. Then it vanished, vanished as it had in the dream, and she couldn't remember anything about it. Jael sat back in the chair and stared into the lake.

"Still with us?" Chris asked.

Jael nodded.

"Have you been to a therapist?" her mother asked.

"No," Jael said, "and unless he makes house calls in Tibet, I'm not about to." When her father tried to speak, Jael cut him off. "As you used to say, Dad, there's no room for negotiation on that point."

So he stood, relighted the burners, and mixed the batter for the crepes. He heated the Henri's sauce in one pan, and butter to fry the crepes in the other, and didn't say a word. Jael's mother stared out into the lake. Chris stared at Jael and shook his head.

"Sorry," Jael said. She sat up briskly and smiled. "Well, after all that, isn't someone going to ask me my personal reason for going to Tibet?"

"We already know it," her mother said. "The same motivation

you've had for everything in the past decade: You want to find Julie."

Evidently it wasn't much of a secret. Her father took her plate, filled it with steaming crepes, and handed it back to her. "Eat up," he said. "They'll be the last you get for a while."

Crepes were her favorites, and she'd miss them, but it was a small price to pay. She was on her way to the Roof of the World. There was no way to tell what secrets were buried in those endless glaciers or hidden among those exquisite peaks. There was, in fact, only one thing she knew for sure: If there was to be an end to her search, that end would be found in Tibet.

FOUR

Kenilworth, Illinois—July 17, 1981

A car sped down the boulevard a hundred yards from the study, but Matt knew it wasn't Bekki. The engine missed on two cylinders, and she wasn't the type to let her car's engine sputter. He rose from the swivel chair and left his notes on the Thornton case in the lamp's white glare. It illuminated only what was beneath it, just a ten-inch dot. It was only good for solitary work, writing briefs or reading cases, not for pleasure. As Matt walked to the window and stared at the darkness beyond the elm trees, a cicada screeched, a sound like sheet metal ripping, then stopped. Maybe it was the night, maybe it was just his mood, but the noise sliced through muscle and sinew and left him shivering. He listened to see if the noise had awakened Dylan.

Thank God, it hadn't.

Matt switched on the floor lamp and gazed at the time: twelve fifty-four. Bekki still wasn't home. Another trip to the city to search for *just* the right antique for Mr. So-and-so, she'd said. Not likely. She hadn't stopped seeing her lover. Despite the promises, she'd probably known she wouldn't from the start. Matt couldn't blame her. Not too much, anyway. The *strange,* he'd called new lovers in college; no matter how good the lover he had was, the *strange* was always better.

God, how sex makes asses of us all, he thought.

He walked to the bar, poured three fingers of Scotch into a tumbler, filled it with ice, then shook his head and threw the drink down the drain. He couldn't afford the luxury of drowning his sorrows. He had two memos due the next day. Number one would be easy enough; it recommended that the firm take a case involving copyright infringement. But the other? He hadn't

48

started on the other. It was a child custody suit, and he didn't know if he was up to that kind of battle.

He did know that he wouldn't let Dylan testify in court, if it came to that. Never. It would rip the boy in two. And Matt had to be careful. He'd talk to Bekki again, threaten her if necessary, but he had to keep his temper, be sure not to do anything that could affect visitation privileges in a divorce case. He tried to shake the confusion from his head. He walked from the study, turned on the hallway light, all the lights in the living room, the kitchen, the pantry, the bathroom, and the sauna, even the outdoor pool lights, then headed for the stairway. He switched on another 250-watter on the way to the second floor and started to feel better. He'd always believed that bad things couldn't happen in full light.

The house glowed.

The light in the upstairs hallway was always on, a concession to Dylan's nightmares, and his bedroom door was kept slightly ajar to allow for rapid escape from the vampires and mummies, werewolves and ghouls, who visited from time to time. In a way Dylan was lucky. His fears still had specific names and shapes.

The cicada screeched again as Matt pushed the door open. He held his breath and waited; Dylan remained asleep. Good thing. Once the boy awoke, it was impossible to get him back to sleep. And his night terrors weren't merely an attempt to get attention: Dylan's pupils would be dilated with fear, his head damp with perspiration. He'd bury his head against Matt's shoulder and cry and say a monster was out to get him, the wolflike thing he'd first drawn at the beach. He'd drawn it a hundred times since then, for some reason even hung the drawings in his room—almost as though they were talismans, graven images to frighten the real thing away.

Matt knelt by his son and brushed a strand of hair from the boy's face. He was a too-beautiful boy: His eyes were too large, his lashes too full. His lips were pencil-thin, and his fingers already long and bony—philosopher's hands, the book on palmistry had called them. Everything about him was so gentle, so very gentle. . . . Matt kissed him and whispered, "Whew,

Cap'n, you sure as hell didn't ask to end up in the middle of this brawl, did you?"

Dylan curled into a fetal position and rolled away from the hall's light. *Leave him alone,* Matt thought, *tonight will be bad enough without Dylan up.* Moonlight poured through the window like strained cream; shadows swayed and weaved and made the images on the wall seem even more bizarre than they were in the daytime. They'd named the monster, hoping that once the unknown had a name, it wouldn't be unknown anymore. The Creepster, they called it, slightly spooky yet not scary enough to terrify anyone.

Anyone but Dylan.

Nothing seemed to help anymore. Perhaps a psychologist would.

Matt kissed Dylan on the lips, something he would never do if the boy were awake, pulled the covers up to his chin, stood, and tiptoed into the hallway. It was thirty feet down the corridor to the master bedroom, the place where he and Bekki had always communicated best. He took off his slippers and let the carpet's soft pile press up between his toes.

The bedroom's decor was Early American, its color light blue: both Bekki's choices. The aromas—the powders, the perfumes, the deodorants—were all too familiar, all too Bekki. The only smell Matt could stand was the cedar chest. There was spring in its odor, pine trees and sunshine and catching yellow perch from a raft: all the best things about being young.

Things Dylan would never know unless they moved away.

Matt opened the lid and saw the gray Icelandic sweater he had ordered for Bekki's first Christmas present when they were both undergraduates at Madison. The first time she had worn it, it was all she wore. *It covers too much,* he'd thought when she stretched it down to her thighs. *It covers just enough,* he'd realized when he pushed it back up to her breasts and kissed the flat plane of her stomach. It had stretched and molded to any situation; it had looked as good on her in her eighth month of pregnancy as it had the first time.

Too bad he wasn't as pliable as the sweater.

He sorted through the old clothing, hoping to jog memories of vacations and parties, plays and concerts, all the things that had been brightest between them. . . .

Headlights flashed through the window, and the sound of an engine approached the house. Matt stuffed all the clothing back into the chest, placed the sweater on top, closed the lid, and sat on the bed. The engine noise stopped. A car door opened, then slammed. A long pause. The front door opened—closed—then, one at a time, the downstairs lights clicked off. There were footsteps on the stairway. Footsteps on the hallway carpet. Matt looked up as Bekki stepped into the frame of the doorway.

"Why all the lights?" she asked.

"I didn't want you to break your neck."

Bekki smiled, a purely Bekki smile with a shrug of the shoulders and a twist of the head, then walked into the room. She stopped in front of the mirror, removed her contact lenses, and shook her head as she ran her fingers through her hair. "When did you get Dylan settled in?"

"Ten. Maybe ten-thirty. He's been out ever since."

"Thank God," Bekki said, closing her eyes. "Maybe the nightmares are over."

"Yeah," Matt said. "Maybe."

Bekki walked to the corner of the bed, bent over, and kissed Matt on the top of his head. The ceiling lamp was directly behind her head, so it was impossible to see her expressions. "Use any new tricks getting him to sleep?"

"He did some math," Matt said. "We played a couple games of Atari, did a drawing of the Creepster. Then he just conked out."

Bekki walked to the full-length mirror; once, years ago it seemed, there had been a time when that would signal the start of a dance. She would turn to him and smile, then begin to dance. It wasn't a striptease, nothing crude like that; something more simple and naive. She had said it was her way of telling him that being seen naked by this one man was simple and natural, and that all the laws that regulated behavior between men and women meant nothing.

Tonight she turned away from him before she unbuttoned her blouse. She almost seemed embarrassed. She unzipped her skirt and stepped out of it. He could see the soft rises of her shoulder blades, the way her ribs moved when she breathed. God, he wanted her even now, even now. When she turned back to him, she wore only bikini briefs with thin ties at the hips and a red designer label on the silky fabric. "Those new?" Matt asked.

No response.

"I asked if the panties were new," he said.

"Matt," Bekki said. She stopped. Her face was drawn up, pursed, as though she were a child who had just tasted something bitter. Slowly, then with gathering speed, she began to nod. She shrugged. "Matt, they were a present."

He rolled out of bed, walked toward her, and took her by the shoulders. He slid his hands from her shoulders to her ribs, traced each bump with a fingertip until he reached her waist, then moved his hands to her hips. He hooked his fingers under the elastic band, then slowly slid the panties down to her thighs, being sure to pause where he was sure she would respond to his touch, then down to her knees. He released them and they fell to her ankles. "Kick them away," he said. "As far fucking away as you can."

But she remained completely still. Then she let her hands droop to her sides and began to shake her head. "No, I won't do that," she said.

"Then I'm leaving," Matt said. "Dylan comes with me."

"You're joking."

"What if I hired a detective? Had some pictures of you and lover boy for the judge? Maybe some eight-by-tens for your folks."

Bekki dismissed him with a flick of the wrist. "You're blowing off steam."

"I've been warning you for months."

"Grow up, Matt. You don't want that kind of publicity."

"I want my son."

Bekki bent over and pulled the panties back up. "But you won't get him," she said sharply, precisely, her eyes clear and hard. She walked across the room, opened the closet door, took out a long bathrobe, and put it on. "There are two reasons you won't get him," she said. "One: I'd be sure there were enough of your old flames in court to even things out." She held up another finger. "Two: You'd never put Dylan through the hell of a custody battle."

"It's hard to say what I'd do to get the chance to fry your ass." He paused and forced a smile. "Griffin's law on divorce cases: The wayward man is merely sowing wild oats, but a woman who would leave a sick son at home for a lover is a sociopath."

Bekki frowned. "You shithead!" Then she glared at him, set her jaw and started to nod, then marched into the closet. Matt's clothes started to fly through the door. "I'm sure there'll be a couch at the office," she shouted as some shoes hit the floor.

"You can stop now."

"Perhaps a room at the Y," she said as more clothing flew from the closet: some ties, a sports jacket, his tux, his hunting jacket. . . .

"I'm not going to lose my temper," Matt said.

It stopped raining clothes. Bekki peered from the closet and stared at him. "You really have grown up," she said.

"If I hadn't, you would have destroyed me long ago." Matt walked over to a pile of shirts and pants, began to sort through them, and placed the ones he would take with him on the bed.

When Bekki emerged from the closet, she was carrying two valises. "It'll go faster if I pack for you," she said.

Matt found his shaving kit and walked to the bathroom for his razor, toothbrush, and shaving cream, then walked back to the bedroom and sorted through the jewelry box for some cuff links and an extra watch. He was careful not to touch Bekki, not even to brush against her. She searched through the drawers, balled up socks, then took some shirts from the closet and carefully placed them in a garment bag so that a single stroke from the iron would remove all the wrinkles.

The cicada shrieked yet again, a sound like the intestines being ripped from metal.

Only this time it wasn't a cicada.

The cry was too hoarse, the pitch too deep. It came from down the hall, from Dylan's room. Bekki dropped the shirts onto the bed. "Christ," she said, "what's that?"

Roaring filled the hallway, a sound like a ship grinding against an iceberg, an airplane skidding down a runway—only it was alive. Matt ran from the room without answering. The hallway light was off and he tripped over some loose carpeting ten feet from Dylan's room. No light leaked from under the door. Matt grabbed the doorknob. It wouldn't budge.

Suddenly the hallway light was on and Bekki stood next to him. "Dylan," she shouted, "open the door!"

The screech kept pouring through the door, constant, deafening. It didn't seem possible that a human could make such a noise.

"Dylan!" Matt shouted. No answer. Matt crashed his shoulder into the door. It was oak, made in the 1880's with the rest of the house, and it didn't budge. He threw himself against it. Pain streaked through his shoulder and arm. "Where's the key?" he asked, gasping.

"The cupboard? The basement? How am I supposed to know? What if the housekeeper has it?"

"Find it!"

Bekki sprinted down the stairs. Matt ran back to the bedroom, tried to lift the cedar chest but found it was too heavy, opened the lid and pulled out the clothes, then lifted it to his shoulder and carried it down the hallway. The door might have been made of oak, but the door knob was old, worn metal. He slammed the chest once, twice into the knob. Nothing. The chest shattered on the third try, and the door sprang open. He flicked the switch to the overhead light, but the room remained dark.

The only light was moonlight flowing through the window; shadows from the swaying tree limbs outside the window made the room flicker, weave, dance. All colors were drained. It was a world of the negative, all black and white and terribly out of focus.

And the sound.

Dylan sat rigidly on the bed; covers were scattered on the floor. He was naked with his head tilted back at a frightening angle, his mouth gaping open. The scream pulled his features into a Halloween mask. His eyes were blank, a phosphorescent white, his lips pulled tight against his teeth. The muscles stuck out from his neck, shoulders and arms like strings, and seemed to knot, to roll in steady ripples.

Matt looked at Dylan's head. It must have been the moonlight. It had to have been the moonlight. An aura, a faint halo, seemed to sprout along his hairline. It was more than a halo, more than a ring; it was a constant glow.

And the sound, the sound: It grated and ripped and tore through Matt's mind.

He slapped the boy. It was like hitting a statue. "Dylan!" Matt screamed. He crawled across the floor and frantically searched for the cord to the night-light. He touched the shade. The switch. The wire. The plug. He dragged it to the wall and found an outlet.

When the lights came on, the roaring stopped.

Dylan lay back, his eyes closed, his sheet soaked in sweat and urine. His body twitched once, then twice, then his tension started to melt, and he curled into a fetal position. A leg straightened out, twitched, then lay still.

Matt crawled back to the bed. *A pulse,* he thought, *God, let there be a pulse!* He took Dylan's hand and pressed his thumb against the boy's wrist.

There was.

It was racing at an incredible speed, but strong. Matt leaned back on his knees and started to sigh, almost weep, with relief. He checked Dylan's breath—rapid and shallow, but it was there. His forehead was hot, at least 103.

Bekki stood in the doorway. The more she stared at Dylan, the condition of the room and bed, the more her face twisted. She gasped and ran into the room crying.

Matt took her hand. "It's okay, Bek," he said. Bekki sat on the bed and pulled Dylan against her. When she touched him, his eyelids fluttered open. Foam caked his mouth. He tried to speak but made no noise.

"What is it, darling?" she asked, rocking the boy back and forth, cuddling him, stroking his matted hair.

It was simple to see the word he was trying to form, *Creepster,* but it came out as two grunts. He started to cry, then swallowed, flinching with pain at each sob. The only sounds he made were harsh raspings.

"He could have hurt his vocal cords," Matt said. "I'll get Dr. Gower." He stood and started to run from the room.

"Please bring some orange juice!" Bekki said. She choked back a sob.

Matt ran down the stairs into the study, dialed, and had to threaten the doctor's answering service with a lawsuit, then assault, before they gave him the number of Dylan's pediatrician. When the doctor answered the phone, Matt left only his name, address, and a short message: "My son may be dying."

Matt slammed down the receiver, walked into the kitchen, poured the orange juice into Dylan's Flintstones mug, and took it upstairs.

Bekki had filled a basin of water and was gently washing Dylan's face and talking to him in whispers, murmurs. "Fucking doctors," Matt said as he handed the mug to Bekki.

She eased Dylan's head into her palm, helped support him, and let him drink; he winced at each sip. "He's coming?" she asked.

"Or he'd better hire a bodyguard," Matt said. He glanced around the room. The drawings of the Creepster had been ripped from the wall, then neatly piled onto a chair. Dylan's collection of stuffed dogs was arranged in a precise circle around its base. It looked like an altar, a bizarre, primitive altar. Matt walked back to the light switch. The mechanism was broken, and the switch flopped up and down.

"What happened?" Bekki asked. In her relief she looked soft, vulnerable, again.

"When I finally found a light to turn on, it was like pulling the plug on Dylan. He slumped over and the screaming stopped."

"What about the switch?"

"He must have smashed it somehow. A chair?" Matt paused while Bekki lifted the washcloth from the basin and wiped some mucus from beneath Dylan's nose. He nuzzled against her. "Did you see it?" Matt asked.

"What?"

"The light around his head."

"Shit, Matt, I'm scared enough as it is."

"It was there."

"This hasn't been an easy night," she said. "When was the last time you had some sleep?"

"It was there." A slight breeze swept through the window, and the tree limbs, silver in the moonlight, brushed against the window like claws. Dylan tensed. His eyes widened and he stared at the window.

Matt sat down on the bed next to Dylan and put his hand on the boy's head. "Relax, son," Matt said, moving his hand to Dylan's shoulder. "We're here and the light's on and everything's all right now."

But Dylan remained tense, alert, ready to scream, although he couldn't scream. He kept staring at the window, staring as though he expected something horrible to burst through the glass and devour them all.

FIVE

Jael turned away from the funeral pyre and let her eyes sweep up a brittle ridge toward a peak so high it staggered her imagination. As beautiful as the mountains were, to stare at them was escapism. The real test was within the monastery, within her mind.

A yellow-robed Buddhist monk approached a brazier and thrust a torch deep into the glowing coals. He bowed first to the compassionate deity Chenrezi, then to the wrathful Mahakali who drank blood from skulls and danced on a carpet of human skin, then turned toward the pyre and set it ablaze. As the flames spread through the wood the pyre became an inverted bowl of flames.

Jael closed her eyes and tried to shake the image of the burning car away. She pulled the damp shirt-sleeve from her wrist. How could she be sweating? The monastery was at thirteen thousand feet, her breath condensed as it touched the air, and she wore only a sweater; her down coat was in the room she shared with Chris.

She took three deep breaths, but the queasiness just would not disappear. Maybe it was the three hundred monks hypnotically chanting *"Om mani padme hum."* Maybe it was the knowledge that everyone in the monastery except she and Chris, and perhaps Yen Hui, the Chinese cultural liaison, believed that the corpse's spirit still hovered above the fire and would be driven toward reincarnation only when the body was destroyed. Maybe it was merely . . . No matter what it was, she had to get control of herself.

Flames jumped from branch to branch and white smoke swirled away. How could the cinders of a two-week-old corpse smell so sweet? Unless Jael put some distance between herself and

58

the event, she'd have to leave. It was time to create a distraction. She slipped a cassette into the tape recorder, pushed a green button, and lifted the mike to her lips: "Yellow, green, and red funeral banners loop from building to building. A toothless beggar with oozing sores spins his prayer wheel, chants his chants, and envies the soul who is free from the prison of its body. There is absolute faith in the nodding of the old man's head, faith in the cadence of his words."

Jael envied the beggar's faith as the beggar envied the soul's freedom. Only an idiot could find faith in this ceremony. There was sham everywhere: The funeral wrappings hadn't blackened, so the sweet smoke couldn't come from the corpse; no, it was from the sacred plants, juniper and sandalwood, not flesh. The pyre had levels and compartments that channeled the fire to a hollow directly beneath the corpse where something, a cache of tinder or a vial of oil, exploded and shot flames through the wood.

Another magician's trick.

Soon the linen wrappings smoked, then burned off the body. Then hair singed and the flesh sizzled and split and blackened and the air filled with the smell of broiling pork.

The world started to spin. Jael stumbled backward.

Chris grabbed her arm. "You gonna make it?"

"Probably not."

He started to lead her away. "I'll take you back to the room."

"Someone has to stay and record this," she said. "It appears as though it won't be me."

"The cremation isn't that important."

"It may be part of my book," she said. "It *is* that important." She took three deep breaths, then shook her head. "Don't worry, I'll circulate and gather some local color."

Chris swept a lock of hair from her damp cheek, then kissed her on the back of the neck. "Be careful," he said, motioning behind her. The cliff. Another three, maybe four steps backward and she'd start the two-thousand-foot plunge to the valley floor. There were no guardrails or warning signs; this wasn't the Grand Canyon. No other westerners had visited the Bod Ombu monastery since the Chinese invasion thirty years before, and the monks showed no concern for the locals. If a villager or monk were killed, everyone would believe it was the result of his karma, the psychic residue of previous lives.

Jael nodded respectfully to Yen Hui, moved away from the cliff, walked through the monks surrounding the pyre, then squeezed through the villagers who packed the courtyard. They smelled of a world of close contact with animals and no water to spare for baths. A wisp of red smoke rose from the fire. More charlatanism. The color change showed the worshipers that the spirit had left the body and was starting the journey toward reincarnation. The monks chanted to the disembodied soul:

> *O nobly born, that which is called death hath come. Thou art departing from this world, but thou art not the first; death cometh to all. Cling not in fondness and weakness to this life. . . .*

Jael sidestepped a yak carrying peddlers' wares, then headed toward the stairway that rose to the top of the courtyard wall. Each step was about four inches high, so she took them three steps at a time, and although she was gasping for air by the time she reached the top, the strain helped her mind to clear.

She stood atop the wall and tried to imagine the world beyond the peaks. To the north lay China, Mongolia, eventually Siberia. To the south Nepal, India, Sri Lanka, then ocean all the way to Antarctica. And either east or west, depending on how far she wished to travel, lay home. Somehow the miles were an inadequate way to measure the distance between a Rush Street bar and a Buddhist prayer cell. No matter how far Chris's expeditions had taken her, she never felt *this* far from home. The Sahara had been vast, but it had no peak high enough to let her see how vast. The Yucatán had been claustrophobic, relentless. No matter what was cut down, carved out, or blown up, the vegetation would return in a matter of months. But Tibet. Tibet. Here she could see forever and still know she saw nothing. Here everything radiated eternity, everything: art, religion, geography. Here all matter and thought was *stong-ba-nyid*, emptiness, solitude, meaninglessness.

Stong-ba-nyid, the perfect way to describe her feelings since Julie died.

Her search had to end here. It was inevitable, just.

She stared up at the prayer cells, twenty caves carved into the granite cliff above the monastery. The hermit-saints lived there, but the abbot had said no, they didn't talk to westerners, particularly not women.

Maybe.

Jael walked across the top of the wall, descended into a lower courtyard, and approached the temple's enormous bronze doors. Four snarling statues wearing crowns of skulls kept watch on either side of the doorway. She tried to sense their power, but to her they were only stone and iron and remained utterly lifeless.

A large hall lay behind the doors. At the far end was an altar that housed a gold statue of the Buddha. Frescoes of gods blessing the faithful and demons torturing the damned covered the walls. As Jael approached the altar, a monk entered through the side door and walked toward her. He stopped by the altar, hesitated, then bowed. He was bald, as all monks were bald, and his ears stuck straight out. One thing about his features was unusual: His skin was cracked from the wind and sun. The other monks had been mushroom-pale, with skin so soft that blue veins throbbed at their temples.

And his eyes.

There certainly wasn't the saintliness she hoped to find. His eyes were too alive, too *knowing;* they moved constantly, assessing her dress, expression, stance. Jael became nervous when he didn't speak. "The abbot allows me to study your temple," she said. When his expression didn't change, when there was no sense of recognition in his eyes, she realized she'd spoken in English. She repeated the phrase in Tibetan.

The monk still didn't answer. There was one way in which he was very like a monk and very little like other men: His eyes stayed locked on her face instead of wandering over her body. "I saw you on the wall," he said in Tibetan. "You stared at the saints' cells as I stared at them when I was a boy."

"Do you know any saints?"

"All killed when the Chinese came," the monk said.

No wonder the abbot wouldn't let her see them.

"People who look for saints really look for miracles," the monk said. Suddenly he scurried up to Jael. A hand covered by warts emerged from the robe and grabbed the sleeve of her sweater. "Come," he said. "I will show you miracles."

The monk led her through a side door into the central courtyard. Seven small shrines were stuck in the wall, each with its own multi-armed deity, each with a notch for offering sacrifices. They entered a building that was rancid with the smell of old yak-butter lamps, walked down a dark hallway, and turned into the monks' sleeping quarters. They were barely sleeping quarters, just mats on the floor. Jael didn't enter but listened for footsteps in the hall. The monk pulled on her sleeve, but she wouldn't budge.

"This is the first cremation since the Chinese," the monk said. "A show for westerners. The monks will chant and burn until midnight." Jael made one final check of the hallway before she walked in and sat down on a mat. She hoped there weren't any lice. The monk dropped into a lotus position in front of her. And sat there. Without speaking. For what seemed like minutes. Finally Jael started to fidget.

"Do you have *yuan?*" he whispered.

Jael started in surprise.

"Yuan," the monk repeated. "Money."

It was the first step in bartering, a game Jael had played regularly since she arrived in Tibet. "How many *yuan* I have depends on the size of your miracle."

And the monk was on his feet. His movements were so sudden that they almost seemed like an illusion. He glided to the doorway and motioned for Jael to remain silent while he listened for footsteps. When he was satisfied they were safe, he returned to the mat, reached beneath it, and withdrew a long, thin object in a red cloth. He crept up to her and whispered, "A miracle."

Beneath the cloth was a dagger, more of a sword, actually. It was curved like a scimitar but narrow at the hilt and four inches wide at the tip. It shined with a peculiar reddish-gold hue in the dust-softened sunlight; the color wasn't from rust but from some process involved in the forging. The handle was made of a single piece of ivory etched with carvings of unearthly animals: the wolf-gods of the Red Bon, the most magical of all the pre-Buddhist Tibetan religions. Legends said the Bon conjured demons, controlled the weather, and communicated with the dead. While the Buddhists coexisted with other Bon sects, they systematically wiped out the Red Bon. Swords like the one Jael held were used by the Red Bon to control the demons they conjured.

"A *phurba*," she said.

The monk nodded.

"But new," Jael said. "The last *phurba* was forged a thousand years ago."

"The *Bonpoba* exist only when there is need," the monk said, staring at her. He was anything but monklike. Now there was violence in his eyes, violence and a clearly distinguishable evil. She might have left—if he weren't a man with miracles. "What do you know of the *chöd?*" he asked.

"A Bon ceremony. A shaman disembowels himself, scatters his blood to the wind, then magically heals himself." She brushed her hand across her face to remove a strand of hair. "The symbolism involves death and rebirth."

"Western nonsense," the monk said. "Men lose their lives. None return to life."

"Human sacrifice?"

"Many benefit from the deaths of a few." The monk shrugged, then rewrapped the sword and placed it under the mat. He paused again. The pounding of drums rolled in from the courtyard. "The Chinese forbid novices to join the monastery, so old men must till the fields," the monk said. "I am fifty-five. I don't wish to till the fields at eighty."

"How many *yuan* for a miracle?" Jael asked.

"Sherpas will take me across the mountains for five hundred *yuan*. For another five hundred, I can travel to Delhi. For a thousand I can buy a hut."

"Two thousand, then," Jael said.

"Ten thousand," the monk said. "I don't wish to beg at eighty."

"Too much."

The monk leaned forward, smiled, and whispered, "And if the Red Bon have a shrine on Sagarmatha?" he asked. "There will be a *chöd* in three days. We can see it if we leave tonight."

Jael leaned back on her hands and looked up at the grease-stained ceiling. A *chöd*, she thought. Not likely. All the magical religions were gone. Civilization had destroyed them. Druidism wiped out by the Romans. Egyptian cults replaced by Islam. The Aztecs slaughtered by the Spanish. To witness a Red Bon ceremony was to take a ride back in a time machine . . . and who knew where the ride would end? If a ticket existed to the other-world, it would probably lie in the *chöd*. "What if the Red Bon catch us?" Jael asked.

"We die," the monk said.

All her trips into the field had been dangerous. The Sahara could dry you up and spit you out, and the Yucatán had more deadly plants, animals, and microbes per square inch than any-where on earth, and they hadn't offered a chance to witness the *One* ceremony. "Your name?" she asked.

"Yum Gyeba," the monk said.

"My name is Jael, and I have ten thousand *yuan*."

"My ass," Chris said calmly as he rose from the cot and stood above Jael. He was a master of changing inflection without changing tone. He swore in the same register he said grace. "First let's consider the chance of the *chöd* occurring, then the morality of your watching it."

"Please sit down," Jael said.

Instead he moved toward the sleeping bags and started to pace. His skin was so pale, he burned whenever he was in the sun: The high-altitude sun had burned his face bright red, and now it was impossible to tell how angry he was. "It's slipped your mind, of course," he said, "that Yen Hui is escorting us to the monastery at Kula Kangri tomorrow."

"Chris, there's plenty of room on the cot," Jael said. He had expressed disappointment in her only once before, when she had questioned his method of dating some Minoan phalli. He had belittled her then, and he would belittle her now.

"You mentioned morality," she said. "Would the good professor be kind enough to explain what is immoral about watching a primitive ritual?"

Chris tugged at the collar of his jacket. "The 'good professor' notes that attending a human sacrifice implies complicity. It implies aiding and abetting a homicide. I'm sure that Yen Hui will provide the fine points of provincial law if we ask him."

"He wasn't coming with *me,*" Jael said.

Chris wasn't listening; he picked at his beard, his surest sign of displeasure. "His job doesn't require brilliance, merely observation. If we see what he wants us to see, we keep our visas and establish the contacts necessary for future trips. To risk that for any mumbo-jumbo?" He spoke the next sentence like a prayer, and its effect was devastating: "Do you realize how offending the Chinese would affect my work?"

The pronoun jumped out at Jael. "So finally it gets down to *your* work," she said. It was her turn to stand and pace. "Well, I have work, too, and a plan: You go to Kula Kangri with Yen Hui while I pretend I'm sick and stay here. As soon as you're gone, I leave for Mount Everest. Yen Hui's a man. Would you question the line 'My assistant has the monthlies and isn't up to traveling'? Just give him a man-to-man wink, a smirk; the Chinese are even more proper than you," she said, then let her voice grow softly sarcastic. "If that's possible."

He ignored the observation. "What happens when we return and Yen Hui questions the abbot about your stay?"

"My monk says the abbot takes bribes."

"You didn't mention your monk's name."

"Neither did he," Jael said. The lie hadn't hurt a bit.

Chris bent over and started to search through the pockets of his backpack. Jael couldn't see his expression. "Your monk is either insane or a liar," he finally said. "We both know the Red Bon were exterminated a thousand years ago."

She sighed and rolled her eyes. "Look," she said, "I know it's a long shot, but how many chances does a person get to step into another world?"

"And find a sister?"

"And find whatever's there," she said.

Chris looked up and shook his head in disbelief. "I suppose he promised to introduce you to a family of abominable snowmen too."

Jael walked over to the glassless window and pointed to the huge peaks, which burned red in the sun. "You could hide a city out there," she said. "Why not some priests and a shrine?" Then she slowly turned back to Chris and pointed a finger at him. "Since when did we start imposing our morals on the cultures we study?"

"It was my way of emphasizing the silliness of your scheme, no more."

There was hurt in his voice. Whether it was a reaction or strategy, she wasn't sure. Either way, Jael didn't feel good. It hurt her to hurt him. "Even if there is no *chöd*," she said, "I'm in no danger. I won't pay him until I'm safely back in this room. If he hurts me, he'll spend the rest of his life tilling fields."

"What if he's interested in something other than money?" Chris asked. There was a mixture of fear, anger, and jealousy in his voice—and a declaration of territory—in his phrasing, the same type of territory that is declared when two high schoolers fight over a cheerleader. Since she cared for him, she didn't point that out.

"Look, he's a toothless celibate whose head comes up to my shoulder." Jael paused and waited for his comeback, but there was none. "The dagger is a *phurba*. The shape's right. The engravings on the handle are right. The blade has the same sheen as the Black Mass daggers that were tempered in blood. Either his connections are real, or he's one hell of a craftsman."

"Or he stole it from a shrine."

"I'm not saying there's no risk," she said. "He could hire some friends and stage the ceremony for less than ten thousand *yuan*. But what price would you put on watching an authentic druid ritual? Or an Egyptian conjuring? Or an Aztec sacrifice? We could learn the master scheme for all the archetypes. What would that be worth?"

"They'd invent a Nobel prize for the social sciences."

Jael hesitated. She had only one strategy left, and she wanted it to sound impressive. "And we'd be the co-authors."

Chris stood by the window; the pale light darkened as the sun dropped behind the peaks. "You're offering me co-authorship of *The* One *Cult?*"

Jael nodded.

Chris walked toward her, stopped, took her by the shoulders, stared at her, then released her and kept pacing.

"Well?" she asked.

"No."

"No what?"

"No, nothing is worth the danger."

Jael didn't want to ask the next question. "Why?"

"Because I love you, and someone has to protect you."

"Chris—"

"I love you," Chris interrupted, holding a finger to her lips.

"Shit," Jael said rather weakly. Chris took her by the shoulders, kissed her forehead, then pulled her against his chest. "Shit, shit, shit," she muttered.

They hadn't made love since they arrived at the monastery—a matter of respecting proprieties and traditions—but there were new stakes. They dragged their sleeping bags next to the doorway so if someone peered in he wouldn't see anything unusual. Jael said she didn't want to be caught by the abbot, so they decided to play a game, a game they hadn't played in months: The first one to make a sound had to answer *any* question asked, *honestly.* Jael had never lost. Before.

Tonight there was a reason.

Tonight she wanted to make him trust her as he never had before, to hold her and make love to her and to sleep soundly all night long. So, after the stroking and kissing, after the coolness of the air was forgotten and the sweat stuck to them and a sweet sliding sounded each time they moved, she rolled on top of him; a little yipping noise escaped her throat when he entered her, and after that it didn't make any difference anyway, so he whispered "I love you" over and over until she kissed him quiet. He pulled down on her hips and moaned. She didn't let him rest but started to move immediately, when he was most sensitive, not as retribution for winning the game, but because it was the most intimate thing she could think of at the time.

Then, while she lay draped over him, he pulled the sleeping

bag over their heads so they breathed the same air. "You weren't really going to go?" he asked. Already his voice was sleepy, thick.

She kissed him on the lips as an answer.

Chris turned onto his right side as he always did, tucked one leg against his chest and his hand under his chin, like an infant. But Jael wasn't finished with him yet. Sex was a sleeping potion for Chris, and she wanted to be sure that he'd be out all night. She snuggled up to his back until they fit like spoons, then nibbled his earlobe. He didn't stir, so she ran a finger down his chest to his stomach until she ran out of stomach, then concentrated her efforts there.

He turned to her. "No stakes this time," he said.

Good thing he didn't know.

The moon was waxing and bright enough to transform the floor of the room into a skating pond of light. Even Chris's red mummy bag was glazed and colorless, and the lumps inside that were Chris looked like a stump covered with snow.

Jael rolled from on top of him, dried the film of sweat, dressed quickly as her body steamed in the cold, stuffed a week's worth of supplies into her knapsack, then laced her hiking boots. She'd been quiet and careful. Chris burrowed deeper into the sleeping bag.

Yum Gyeba would be waiting at a slope of shattered rock outside the monastery. They would climb a thousand-foot ridge in the dark, drop into a valley by morning, and after that . . . ? She'd never ridden a yak before, but from what she'd heard, their backs were so wide that she couldn't fall off, and they were surefooted enough that she could trust them on the narrowest path.

It hadn't been easy to set Chris up, at least not emotionally, but it was even harder to write the letter. After stuffing three attempts into her pocket, she wrote a fourth:

Dear Chris:
    There are things I have to find out, things I'll never be able to explain to you. Imagine never being alone. Never being afraid of anything by yourself. Imagine sharing happiness, hope, in a way which doubles, triples, the joy.

If you were capable of understanding, you would have patted me on the head, smiled that paternal smile of yours, and wished me luck.

Then, things always seem to work out better in dreams than in reality.

This is getting harder. Yen Hui will never fathom what I've done if you stick to the alibi.

I do love you,
Jael

She removed her parka from the peg on the wall, pinned the letter to Chris's pack, walked across the room, and bent to kiss him—but that was too risky. Instead she tiptoed past him and blew him a kiss from the door. She slipped the knapsack onto her shoulders, took a deep breath for courage, then moved from the doorway into the tunnel of darkness that was the hallway.

SIX

Chicago, Illinois—July 20, 1981

If the Miró on the wall and the Alexander Calder mobile hanging from the ceiling of Dr. Ruth Velde's office reflected her skill as accurately as the size of her fees, Dylan couldn't be in better hands. Not that it made things any easier for Matt. He never had been any good at waiting; it was the most helpless feeling in the world. He glanced at the oak paneling, the ultramodern glass and chrome desk, the huge window that filled the room with sunlight, then searched through a pile of magazines on the end table. When he discovered he was too nervous to read, he drew figure eights in the carpet with the toe of his shoe.

Bekki sat across the room, smoking a cigarette and carefully reading a copy of *The New Yorker*. Matt shook his head and looked back at the swirling mobile. *All those years together,* he thought, *and there's so little left to say.*

"Bek?" he asked.

She raised her eyes without raising her head. "Please, Matt, the more we talk, the harder this is going to be."

"There's a lot to straighten out," Matt said. He lifted his chair and moved it across the room next to her. When she continued to read, he gently took the magazine from her hands and set it on the floor behind him. *Then* she looked at him. Matt spoke first. "What if we're the cause of this?"

"What are our options?" Bekki asked, tilting her head and straightening her skirt. "Would it help him to live in a house where every word led to an argument?"

"I don't know," Matt said. He closed his eyes, rubbed his forehead, then looked back at Bekki. "Would it be easier on him to end up in the middle of a court battle?"

She made a wry face. "You'd put him through that?"

"Not unless I was damn sure I could win," Matt said.

Bekki crushed her cigarette and immediately took another from the pack. She put it to her lips and lighted it—or tried to light it. The butane flame didn't catch. Matt took a small box of wooden matches from his pocket, struck one, waited for the sulfur to burn, then held out the flame to her. "You're smoking?" she asked.

"They let me be chivalrous to pretty ladies."

"Please, Matt, it just won't work." Bekki leaned back, stared at the ceiling, and inhaled deeply. She held the smoke for a short time, then exhaled. Matt handed the magazine back to her, moved his chair across the room. He picked up an *Esquire* and tried to find something interesting; he just wasn't in the mood. This time when he looked back at Bekki, she was absently flipping through her magazine too.

Then a door opened.

Bekki and Matt were both on their feet and moving toward Dr. Velde before she entered the room. She was short, with white hair tied in a bun, wire-framed glasses, and a crisp print dress. She looked more as though she should be stirring a kettle on a wood-burning stove than running the most prestigious psychological clinic in the Midwest.

"Where's Dylan?" Bekki asked.

"With an assistant," Dr. Velde said. She gestured for them to bring the chairs to her desk. "Please sit down."

"How is he?" Matt asked.

Dr. Velde smiled. "I think he'll be all right." Her smile grew wider, wide enough to be convincing. "I need some questions answered before we start the next series of tests." She walked behind her desk and sat down.

Matt carried two chairs to the desk. He held one for Bekki, then sat down. Dr. Velde took a pack of cigarettes from the desk, offered Bekki and Matt one, and, when they refused, asked, "Mind if I have one?" She lit one, took a deep puff, and leaned back. "When did Dylan's nightmares begin?"

"He's always had bad dreams," Bekki said. "They've only become unbearable in the last few months."

"Any falls or blows to the head?"

71

"Nothing we know of," Bekki said. "Nothing that left marks."

Dr. Velde leaned forward and rested the cigarette on the lip of an ashtray. "When was the first time you noticed this creature?"

"Four, four and a half months ago," Matt said. "He drew it at the beach."

"Did either of you suggest it to him? Even accidentally?"

"You're joking," Bekki said.

"He was alone," Matt said. "Bekki and I were arguing."

Dr. Velde shifted her weight and leaned back. "What is the status of your marriage?"

"We're going to be divorced," Bekki said.

Matt leaned forward and asked, "Can we hold the background information for a second?"

"Of course."

"What happened to my son?"

"You're referring to the unusual screaming?"

"For starters," Matt said.

Dr. Velde nodded slowly and stroked her chin while she organized her thoughts. "Abnormal strength, intelligence, and the like aren't uncommon during hysteria."

"Which doesn't explain the glowing."

"No, it doesn't," Dr. Velde said. She rested a hand on her hip, then raised a finger to emphasize a point. "You were under tremendous stress."

"I saw it."

"I'm sure you thought you did. . . . Dr. Gower's report shows only evidence of a strained larynx."

"And a child radiating light doesn't fit into any of your theories," Matt said.

"There are a number of things about Dylan that are unusual," Dr. Velde said. She pushed herself away from the desk and drummed her fingers on one of the drawers. When the light from the window crossed her face, she squinted and moved forward again. "Are either of you familiar with the Rorschach test?"

"Only that it involves inkblots," Bekki said.

"There's a bit more to it than that," Dr. Velde said. "The first thing the evaluator must do is gain the patient's trust. While that normally takes awhile, Dylan is a very trusting young man." She paused long enough to let the compliment register. "When I was fairly sure I could trust his responses, I handed him a card with an inkblot on it and asked him if it reminded him of anything. When he finished his response, I took the card back from him and went on to the next. After we finished all ten, I handed them back to him one at a time and asked him to repeat his answers and discuss them in more detail."

"Sounds a tad complex for a six-year-old," Matt said.

"The test is equally valid on three-year-olds and eighty-year-olds," Dr. Velde said, tapping the ash off her cigarette.

"What does all this tell you?" Bekki asked.

"That depends on what I'm looking for. In this case, Dylan's developmental level and his level of anxiety." She paused and glanced at the note pad on top of her desk, then back at Matt. With the cigarette wedged between her middle and index fingers, her glasses resting on the tip of her nose, and her eyes evaluating every word and gesture, she looked a lot less like a granny and a lot more like a psychologist. "Dylan gave me some very interesting responses."

"Abnormal?" Bekki asked.

"I'm not sure *abnormal* applies to Dylan." Dr. Velde waited for questions before she continued. Bekki didn't say anything; Matt had nothing to say. "Are either of you mythologists?" she continued. "Perhaps archaeologists?"

"I'm a lawyer," Matt said. "Bekki's an interior decorator."

"Any unusual hobbies?"

"I paint, if that's unusual," Bekki said.

"Do you incorporate mythological themes into your works?"

"If I borrow from anyone, it's the Impressionists."

Dr. Velde pushed her glasses up to the bridge of her nose and wrinkled her brow. "You seem surprised," Matt said.

"Mildly." Dr. Velde started to rock again and tapped her fingers on one of the chair's arms. "And you have no friends who are experts in Assyrian or Babylonian culture."

"What are you getting at?" Bekki asked.

Dr. Velde took a final deep puff from the cigarette and let the smoke escape through her nose. She crushed the stub in the ashtray, then removed a stack of cardboard squares from the top drawer of her desk. "Dylan's responses show an unusual degree of developmental inconsistency."

Matt whistled and held up his hands. "You'll either have to be more simplistic or slow down."

"I can do better than that: I'll show you what I mean." She took two cards from the pile and laid them faceup on the desk.

Matt was disappointed when nothing came to his mind as she laid down the first card. It was a blob, nothing more. The second card was easier: he immediately saw a four-legged bird sitting on a bearskin.

"We measure a patient's development by ranking the complexity of his responses," Dr. Velde continued. "For this card Dylan's responses were 'a bat' and 'a sea creature.' For number six, 'a star' and 'an explosion.' Note how he responds to the shape as a whole. A very simple set of responses."

"Anything wrong with that?" Bekki asked.

"Hardly. It's called a W-minus response, and it's exactly what we expect from six-year-olds." She took two more cards from the stack and laid them on top of the desk.

Dr. Velde traced the outline of the first card with her index finger. "But Dylan's response to this—and it was instantaneous—was 'two lions with wings carrying Mom away.'"

"He said *that?*" Bekki asked.

"It's not necessarily hostile. It could express the fear of your leaving. Children whose parents are breaking up often have an inordinate terror of being left alone."

"I moved out the day after the incident," Matt said. "I'm living downtown. I only get to see him on weekends."

"That could account for part of it," Dr. Velde said, nodding slowly. "But what's most interesting is the complexity of the response." She traced the lions, their wings, then the woman in the blot's center. "Note how he divided the blot into three distinct segments, then reunited them into a single concept. It's called the W-plus-plus response, and it shows the highest level of conceptual ability."

"He's always been precocious," Matt said.

"There's something beyond precocity here, Mr. Griffin. Mythology has a name for winged lions: griffins. There was a possibility that Dylan was punning on your name." Dr. Velde turned toward Bekki. "Has he shown this level of sophistication before?"

"Not that I know of," Bekki said.

Dr. Velde held up card number three. "A typical response for an anxious six-year-old might be a crab or a spider. Dylan said: 'Two people with knives standing over a table. They just cut the heart from something.'"

"God," Bekki said. "That sounds like a sacrifice."

"My conclusion also," Dr. Velde said.

"Dylan's sacrifice?" Matt asked. "With Bekki and I as high priests?"

"We have no way of knowing that," Dr. Velde said. "All we know for sure is that the impending divorce accounts for his anxiety. But the W-plus-plus responses? He had seven. An intelligent adult might have one or two."

Bekki pointed to the cigarettes. "All of a sudden I need one," she said. Dr. Velde held out the pack, then the lighter. Bekki took a deep drag and released the smoke in puffs. "What about the Creepster?"

"I asked Dylan to draw whatever was on his mind. He made pictures of your house, a sailboat, his hamster. They were clearly the work of a child. Lines wobbled. The sense of proportion was off. Everything was flat. Then he handed me this."

Dr. Velde took a piece of lined notebook paper from the top of her desk and handed it to them. It was one of the most sophisticated line drawings Matt had ever seen. The square ears, the pointed snout, the erect tail and long fangs, everything flowed together as though it had been done with a single line. There was even a sense of personality, not like Rembrandt or Vermeer—more as if Picasso had tried to emulate a sketch from an Egyptian tomb.

"The Creepster," Bekki said.

"Note the incredible steadiness of hand, the way he merges the features of real animals with imaginary ones. Even the sophisticated way for making it look sinister—two simple lines extending from the eyes."

"How did he do it?" Matt asked.

"I have no idea. A better question might be *why* with just this one picture?" Dr. Velde rested her chin on her hand and shook her head. "Right now I just don't know."

Bekki sat up rigidly and frowned. "Exactly what *do* you know?" she asked. Her voice rose and broke in frustration.

"That I can help him adjust to the anxiety of his parents' divorce. I'd like to see him once a week. Maybe more later."

"When can we see him?" Matt asked.

"I'd like to administer one final test. It's called diagnostic play therapy. It allows him to express the causes of his anxiety through his play."

"I want to be with him," Bekki said.

"That would invalidate the test. There is an observation room available." Again she pushed the glasses to the bridge of her nose. "Here's a warning: A child's play can be painfully revealing."

"We want to be there," Matt said.

The playroom was like a Disney movie in which the toys are as big as the actors. Mobiles hung from the ceiling, rocking horses and trains were scattered across the floor, and posters and a large mirror decorated the red and yellow wall. The room even smelled like candy. A large dollhouse stood in the center of the floor. It was more than four feet tall, with a dining room, a living room, a kitchen, bedrooms, and a game room. It had been cut in half so all the rooms were accessible. It was a dream house for all the eight-inch dolls deposited in a nearby toy box. A zoo's worth of stuffed animals were bulging from a box by the wall.

Dr. Velde nodded toward the dollhouse. "It will allow Dylan to establish family relationships, softened by the fact that the participants will be dolls instead of real people. He may exaggerate some things—wish fulfillment. It can seem rather silly at times." She led them across the room and opened the door by the large mirror. The observation room was small, scarcely large enough to hold five chairs. "Feel free to talk; the booth is soundproof." She raised her hand and emphasized her words by pointing with a finger. "Don't enter the playroom until we leave. And don't mention that you watched him. It's crucial that he trusts me." She stepped into the playroom and closed the door.

As soon as she left, the silence began.

There had been too much silence for one day. "Everything she's said so far blames us," Matt said.

"Obviously," Bekki said.

"So now what?"

"Now we watch," Bekki said. "Then we talk about what we see. Then we make the most adult decision available."

"I mean about the three of us?"

Bekki bit her lip, put her hand on Matt's shoulder, and said gently, "You really are a good person, and I *loved* you once, but no matter what happens, you and I are done."

"And Dylan?"

"I'm not saying the first months won't be hard on him. But you love him. I love him. We'll help him through."

The sound of a slowly opening door filtered through the speakers. Framed by the mirror, the playroom looked as though it were on TV. It reminded Matt of soap operas, and for the first time all day he was embarrassed, embarrassed that a thirty-four-year-old man with a room full of degrees had to go to a shrink to tell him what he knew all along: that his son was tortured by the fact that Matt couldn't keep his wife.

Dr. Velde entered the playroom with Dylan holding her hand. As soon as they were inside, Dylan pressed his shoulder tighter against her leg. *So even the colors and toys aren't easing his fear,* Matt thought. She led Dylan around the room, pointed out a panda here, a caboose there. Then they moved along the wall and stopped at the poster: a smiling sun; an orangutan that looked like a sumo wrestler. Dylan stopped when they arrived at the mirror and ran his hand over the glass. He didn't seem to focus on his reflection, but at something beyond it.

"He knows we're here," Bekki said.

"It's a one-way mirror," Matt said.

"Mom and Dad gonna get here soon?" Dylan asked, his voice sounding scratchy over the cheap speakers. His face moved closer to the mirror and he tapped the glass hopefully with his fingers.

Dr. Velde's face showed no surprise. Which surprised Matt. "I want to keep you to myself for a little longer," she said.

Dylan continued to stare at the mirror, then nodded and, evidently satisfied, turned and led Dr. Velde to the dollhouse. He bent over and looked inside. "Think Mom and Dad are going to get back together?"

"I don't know them well, Dylan. I won't tell you things that I can't be sure of."

Then Dylan led Dr. Velde to the toy box and finally released her hand. The more involved he became with the toys, the better Matt felt. Dylan dropped to a squat and rummaged through the stuffed animals. He picked up a cat, one with a chewed-on ear and a pulled-off tail, and frowned. "The Creepster got this one."

"Does the Creepster ever say if he's going to hurt you?" Dr. Velde asked.

"Not me."

"What about your mom and dad?"

"He doesn't talk . . . not really."

"Then what does he do?"

"I don't know," Dylan said, "but I know what he wants. He wants to get away from where he lives and come live with me."

"Where does he live?"

"It's cold and lonely and . . . it's different," Dylan said. Then he shrugged. It was such an adult, apathetic shrug that it tore out Matt's heart. Dylan selected a stuffed dog and a crocodile, laid them next to the dollhouse, then walked to another toy box and pulled out one doll dressed in a business suit, one in a wedding dress, and a naked baby doll. He looked up at Dr. Velde. "I told them not to get divorced," Dylan said. His head drooped against his chest. Because he faced away from the mirror, there was no way Matt could see his face, but Dylan had a way of tightening his shoulders and shuddering when he sobbed that was unmistakable. He gasped for air. "When they're together, they don't even look at each other."

"Satisfied?" Matt asked.

Bekki turned to him and gave him a look she might have given to Dylan if he were misbehaving.

Dylan hugged the dolls as he cried. Dr. Velde placed her hand on his head. He looked up and said, "Don't tell anyone that they're getting divorced."

"There's no reason to be ashamed," Dr. Velde said. "You're probably the reason they stayed together as long as they did."

The boy's tears slowed, then stopped, although he still shuddered when he spoke. "Just don't tell anyone." He stood and walked toward the dollhouse, then picked up the crocodile and dog and threw them down. "Sometimes I get angry."

"You wouldn't be normal if you didn't."

"Some pretty bad things happen at night," Dylan said.

"What kind of things?"

Dylan looked vacant, incredibly distant. Matt had seen that look too often in the past months: It was the look of a sixty-year-old instead of a six-year-old. Matt turned to Bekki. "If anything happens to my son because you *had* to fuck around . . ."

Bekki turned to him, nodding and frowning. "Did it ever occur to you that you might be the reason I fuck around? Did you ever even ask?" She began to shake her head. "There are times I think Dylan has more sense than you."

Dylan placed the man, woman, and baby dolls in the bathtub together. He smiled as he pretended to turn on the water. He took them out, used one of the miniature towels to dry them, then set them around the dining-room table. The smile faded and was replaced by wide eyes and a grimace. He took all three dolls, placed them in the master bedroom, all in the same bed, then took the furniture from the dining room and stacked it inside the master bedroom's door. He found as many sheets and blankets as he could, even removed tablecloths from some of the other rooms, and piled them on the bed, completely covering the dolls.

He picked up the stuffed dog and forced it down onto the back of the crocodile. He tinkered with the dolls until they stayed together.

"What's that?" Dr. Velde asked.

"The Creepster."

And slowly, ever so slowly and carefully, Dylan walked the Creepster up the walls of the house, across the roof, then through every room but the master bedroom. Then he walked it up the chimney and stuck it on the peak of the roof, directly above the bedroom. And he left it there, perched high, glaring down from where it could threaten and dominate everything that lay beneath it.

SEVEN

A Trail Near Mount Everest—July 22, 1981

There was something insane in the Himalayas, something not sane about their vastness and their silence. The silence went beyond Jael's dreams. It was a silence that wasn't so much an absence of sound as the presence of a feeling. Jael definitely heard things. Wind ripped snow off the high ridges and avalanches rumbled down the far side of the valley, but the peaks were so enormous, the glaciers so endless, that any sound was dwarfed. No wonder the Sherpas thought the mountain was a goddess. In every culture Jael studied, there was a myth about a person who saw the naked face of a god and died. There was terror in too much beauty, and Jael knew that the goddess of the Himalayas had turned toward her. She wasn't sure how long she could resist the glance that could devour her.

She opened her eyes, saw the yak's brown-blue fur above the saddle pad, then glanced to Yum Gyeba, ten feet ahead of her on the trail. The back of his head reflected the sun as brightly as the snow. "How much farther?" Jael asked.

"We must be above the shrine and hidden by dark," the monk said without turning around. The acoustics of the gorge made his voice sound as loud as if he were facing her, all around her, within her. "Soon," he said. "Very soon."

Yum Gyeba's statement wasn't that comforting. There had already been 113 zigs up the path, and there were at least that many zags left to go. His yak turned up the next switchback and kicked a rock over the cliff. Jael counted, and after fifteen seconds it still hadn't struck bottom. Fifteen seconds at how many feet per? She couldn't remember the formula. This was no time to get mountain sickness. *Concentrate on breathing,* she thought, *deeply in, deeply out.* Just a bit more oxygen and she'd be fine.

Maybe. Her eyes bounced with the yak's rhythmic gate.

"Bon country," the monk said.

Jael sat up and tried to shake the fog from her head. Brightly colored stars made of sticks and yarn dangled the entire length of the overhang. There was something peculiar about them: They hung heavily, like meat in a butcher shop, instead of like the gay ornaments they resembled.

"Spirit traps," Yum Gyeba said. "The shape attracts evil spirits and the yarn snares them." He touched one with his bamboo rod, and it shuddered as though it were alive.

All at once the air was stale, rotten. At seventeen thousand feet there was nothing left to rot. The last wildlife Jael had seen was a marmot at fifteen thousand feet the day before. She dismounted, took her Swiss army knife from its case, and reached for the spirit trap. Her fingers snapped back as though they had touched dry ice. It felt as though all the chill in the mountains had condensed and settled in that one spot. She stared up at him. "What is it?"

The simplicity slipped from the monk's eyes. "Imagine existence without time. All time as *now*. Imagine form where there appears to be nothing. Imagine having all knowledge. . . ." He lifted a hand, then smiled, shrugged, and said, "But how does one explain the gods to a westerner?"

"Try."

He shrugged again. "You would probably call it the weather."

There *was* something unusual about this atmosphere: No doubt a ravine channeled cold air down from a snowfield. Perhaps there was an ice-fed stream nearby, something that altered barometric pressure. Whatever it was, it created an ideal spot to manufacture the occult. Jael opened the largest blade on her knife, reached through the cold, and, although her fingers were numbed, cut ten stars from their threads. She brought them back to her pack, carefully arranged them among her sweaters, then remounted the yak.

Yum Gyeba touched his yak's flank with the rod, but the animal wouldn't move past the spirit traps. Yum Gyeba struck it. Still nothing. Finally he took a carrot from his pack, tied it to the rod, and dangled it in front of the yak's nose. The animal hopped forward, lured by its appetite. Jael laughed. Almost. Maybe it wasn't so funny after all. She was just like the yak, only her appetites were different. The carrot Yum Gyeba dangled in front of her nose was the Bon, the afterworld: a mystical carrot.

The monk bounced up the path. As soon as Jael entered the shadow of the overhang her perceptions changed. The peaks that had been awe-inspiring were suddenly bloated and grotesque; Yum Gyeba's head was maggot-white instead of snow-white . . . and suddenly the invisible threads, the closeness she hadn't sensed in a decade, were in place and she shared the images of a fountain of fire, an intricate net of bright blood, red hair sizzling in a white-hot explosion. . . .

Jael jumped so abruptly that her yak bolted, hopped, and ran two strides before it slowed down. She looked up the path. Yum Gyeba stared at her, smiling.

Jael whistled and shook her head. Her symptoms were nothing like what *The Merck Manual* listed for oxygen starvation. She was supposed to experience headaches and insomnia, not hallucinations that took her back to Julie's death.

As soon as she left the shadow of the overhang, as soon as the spirit traps were behind her, she welcomed the sun's warmth, shivered away the cold, and laughed when the monk let his yak nibble—barely—on the carrot.

She stared at the steep rockslides. How many shades of black there were in the full sunlight: ebonies, grays, charcoals. There were almost as many words for black in Tibetan as white— plenty. Tibet was a world of extremes, black/white, high/low— there was very little in between.

The yak's gait eased her eyes shut, and Jael didn't open them again until she perceived a change in the path. They'd moved off the switchbacks. Although she couldn't distinguish the new path from the rest of the slope, the yak moved steadily, evenly, winding around boulders, wading rivulets of snowmelt, dropping into saddles and struggling up crests, until it reached a bridge. The cat's cradle of rope and twigs stretched across a chasm and swung back and forth in the wind. Over the edge, two, maybe three thousand feet below, was a gorge packed with ice slides.

Jael looked up at Yum Gyeba. He twitched his nose, then scratched it. "You search for the dead," he said. From his inflection she couldn't tell whether he was making a statement or asking a question.

"But I don't wish to join them," she said. Jael looked into the chasm, breathed deeply, then looked back at the monk . . . and when he smiled the dizziness was gone and her perception was so clear, she could see a vein throb on his forehead. "Lead on," she said.

She dismounted and, instead of leading the yak, let it lead her. Its hooves fell one in front of the other, a perfect line, on the wooden slats. She followed it, placed one foot in front of the other, and didn't look to either side until the bridge was behind her. They didn't remount but led the yaks onto a footpath that was worn into the granite. They stayed on it as it narrowed at a ledge, then widened as it curved around a boulder.

When Jael looked up, she knew they had arrived.

A crag jutted over the ice slide, sheer, black, half a mile above the valley floor. The luminous ice contrasted with the black stone; the view was as disturbing, as surreal, as a three-dimensional negative.

And the stench.

It was a dead place, dead like a battlefield. She could smell, *feel,* the things that had died there—no, that had been killed there, and there was little doubt that those things were human. There was a small pyramid carved directly from the granite, a single slab perhaps a hundred feet high; it had seven terraced levels and a central stairway that rose to the shrine, four pillars and a roof covering a granite altar. Yum Gyeba said that the Bon could arrive at any time, so he led her past the pyramid and into a huge field of boulders. They followed the yaks through the loose rock up to a cliff that was slightly above and two hundred feet from the shrine—close enough for a good view, yet with enough cover so that they wouldn't be seen.

Jael took her binoculars, cassette recorder, tripod, and Nikon from her pack, prefocused the camera's five-hundred-millimeter lens at the altar, loaded the camera with 1600 ASA film so she could take pictures in firelight, then set the shutter and advance for thirty seconds. By the time she finished, her hands were so weak she could scarcely close the camera.

She sat down, giddy with fear, almost nauseous from the sickness, and leaned against the boulder to watch the sunset. She was drowsy but didn't want to sleep. Just rest.

Just rest.

Jael had no idea where the fire had come from, and even less of an idea why she was running toward it. At least it was a dollhouse and not a car—or it seemed like a dollhouse. It was more an impression, a feeling, than an object. Jael dropped to one knee and peered through the scaled-down window. Julie was inside, trapped by flames. Jael tried to open the window. It wouldn't budge. The door, small as it was, was impossible to break down. Instead, Jael reached into the chimney, squeezing her hand past the cinders and bricks until her fingers opened into the room. She searched for Julie, groped until something wiggled in her hand. Jael cradled it like an infant and eased her hand up the flue. . . . Julie lay sleeping in her palm. Then Julie stirred and started to grow. Then she was full-size and her face began to blister and blacken and there was something inside her skin, something with yellow eyes, a curved snout, and fangs, and the charred hands became claws that reached out for Jael and pulled her forward. The bubbling lips puckered into a kiss. Jael screamed as she tasted flesh as salty as pork.

"Quiet," Yum Gyeba whispered. When Jael's eyelids fluttered open, he lifted his hand from her mouth. He nodded toward a line of orange dots that twisted up through the darkness. "Bon," he said.

Jael nodded that she was all right, that the dream was finished, and he helped her to her knees. *I am in the Himalayas,* she thought, *not on the North Shore. I am sick and dizzy, but if I make noise, I'll die.*

Jael took long, deep breaths, but they didn't seem to help. Everything hurt, every bone, muscle, tendon. . . . Maybe it was the sickness, but the frigid granite drained her body heat, and that was even worse. God, it was cold. Despite her three sweaters, duofold underwear, and down parka, the cold seemed to originate in her heart and radiate outward.

The noise from the Bon procession wound its way up the gorge like a serpent. Thighbone trumpets blared. Drums beat, throbbed, like a universal pulse. There was chanting, but the words were blurred by echoes and time. The language was a Tibetan dialect; Jael could distinguish the root words for wolf and death, but it was from an earlier time, a time as incomprehensible as the crag itself.

"What are they saying?" Jael asked.

"They awake the ancients of the gorge."

Jael reached for her binoculars. By the time the Bon reached the rope bridge, the orange dots weren't just bright points in the night but torches that bounced with each step and threw mushroom-shaped shadows across the chasm. Jael wondered if any fire could ease her chill. And the cold kept growing, and the pounding of the drums throbbed in her head, and she wasn't sure if the noise was drumbeats or another symptom of the sickness.

Get control, she thought. Without control, there would be no reliable data. Without reliable data, Chris would have the right to be as mad as he was probably going to be anyway. . . . But the cold—it felt so intense, so maliciously intense, that it seemed almost alive.

The first torches swung around the large boulder, and the Bon were people instead of shadows; conical hats, sleeveless robes, and masks covered their bodies. Time to become a scientist. Jael picked up the tape recorder's mike and pressed the record button: "Ceremonial robes like the druids. Staffs and torches. Long hair sticks from their hats in braids. Most of the masks simple, folds of skin with eye slits."

Four persons had no clothing or torches. There was little doubt what their role in the sacrifice would be. The priests around them wore different masks. One was humanoid, but gradually, one mask at a time, they transformed: The noses elongated and curved; the ears grew up and sharpened; the teeth became fangs. "There's an attempt to express a metamorphosis," Jael whispered into the mike. "Man becomes wolf-god. Could this be the source of the werewolf legends, all the myths of shape changing?"

Jael moved so she could get a better view of the pyramid. One by one the torches crawled up the stairway and gathered under the shrine's roof. The Bon stacked wood and started a fire. In the smoke and flickering light, the Bon were red on one side, black on the other like demons emerging from brimstone. The height of the cliffs amplified the drumbeats; Jael could scarcely hear the chanting. Four priests carried a star-shaped frame up the stairs. A prism hung from its apex and refracted firelight into the darkness.

Jael activated the camera and reached for the mike. "Could this be the prototype of all religious ceremonies?" she whispered. "The star could be the pentagram of satanic worship. The chants the conjuring. The trance demonic possession." She paused. "Could the *One* ceremony be a variation of the Black Mass?"

Again the cold washed over her and she started to gasp and wheeze. "It's so bleak," she whispered. "Horrible. Everything black and white in the moonlight."

There was no need to record hallucinations; better to let the mike pick up its own impressions. Jael turned the volume up and pointed the mike toward the altar; she activated the camera. The tape would last forty-five minutes. Too bad the film wouldn't: only thirty-six shots at thirty seconds between each exposure—eighteen minutes.

The drumbeats stopped and the priest with the wolf-head mask stepped onto the altar. He removed the mask, stiffened, looked toward the sky, and opened his mouth. A metallic roar filled the canyon. The air around him glowed. He didn't pause for a breath, just kept screeching and screeching, and the *phurba*'s blade gleamed red in the firelight. A fountain of flames exploded, shot sparks as though the fire were being squeezed at the base. The priest started to dance, waving the knife in tight circles around his head, and Jael's breath grew rapid and shallow. One of the naked men knelt, took a piece of charcoal, and traced an incision line across his abdomen, arms, and legs, aiding the priest as thousands of druid, Babylonian, and Aztec sacrificial victims had done, and the mountains seemed to close in, and the priest threw powder in the victim's face, and Jael tried to pull the parka's hood tighter to ease her chill, and four men held the victim down, and Jael felt all the fascination and self-revulsion of a peeping Tom, and the blade flashed down, and the night was clear and dark and brittle as crystal.

The priest continued to roar as he skinned the man, flayed him alive, then put on the steaming skin and started to dance.

"They become their wolf-god Htamenma," Yum Gyeba said. The hacking began.

And the Bon caught the blood, and their drums mimicked the death spasms, and the cold started to grow, and Jael thought, *What I need is objectivity and distance,* but the air was heavy with blood, heavy with sulfur and fire smell, and everything was dreamlike, hazy. The Bon started to howl.

There was something in the air, something cold and unclean. It was as if pure evil had come to life and was moving among them. Jael wanted to whimper . . . or was she whimpering already? Quiet. She had to be quiet. Whatever was out there hovered nearby, listened for her voice, her breath, the beating of her heart, watched and waited to single her out for something deadly and seductive.

Jael raised her head and looked down at the altar. A mist condensed in the clear sky and dropped down, a swirling fog that spun like a cyclone. There was a burst of light so brilliant, it illuminated the crevices on the far side of the canyon, and a roaring, a sound like a living siren, swallowed all other noise. Something emerged from the smoke and it bent to the victims like a ghoul.

And just before the pounding in Jael's head blotted out her sight, pushed her into darkness, her last thoughts were regrets. Regrets that she couldn't comprehend the terrible beauty. Regrets that she couldn't tell whether the goddess's eyes and face were Julie's.

At first Jael thought she was asleep on her waterbed and that if she could just grope her way to the drapes, the sunlight would clear her grogginess. The stench of sulfur told her she was still in Tibet. She saw images of the fog and the fire and the blood, but she didn't know where the ceremony ended and the dreams began. She opened her eyes. The light was so intense that she had to roll onto her side to focus. Judging from the position of the sun, she'd had her longest sleep in months.

A wool blanket covered her, and someone had tucked a goatskin pack under her head. Where was Yum Gyeba? The yaks were still tied to the boulders, the gear was still there, but the monk was gone. Her heart raced and her mouth was dry. She wasn't dizzy, and the headache, nausea, and hallucinations were gone, but something had replaced them: A feeling of dread settled into her like a disease.

When she remembered the Bon, she fell to her knees. What if they'd captured Yum Gyeba? What if they were still at the altar? She crawled to the rim of the cliff and peered over.

Today, with the sun high and the sickness in the past, she could see the temple for what it was: a miniature of the Aztec pyramid she'd helped Chris excavate in the Yucatán. Then she remembered reading about a ceremony like the one she'd watched: Before the Spanish arrived in the New World, the priests of Xipe Totec, the Aztec flayed god, would wear the skins of freshly killed captives to perform their ceremonies. With the ceremony and the pyramid as proof, the final chapters of *The One Cult* began to take form. No odds could account for this degree of coincidence.

She picked up the binoculars and looked at the base of the pyramid, then let her eyes follow the stairway toward the shrine. Yum Gyeba stood on the stairway, motioning for her to join him. But she wasn't going anywhere without her camera.

The cassette recorder had shut off automatically when the tape ended, but the automatic shutter on the Nikon still clicked dutifully, clicked until she turned it off. She opened the camera and unloaded the film, carefully tucked it in her pack, then reloaded with color film. She looped the camera and bag over her shoulder, walked through the twisted boulders, and listened for something she prayed wasn't there.

Yum Gyeba met her at the pyramid. His eyes blinked constantly; his face contorted as though he were living a nightmare. He held the *phurba* so tightly, his hand sweated. "Your eyes have cleared," he said. His voice broke. "Sometimes the mountains change their minds about sickness."

Jael glanced around her. No torches or robes remained. She closed her eyes and tried to sort through the flood of images from the previous night. "What was the burst of light?" she asked.

"Torches?" he asked.

"More like an explosion," Jael said. She pointed to the crags on the far side of the canyon. "Whatever it was, I saw those cliffs as clearly last night as I see them today."

"The light of too much sickness."

"And the roaring?" Jael asked.

"The roaring of brain that has done too much work with too little air." A rock bounced down the talus slope. Yum Gyeba snapped the *phurba* above his head as he turned toward the noise. His hands, his entire body, trembled.

"Just a rock," Jael said.

"We go."

"I need some pictures," Jael said. "Ten minutes. It will take you that long to bring down the yaks." As soon as she said it, Jael wished she hadn't. But pictures were proof.

Yum Gyeba opened his mouth to argue, then turned from Jael and scurried among the boulders. She looked up the pyramid and tried to see the shrine. Impossible. It played tricks with perspective, was designed to look as though it vanished into the sky. She started up the stairway. Her muscles ached with each step, but the sweat on her face was more the result of fear than exertion. It was like walking up the tongue of an enormous serpent. The flat surface of the shrine was slick with blood, blood that had frozen during the night and was starting to thaw. She snapped several shots of the carvings and inscriptions on the steps, then braced herself for the altar. No real surprises. Blood. Sinew. Bits of flesh. Then she saw a huge surprise.

The blue star.

It was the most exquisite piece of primitive art she had ever seen. Transparent, three-dimensional, just large enough so that she couldn't hold it in one hand, it caught and refracted the light in all directions. Almost hypnotic. There were no mold marks, no signs of carving. It was too large to be a diamond—perhaps a crystal or some indigenous material she didn't know.

She snapped a half-dozen pictures of the altar, then edged as close to the abyss as she could, set the focus on infinity, and snapped a shot of the ice slides below. Ceremonies had probably been conducted there for three thousand years. How many bodies lay scattered beneath her?

Something echoed through the canyon. Laughter? A scream? The surge of cold rushed through her again and her knees trembled. She had to get away. As she walked toward the stairway the star caught sun rays and scattered a thousand spots of light. It drew her to the altar. It would be common thievery to take the star—worse: desecration—but somehow it was soon nestled in her camera bag. She covered it with a lens cloth and hurried to meet Yum Gyeba.

"We must leave!" he shouted.

"A few more shots of the pyramid," Jael said.

"Now!" He struck his yak with the bamboo rod and bounced down the trail. Although Jael mounted immediately, he was around the first boulder before she could get her yak to move. She trembled without knowing why. As she walked over the rope bridge and remounted on the far side she felt the monk's eyes, something's eyes, move across her, although Yum Gyeba continued to stare down the trail. The eyes had emerged from nowhere, from within her.

The nausea and chills had returned. Boulders sprouted fangs. Each shadow seemed to breathe. The wind wheezed her name over and over and over. The terror was a part of the mountains. She had to get away, run and leave whatever was following her in the chasms, prowling the trails.

Even as she stared off the cliff and tried to keep her mind on the terrors of *this* world, she started to compose a letter to Chris, searched for the right words to explain why she couldn't wait for him at the monastery but would meet him in Peking instead.

EIGHT

Kenilworth, Illinois—August 15, 1981

Matt would have loved to give Dylan a hug, to toss him up in the air, catch him, and deposit him in the convertible's passenger seat the way he would have done the previous summer. But Dylan had grown up. The only response Matt would get now would be an exasperated *"Dad,"* a one-word scolding, then ten sullen minutes. Now that he only saw the boy on weekends, even ten minutes of sullenness was more than he wanted. More than he could stand.

So Dylan opened the Mercedes's door himself, climbed into the red bucket seat, and fastened his shoulder harness like a scaled-down adult. Matt sat behind the steering wheel, started the engine, and turned toward the boy: Dylan was wearing his Cubs hat backward.

Matt lifted it from Dylan's head and turned it around so the red *C* faced forward. Dylan reached up and twisted the cap so the bill was in the back.

"When I was your age . . ." Matt paused, thought of the echoes of that phrase, of how often *his* father's lectures had begun that way, then smiled at the inevitability of it all. "When I was your age," he continued, "only yo-yos wore their baseball caps backwards."

"What are they?"

Matt searched for just the right word. "Dummies," he said.

The boy looked honestly worried.

"You know Goober on *Andy Griffith,"* Matt continued. "Well, he wasn't the first. There was Rootie Kazootie. . . . Maybe it was Howdy Doody. Anyway, they all wore their baseball caps backwards."

Dylan laughed at the names. "There you go," Matt said. "A

backwards baseball cap makes you look just like them. Rootie. Goober. Doody. You want me to start calling you Spud or Aloysius?"

They both laughed, but when Matt reached to turn the cap around, Dylan started to frown and let his mother's big doe eyes get all serious. "Mom said that when you were a kid, you used to wear you hair down to the middle of your back."

Touché. There was no getting around one fact: Dylan was a precocious little snippet. Matt fastened his shoulder harness and pulled out of the driveway. Dylan, always the diplomat, immediately switched subjects. "What are we doing today?"

"I just steer this thing," Matt said. "You're in the navigator's seat. Anyplace in particular sound good?"

Dylan shrugged, just as Bekki would have done if her mind were made up but she wanted Matt to pry the information from her. And, as he would have done with Bekki, Matt played along. "The Mets are in town," he said.

"The Cubs always lose."

"That's their charm," Matt said. "They've been losing since before *I* was born."

There was a smaller shrug from Dylan, one that meant *If we can't do any better than the Cubs, we may as well stay home.* Matt couldn't blame the kid much either.

Matt glanced away from the road and said, "We could go to the beach so you could help your dad watch girls."

Dylan looked out the window. "Why isn't Mom coming with us?"

"No fair," Matt said. And for the first time he felt only moderately guilty. "We've been over that plenty."

Once that obligatory question had been disposed of, Dylan looked back at Matt and said, "The zoo. Brookfield."

"Lincoln Park Zoo is closer. If we don't spend all day driving, we can take in some rays in the afternoon."

Dylan nodded when he heard the compromise and hunched as far over the dash as he could so he could see out of the windshield. Within a few miles Sheridan Road became Broadway. The farther they drove into the city, the more city-smelling things became: pizza parlors and delis, auto exhaust and garbage, industry and sweat—nothing like the sterile suburbs. The smell of people piled one on top of another had both an alienating and a seductive quality. There was the sense that things were damn tough in the city but that it was the place where things happened.

When Matt turned onto Lake Shore Drive, a lake breeze filled with fish and water and seaweed swept into the car. It was a purely adult smell. No wonder Dylan wasn't crazy about the beach, but his complete silence was disquieting. "How's the Creepster doing?" Matt asked. "Still visiting?"

"Sometimes," Dylan said.

"How often is that?"

"Every night." Dylan glanced at the lake, stuck his arm out the window, and moved his hand up and down like a wind foil . . . just as Matt had done throughout childhood. Matt gave the mandatory warning: "You could lose an arm doing that."

"Not if I'm careful," Dylan said.

Which was true enough. When Dylan started to stare at the lake, Matt extended his left arm, flattened his palm, and let the wind push his hand like a river current. Dylan sat straighter as they passed Belmont Harbor, straight enough to see Matt's arm if he looked, so Matt rested his elbow on the door. "Want to go sailing next weekend?" Matt asked. "I'll get the weekend off so we can spend the whole night out."

"Think the Creepster can swim?"

"Has your mother been going out and leaving you alone at night?" Matt asked, perhaps too harshly.

"No," Dylan said. "She's always there." He looked at Matt as though he were sizing Matt up for something, then looked off into the lake again. "Sometimes there's a man with her."

Matt's hands started to sweat; his heart beat frantically. Anger. Irrational anger. Anger over the amount of time Bekki had to spend with the boy. Anger for the advantage she had in making Dylan love her, that she'd slowly steal the boy's affection; more: territorial anger—the old puff-out-the-chest mentality, as Bekki put it. *Stupid, stupid,* Matt thought, *I want her more than I love her.* Not that it made things any easier. He touched Dylan's cheek. "What does he look like?" Matt asked, not really wanting to know.

"I see him in the day when I'm playing or reading," Dylan said. His face turned red, and he began the shallow, arhythmic breathing that would lead to tears.

"The man?" Matt asked.

"No," Dylan sobbed, "the Creepster!"

What would a psychologist call the combination of daydreams and nightmares? Daymares? Whatever they were, they weren't good. "Do you still like to go to Dr. Velde?"

Dylan nodded and sobbed, unbuckled his shoulder harness, and lay his head in Matt's lap. The shuddering and sobs were contagious, even if their origins were different. So Matt sat in the bucket seat, one hand on the steering wheel, the other running through his son's hair, caressing Dylan's neck, wishing to God he could think of some way to share the boy's torment.

They took a right at the Fullerton Street exit, coasted over the road through the lagoons, and turned into the zoo's parking lot. "Chin up," Matt said. "You don't want the baboons to see you with a face full of tears." And then Dylan was up and his red face started to return to normal. His blue eyes sparkled. Matt took a handful of his polo shirt to dry the boy's tears. "Good as new," Matt said. "If Dr. Velde doesn't start to help you soon, I'll find a doctor who will."

"Promise?"

Matt lifted the boy and hugged him. "Where first?" Matt asked as they snapped through the turnstile.

The zoo, unlike the lake, possessed smells that belonged to kids regardless of their ages. The hot dogs. The mustard. The peanuts. And most of all the shit—the thousands of varieties of shit created by the thousands of different digestive tracts processing thousands of different types of food. They all smell earthy, fertile. All but one, anyway. Matt didn't like the ape house, unless it was out of smelling range. "Where to, Cap'n?" he asked.

"The chimps," Dylan said. "They know me."

"Interested in visiting your relatives, eh?" Matt said. He started to tickle Dylan, but the boy squirmed away and began to laugh. He came back as soon as Matt stopped to buy some cotton candy.

Fortunately it was summer and the apes had been moved to

their outdoor cages. Matt could stay in the sunshine and watch the girls walk past. Dylan stuffed a handful of cotton candy into his mouth as they approached the cages.

A bizarre thing happened. First one monkey, then another, then all the lemurs and rhesus monkeys, gibbons and chimps, stopped their screeching and swinging, their monkey things, and turned toward Matt and Dylan.

And stared.

Dylan didn't seem to be upset or surprised by their behavior, so Matt decided to play along. "Maybe they *are* your relatives," Matt said. "Think they'll invite us in for dinner?"

Dylan giggled.

There were a hundred, perhaps a hundred and fifty persons clustered around the cages, but all the apes crowded to the side of the cage where Dylan and Matt stood. Although the monkeys looked like monkeys, they moved more like machines than living things. Something was different about their eyes. They seemed to have purpose. Other people noticed it too. They grew uneasy and backed away.

Suddenly a chimp with a long face and gray whiskers began to chatter in a rhythmic cadence, almost as though he were speaking. Other apes dropped from their swings and perches and picked up something from the floor: shit.

Matt had read how monkeys, too intelligent, too bored with their cages, would masturbate or hurl food or feces at spectators merely to see them react. Matt reacted. He grabbed Dylan and carried him away. Just in time. A wave of feces shot through the bars and fell about three yards short of where he put Dylan down.

Not everyone was as lucky.

Amazingly, Dylan laughed. "They know me!"

Matt didn't know what to say. He just knew he didn't want to upset the boy. Despite the fact that apes kept howling and jumping up and down, Dylan continued to laugh. "Sure you didn't make faces at them last time you were here?" Matt asked. "Maybe pulled their tails?" The apes continued to screech. "Let's split this scene."

"With Goober and Rootie?" Dylan said, giggling.

"Yeah, all of us," Matt said as he led Dylan away. "Where next?"

Dylan motioned for Matt to bend over. When Matt's head was at child level, Dylan said, "Snakes." Matt squirmed at the word.

"Sure they won't scare you?"

"Sure."

They both knew that the snakes would give him a small dose of the chills, just as late-night horror movies had given them to Matt when he was a boy. But that hadn't stopped him from turning on the tube long after his parents went to bed and sitting in the flickering light as Boris and Lon and Bela did things too horrible to mention. Besides, contact with some smaller fears might evict the Creepster for a night or two. Judging from the circles under Dylan's eyes, he could use a few nights off.

Matt glanced over his shoulder at the monkey cages. As soon as Dylan left, the monkeys returned to being monkeys, mindlessly chattering, eating. There was no sign that there had ever been a battle plan or organized assault.

Dylan and Matt stayed in the shade of the huge elms as they approached the snake house. Matt thought that a cloud should cover the sun or some distant thunder should rumble as they entered it. But there were certain advantages to snakes, certain things that Matt could always count on. They'd even scare him as they lay in their cages, looking dead. They'd scarcely have a smell. They wouldn't throw anything at anyone. For the latter two reasons only, Matt preferred them to other animals.

Matt knew that Dylan liked the snake house because it meant a shoulder ride; Dylan was still too short to peer into the cages. So it was up on the shoulders, past the huge pit where the big snakes —pythons, boa constrictors, anacondas—were kept. Matt looked into the pit just long enough to know that he didn't want to see any more: slithering bodies more than twenty feet long, thicker than his thigh, with heads as large as Dylan's. One must have eaten recently: A rabbit-size lump distended its body a third of the way down. To think that those coils and jaws could reduce a child to a shapeless mass . . . Matt veered away from the pit.

"Quit squirming, Dad!" Dylan demanded.

"Sorry, Cap'n."

Matt steered toward the cobras. They had a mystique all their own: the regal hoods, the deadly venom. And the magic of horror movies, the *Cult of the Cobra* this, the *Curse of the Cobra* that. Good thing that there was an inch of glass separating them from the spectators.

"That one knows me!" Dylan said, pointing toward the spitting cobra.

"Storm's a brewin', Cap'n," Matt said. He walked toward the display case, swerving and bouncing, trying to give Dylan the impression he would shake the boy off while holding firmly to his knees. Dylan took the ride calmly. A year before he would have squealed in delight.

When they were within a yard of the case, a gray-brown line stirred and raised its head. Even that much activity was surprising. *Spread that hood, you sucker,* Matt thought, *spread that hood.* As if by command, the snake jerked upright and spread its hood. Matt thought of all the years he'd tapped on the glass, made faces and jumped up and down, and never evoked a reaction from a cobra.

"It's looking at me," Dylan said.

"It's following our movements," Matt said. "We are eight feet tall, after all."

Dylan's legs tensed. "It knows *me!*" There was a flash, and a streak of yellow ooze dripped on the inside of the glass. *"What's that?"* Dylan shouted.

"Poison. That snake spits at its prey."

"It knows me."

It did seem preoccupied with the boy, but Matt didn't want Dylan to know that. "Come on," Matt said. "You know better than that. Want proof?"

Dylan nodded. Matt held him at arm's length, which wasn't easy anymore. "Jeez, you're getting heavy," Matt grunted.

The snake's head followed the boy. "Let's get out of here," Dylan said.

What was happening couldn't be happening. Matt was a rational man; he'd wait until the irrational disappeared. "We'll be okay," he said. "There's no way it can get through that glass."

A thunk. The snake had glided to the front of the cage, struck, and hit the glass. It kept watching Dylan. Another thunk. Again. Again. Dylan was shaking, and Matt stood in fascinated horror. Again and again and again it struck the glass, and red smears blended with the yellow venom, and the cobra's head and mouth must have been crushed, its fangs smashed, but it struck again and again and bits of bone stuck to the glass and the spasms began and the snake stretched out in death and twitched and writhed and continued to strike in spasms—spasms directed at Dylan.

Matt pulled the boy close and hugged him tight and said "It will be all right, things will be all right," then tried to take him into the sunlight before the screaming began.

Again he was too slow.

NINE

Peking, People's Republic of China—August 18, 1981

Jael rewound the tape, arranged into an ordered pile the photos that had been scattered on the bed, then slipped them into her portfolio. She leaned against the stiff pillow. Her eyes hurt, her head spun, and what was worse, nothing that had happened in the past two weeks made any sense. None of it. Not the distortions in her eyesight, hearing, or smell—or, worse, the nightmare. It was back, only more graphic. And it came almost as soon as she closed her eyes.

She'd started sleeping with the lights on.

Even during the day, during the brightest sunshine, the terror from the mountains would cling to her like seaweed to a drowning man; it wrapped around her limbs when she moved, entered her mouth and nostrils with each breath, and dragged her into a darkness she thought was insanity.

She squinted and tried to shake the grogginess from her head. The harsh ceiling light made the hotel appear even cheaper than it was: a basic bomb shelter—four windowless cinder-block walls painted off-white. She had transferred to this hotel precisely because she could get a room with no windows. There was no way the evil could crash through a pane of glass or gently lift a window latch to sneak inside. No matter how crazy the move seemed, it would help her keep sane until Chris arrived.

If Chris arrived.

She needed to talk to him, to rationally explain the craziness of the pictures, to clarify the impossible noises on the tape. He would put his hand on her head and remind her that they were in a civilized country, that a locked door meant security, that room service was only a phone call away, and that things were as they always had been.

Jael buried her face in the pillow. Even on the fourth floor, the traffic shook the walls. She stared at her wristwatch: seven-ten P.M. The sun would still be bright, the vendors in the People's Market would hawk vegetables and meat, and she could take a tour of the Forbidden City. She'd be safe outside. Nothing would be able to get at her with so many people around.

A scratch at the door.

Jael's attention snapped back into the room, concentrated on the sound. It was nothing, nothing but nerves.

She wiped the perspiration from her forehead. Maybe Chris was just late. Maybe he'd missed the note she left when she checked out of the Peking Hotel.

Maybe he was simply ignoring her.

No, that wasn't Chris. No matter how angry he was, he'd want to see her one last time so he could lecture her, tell her—

Something was scratching at the door.

Dream images returned, half-thoughts of flesh being torn and swallowed, of bones being cracked for marrow, of long fangs and yellow eyes and . . . her mouth felt as though she'd chewed a box of Kleenex.

"Hello?" she said. Her voice cracked.

No answer.

"Who's there?" she asked.

"They gave me the wrong fucking key!" Chris shouted.

Jael jumped from the bed. And stopped. She had to control herself. She took one, two deep breaths, waited for her heartbeat to stabilize, then reached for the lock. Her hands shook so badly that she could scarcely turn it. She slid back the bolt and opened the door.

Chris's face was peeling; his eyes were red from too much sun and wind. His beard was two weeks beyond its normal sculpted state. Jael reached for him, tried to hug him, but he pushed her away.

"I deserved that," Jael said. She had to concentrate to keep her voice from quivering. "Go ahead. Get it all out of your system."

"I want an explanation," he said calmly.

"I won't grovel."

"Explain!"

Jael walked slowly back to the bed and lay down. The thin mattress barely softened the plywood that the hotel had substituted for box springs. She looked at the bedspread, which was yellow-white, then at the wall, then back to Chris. He frowned, shook his head, and turned toward the hall.

"Don't leave," Jael said. "Chris?" He stopped, nodded, and came back into the room. He closed the door. "Lock it," Jael said. "Please." He raised his eyebrows, then slid the bolt into place, walked to one of the stiff wooden chairs by the bed, and sat down.

"Now I know how a stuffed head on a wall must feel," Chris said. "What number trophy am I?"

She was too tired to fight, so she rolled onto her side and let her mind wander to the voices in the hallway. A couple argued in French, something about a jade necklace the woman had bought in the Friendship Store. . . .

"Your move," Chris said.

Nothing she could say would be enough. At best he'd be patronizing; at worst, self-righteous. Just having him there was enough. Let him shout, stamp his feet, jump up and down, just so long as he didn't leave.

"The silence designed to make me feel like a bully?" he asked. "We're supposed to be *exchanging* insults." She trembled when she breathed. He walked to the bed and sat down, then touched her forehead with his fingertips. "Jesus," he said, "you're drenched." He took her by the shoulders and rolled her onto her back. "How can I give you the shit you deserve if you get sick on me?"

The anger drained from his face. Suddenly he looked concerned. He took Jael's chin and placed the back of his hand against her forehead. She tried to speak, but Chris put a finger to her lips and shushed her. "No fever," he said. He placed his thumb against her wrist. "Pulse twice normal." He gently lifted her eyelids. The light was white, painfully white. "Your pupils are dilated." He sat back and stared at her. "When was the last time you had a decent sleep?"

"Remember the incubi," Jael asked, "spirits that suck the life from maidens? I may not be a maiden, but I have one hell of a bogeyman."

Chris pushed down on the mattress. "It's no wonder: You can't sleep on this."

"I wish it were the bed," Jael said, her voice quivering. A single sob escaped. "What if the nightmares never stop?"

Chris wrapped his arms around her, then moved back. "I still haven't made it clear how utterly pissed off I am," he said. "I have an hour's worth of screaming built up."

"Scream away," Jael said. "Just don't leave."

He cupped his hand behind her head and she nuzzled against his thigh. "Don't worry," he said. "You're going to be all right." He paused. Jael could feel the movement in his body as he shook his head. "Jesus," he said, "what a stupid thing to say."

"Keep it up. It helps."

He began to rock her, to whisper nothing in particular, to rub her back as he tried to think of something to add. "Your bribe worked," he finally said. "Whatever your monk told the abbot to tell Yen Hui got me from the monastery to Lhasa to Peking without a hitch."

"All the provincial authorities are on the take," Jael said. "I paid the abbot enough so that he could bribe Yen Hui."

"You?" Chris asked. "What about your monk?"

"That's part of the problem; there *was* no monk." Chris poured her a glass of water from the pitcher on the bedside table. She sat up, took a sip, and lay back down. "As we came down from the pass he stopped at a shrine and said that he wanted to say a prayer of thanks, that he'd meet me in the monastery." Jael swirled the water in the glass, but the cloudiness wouldn't dissipate. "I hadn't paid him, so I was sure he would follow. I went straight to our quarters and waited. And waited. In fact, I waited until some monks arrived to take me to the abbot."

"What happened to the monk?"

"I'll get to that," Jael said. She paused to gather her thoughts and some strength before she continued. "As soon as I entered the abbot's residence, he began threatening me; he said he'd inform the Chinese that I'd disappeared for a week. Even after I offered him a hundred *yuan,* he continued to threaten. At five

102

hundred he was merely scolding. At a thousand he was remembering all the walks we'd shared in the courtyard while you were gone. When I offered him fifteen hundred, he radioed Lhasa and told them I was suffering from altitude sickness. A helicopter ride, a military jet, and I was in Peking by nightfall."

"You never saw the monk again?"

"Worse," Jael said. "He wasn't a monk. If his name was Yum Gyeba, the abbot never heard of him."

"And his sleeping quarters?"

"They belonged to a monk who had spent the day at the cremation ceremonies."

Chris reached for the water. He poured a glassful, refilled Jael's glass, then put the pitcher back on the stand. He emptied half his glass with a deep gulp. "Did this Yum Gyeba sell you the *phurba?*"

"Sometime during our last day, he slipped it into my pack, unnoticed and unpaid."

"None of this makes any sense," Chris said.

"You've always had a gift for understatement."

Chris glanced around the room, then spread his arms in a sign of disbelief. "Since we're talking about the inexplicable, why would you trade a suite at the Peking for this dump?"

"The Peking had windows."

"Christ, Jael, you might as well be speaking Tibetan."

"Now that I have someone to take my mind off the *chöd,* what seemed logical is too silly to admit."

Chris drained his glass and leaned against the bedpost. "The *chöd?*" His voice perked up.

"I saw parts of it . . . I think." The more Jael talked, the more solid the room became, the more she could trust the walls, the furniture—her hand—not to melt, vibrate, or evaporate. She swung her legs over the side of the bed, then reached for the portfolio and tape recorder. "I can't try to tell you what I saw, but these should help you understand." She handed Chris a color photo that she had taken of the pyramid the morning after the ceremony.

"That's Bon?" he asked.

Jael nodded.

"Without the snow-covered mountains in the background, I would have sworn it was Aztec," he said.

"There's more." Jael handed him a picture of the altar. Inscriptions, intertwined vines and snakes, animals, and stars were etched into the stone. "Sure look Celtic, don't they," she said. She handed him a third picture, a close-up of an animal carved in stone. "Yum Gyeba said the *chöd* was for their wolf-god Hta-menma."

"That's like no wolf I've ever seen," Chris said. "More like a predatory anteater."

"That occurred to me," Jael said. "From what I could find out, there never were anteaters in Tibet."

Chris began to stroke his beard; he pointed to the red splotches on the altar. "How many people did they sacrifice?" he asked softly.

"Four," Jael said. "At least I think four. I only saw one." The next photo she handed him was of the blood-glazed pyramid top. Footprints showed in the slush. "One person couldn't bleed that much."

"You certainly kept your critical distance."

"I wish I had," Jael said. "I was sick from the moment I left the monastery. At first I thought it was altitude sickness; now I doubt it. The symptoms weren't the same, and it hasn't disappeared at sea level." She paused to rest. She took a sip of water, then leaned back on her hands. "Since I couldn't trust my observations," she continued, "I let the camera and tape deck do my observing for me." She swallowed the rest of the water, then motioned for Chris to sit in the chair. "I tried to get the most important part. I noted what I said when I activated the camera, so I could synchronize the photos and tape. I'll hand you a photo every thirty seconds, so you'll be able to hear *and* see what took place."

"Good as an instant replay."

"Hardly," Jael said. "They have the continuity of the Nixon tapes." She handed him the first of the photos she'd taken that night. It was black and grainy from the Royal-X film, but the objects were clearly distinguishable: men in robes and masks; torches and a fire; a star-shaped frame being carried onto the shrine. Jael pushed the button on the tape recorder. Drumbeats, chants; then Jael's voice came through the speakers: ". . . horrible. Everything black and white in the moonlight."

"I've never heard you sound like that before," Chris said.

"I hope you never hear it again." Jael pointed to the litter. "Note the star. Star symbolism dominated the ceremony."

Chris stared at the photos. "I've seen those masks before." He paused and rubbed his mouth. "They're Babylonian. The priests of Baal."

"That's not what I had in mind, but you're probably right," Jael said. "And there's plenty more to come." A noise, the sound of ripping metal poured through the speakers.

"Equipment malfunction?" Chris asked.

Jael handed him the next picture, one of the high priest with his head thrown back, his mouth straining open. "It came from him."

"Impossible."

"Look at the aura around his body," Jael said. "You just tell me something bizarre isn't happening there."

"It's explainable," Chris said. He hesitated. "Everyone in the picture is suffering from group hysteria. In a ceremony like this, it would be unusual if they weren't. Hysteria doesn't seem to account for a sound that can't be produced by human vocal cords."

"And his glow?"

"Had he been dancing?"

"Naturally."

"Was it cold?" Chris asked.

"Cold doesn't begin to describe what went on up there."

"Then his body would be steaming," Chris said. He started to emphasize points by gesturing with his finger. "The camera caught the firelight filtering through his body steam. What you call an aura is an illusion."

"Maybe," Jael said. She looked at the photo of the sacrificial victim drawing incision lines on his body, then handed it to Chris. "This one is mind-boggling."

"Drugged?" Chris asked as he stared at the picture.

"Probably. The priest blew some powder into his face. The

victims acted as though they were in a hurry for the ceremony to start."

"Imagine five thousand Aztec captives patiently waiting in line for their hearts to be gouged out with a flint knife," Chris said.

Jael merely glanced at the next picture: the priest slicing along the incision lines. Other Bon were frozen on film, dancing, pounding drums, chanting. When the roaring on the tape stopped, Jael handed Chris the picture of the man being skinned.

"Astounding," Chris said.

Jael pulled a photo from partway through the stack and passed it to him. The priest wore the skin as he danced.

"I've never heard of anything like it," Chris said.

"What if I mentioned 'Our Lord, the Flayed One'?"

"Xipe Totec," Chris said. "The reliefs in the temples in Mexico."

"That's what I was thinking."

Chris held the photos in one hand as though he were judging their weight. "Put all this together, and you may also be talking about the final third of your book."

"I wish it were that simple," Jael said. Howling crackled through the speakers, howling and drumbeats and a sudden, unimaginable screech. It was like the earlier metallic noises, only louder, much louder. It swallowed all the background noises. Jael turned down the volume to keep it from hurting her ears. "This is when I passed out."

"Next photo," Chris said.

"That's the problem," Jael said. She handed him the next photo. And the next one. And the next one. Each was completely white, completely useless. "The next seventeen shots, the next eight and a half minutes, are overexposed. Totally."

"Who developed the film?"

"Me. At Peking University." Jael paused to pour more water in her glass. "I didn't want to take any chances."

"Was it on the reel properly?"

She handed him the negatives: black exposures within clear frames. "There's nothing wrong with the film. I mixed fresh chemicals. Whatever's wrong with these photos took place at the altar."

Chris ran his fingers through his hair and shook his head. He looked back at her. "The tape?"

"The roaring continues for eight minutes and twenty-six seconds," Jael said. "What are the odds against the tape and the camera malfunctioning at exactly the same time for exactly the same amount of time?"

Chris didn't answer. He merely sat in the chair and tapped on its arms with his fingertips. Finally he said, "What happens after the eight and a half minutes?"

"You can hear the chanting and drums again, and the photos are crystal clear." She pushed the fast-forward button and advanced the tape to the premarked spot. She pushed the play button. The chanting and drums returned. She handed him the last photos: The Bon were arranged in a star-shaped formation around the altar. Their masks were off, their faces smeared with blood.

"Are you sure this disappearing monk didn't drug you, then tamper with the film and tape?" Chris asked.

"He had the opportunity but no expertise."

Chris shrugged, then sat on the bed next to her and placed an arm around her shoulder. She realized it was time to be patronized. "You did just fine," Chris said.

"Which means the heart of my research consists of blank photos and a roar on the tape."

"Hardly. Just finding and photographing the Red Bon will make academic waves."

"This may amaze you," Jael said, "but there are things more important to me than a reputation."

"It's a start. . . . It means grant money next year." He paused and smiled. "Any more surprises?"

Jael pulled the suitcase from beneath her bed, opened it, pulled out the blue star, and handed it to Chris.

He whistled as soon as he saw it. "Where did you get this?"

"Go back to pictures two and three," she said. She waited until he found them. "The object in the middle of the frame reflecting light?" She pointed to the glow. "I'd guess this is it."

"Your monk didn't deposit *this* in your pack."

"It sounds ridiculous, but it jumped into my camera bag," Jael said. "I was alone on top of the pyramid. It lay on the altar. I kept telling myself I had no business taking it—"

"But you took it anyway," Chris interrupted.

"Strip the self-delusion away," Jael said, "and that's what it comes down to." She glanced at him and saw he wasn't angry, so she smiled and shook her head. "For some reason it seemed more complex than that at the time."

"Was it part of the altar?"

"I didn't take any pictures before the *chöd*. I don't remember seeing it, but I was so sick, I scarcely remember seeing the pyramid."

Chris turned the star over and over in his hands. "It's exquisite," he said. "The only lapidary pieces that come close to it are some Nineteenth-Dynasty Egyptian stellae." He held it at a distance. "What's it made of?"

"You're the first one who's seen it. I doubted the Chinese would give it back." Jael expected a lecture, the bawling-out she'd deserved earlier. Chris acted as though he hadn't heard her.

He held the star up to the lamp; it refracted light all over the room. "I can honestly say that I've never seen anything like it." Chris paused and smiled. "And there aren't many things I can say that about."

"What do we do with it?"

"We take it back to Chicago, where the university's resources are available, and evaluate it." He handed it back to her. "Where's the *phurba?*"

She took it from the suitcase and handed it to him.

He studied the dagger, slowly turning it over and over in his hands. "Your old friend, Htamenma the wolf-god, makes an appearance here too," he said, pointing to one of the carvings on the handle. "We'll have no problem getting this out of the country. Just tell the customs folks that it's another Buddhist ceremonial dagger. It's so shiny, they'll never know the difference." He pulled at his beard. "The star will present more problems, but we'll find a way."

"What if we get caught?" Jael asked. "As you phrased it at the monastery, how would such a breach of faith affect *your* relations with the Chinese?"

"Sorry about that," Chris said. He ran his finger along the *phurba*'s blade, smiled, then looked up at her. "With a little luck and a lot of hard work, that Nobel prize for the social sciences might not be so far away after all."

TEN

Chicago, Illinois—October 11, 1981

Matt leaned against the building that housed the faculty club and looked up to where fog swallowed the soot-stained bricks, then down a long flight of stairs to the street. A car emerged from the mist, its headlights like blind eyes, blank, rigid, and lost, ever so lost. He breathed in the wet air and shook his head. He wasn't there to philosophize or be depressed; he was there to be informed about Dylan's condition. Matt hadn't learned much from Dr. Helmut Meier's paper presentation, "Insights on the Dream of the Bad Animal"; there'd been too much alien vocabulary, words like *numinosum* and *hierosgamos* that meant nothing, nothing at all. With some luck the psychiatrist would be more comprehensible at the postlecture party.

One final glance at the street—the fog deadened even the engine sounds—and Matt pushed on a heavy oaken door and stepped inside. He walked into the anteroom, then the cloakroom, found a hanger for his coat, then hurried down the long corridor and winced as he entered the lounge. He'd forgotten how much he hated academic gatherings, their pretension, their obligation to perform.

He needed a trip to the bar.

The people, mostly professors, judging from their tweed jackets and the clouds of aromatic smoke, gathered in clusters. One group was psychology, the next anthropology, a third religion. They didn't have identification tags, but they didn't have to: Their vocabularies gave them away. Matt leaned against a bar that matched the mahogany wall paneling, ordered a martini, then reached for the hors d'oeuvres. He picked some shrimp and oysters from the soggy bread and used them to ease the sting of the gin.

Meier stood behind a podium surrounded by a large crowd; he was the type of man who drew crowds. Matt finished the drink in a gulp, pardoned and excused himself through a mass of people, and emerged in the first row between a rubber plant and the leather sofa. An informal gathering? Symphonies and funerals were less formal. Hands were raised. Meier would acknowledge someone with a nod, then abruptly move on to someone else. Matt wished he were elsewhere.

But what choice did he have? A psychiatrist of Meier's reputation—if there were others of his reputation—didn't come to Chicago often. Matt raised his hand with the rest of the sheep.

Meier's silver hair was styled and matted to his head as though it were wet. His forehead looked as broad as his shoulders. He nodded at a bald man in the front row.

"I have a patient," the man said, "a Catholic girl with a recurrent dream." He paused, evidently awaiting some sort of recognition, but Meier remained silent and kept staring at him. "A woman wearing a black dress and veil comes into the girl's room, sits on her bed, and offers to play. The girl is terrified without knowing why. The woman edges across the bed. The girl tugs at the veil; it is the Virgin Mary. At once the girl feels safe and reaches up to hug her. When the woman smiles, vampire teeth appear. She begins to devour the girl's arm."

"How old is she?" Meier asked.

"Eleven."

Meier pulled on an ear, which was small and tight against his head, raised a glass of water to his lips, then set it back on the podium. "The dream suggests what Jung calls a 'big dream,' one which expresses universal as well as personal concerns. Such dreams often appear at puberty." He stopped for a drink of water. "The woman is the Terrible Mother. When a woman gives birth to a child, she guarantees the child will die . . . a sad irony," he said. "The subconscious often emphasizes this death-giving aspect of motherhood. The Terrible Mother exists in all religions. To the Hindus, she is Kali. To medieval Christians, the Black Madonna. This girl senses the dark side of her role as woman, the dark side of her sexuality. It is only natural she should feel threatened—'devoured by adulthood,' as it were."

111

The man tried to speak again, but Meier held up his hand and said, "Please, there are many questions tonight."

Matt raised his hand, but Meier looked toward the other side of the room and nodded at a tall woman with long, coppery-colored hair. "I know a woman who's plagued by a dream," the woman said. Her voice was rich and startlingly self-confident. "She's sitting at her piano, playing a bizarre piece of music, and suddenly sees a flash of light from her balcony. She's drawn to the window and opens the drapes. There's a creature on the balcony, a cold, deadly, seductive . . ." The woman's voice trailed off.

"What does the creature look like?" Meier asked. "Does it threaten her?"

The woman shrugged. "I'm sorry. The image remains in the dream. She can't retrieve it when she's awake."

"She's repressing it," Meier said. Then he shrugged and raised his eyebrows. "Without a case history, without knowing more about the creature, I'd be speculating." He paused and smiled. "Speculation will help neither your friend nor my reputation." Then he abruptly turned in Matt's direction, looked past him, and nodded to a man in a black herringbone jacket who sat on the arm of the couch.

After the first half hour Matt began to notice the heat and sour smell of the packed bodies. *Too many tweed coats,* he thought. He raised his hand again. And again. Meier answered questions comparing Jung to Freud, explained the role of amplification in dream analysis, and analyzed the process of individuation, whatever that was. Matt raised his hand, lowered it during the responses, then raised it again. There was something hypnotic about the routine, something so dulling, in fact, that when Meier finally looked at him and nodded, Matt lowered his arm and was silent for an instant.

"Yes," Meier prodded.

"What can you tell me about wolves in dreams?" Matt asked.

"A great deal," Meier said. A bland, expressionless smile lifted the corners of his mouth. He refilled his water glass, then looked up. "The wolf plays a similar role in most mythologies and dreams." He reached to the podium for his glass and sipped the water. "Often it is a symbol of the night, of the unconscious as devourer. Sometimes it is the messenger of the Wild Huntsman who transports souls to the realm of the dead."

Meier turned away and nodded in the other direction.

"Excuse me," Matt said before anyone could respond. "You're saying the wolf could prophesy death?"

Meier's broad face turned back to Matt. Deep furrows appeared in his brow. "I am sorry, but I must continue. There are other questions." He turned away.

"I'm sorry, too," Matt said, "but you haven't answered mine."

There were whispers in the audience.

"The creature isn't really a wolf," Matt continued. "It has a snout like an anteater and the ears of a donkey."

"Anteaters?" Meier asked. "Donkeys?" He smiled and tapped his fingers on the podium. He nodded as if to acknowledge Matt's little joke, then turned away and nodded toward a bald man in the first row.

Matt could feel the roaring in his blood, the heat rising through his neck to his face. His hands clenched and unclenched. "I admire your ability to abstract," he said loudly, "but I'm talking about my son, real flesh and blood."

Instead of moving only his head, Meier turned his entire torso. He removed his glasses and used them to point. "I'm not a man who banters with his audience."

"No," Matt said, trying to keep from shouting, "you're a doctor who's going to answer some questions about my son."

This time Meier didn't look away.

"It's hard to believe the things that have happened to him," Matt said. "His vocal cords were injured making a roaring noise that is impossible for a human to make . . . like metal ripping or something."

"He's undergoing treatment?"

"Of course."

"Then you're familiar with the term *hysteria?*" Meier said impatiently, his face growing redder and redder.

"It's a familiar line," Matt said. "But he glowed. A reddish aura. And when he was at the zoo, animals started throwing things at him; a cobra kept striking at him until it killed itself, as though it had singled him out for—"

Meier cleared his throat and stopped Matt's rambling. "Your son has a very active imagination," he said. Then he nodded with finality at Matt and turned away.

"I saw it!" Matt shouted.

A loud murmur spread through the audience. Meier turned to Matt and said, "Then perhaps you should join him in treatment."

Someone touched Matt's arm. "Now wait a minute," a voice said. "I think—"

"Don't," Matt said. He slapped the hand away and let his voice grow cold and lifeless and crazy-on-the-edge. "Don't think. Don't touch. Just back off." The man did. Matt stared at Meier and continued in the same tone, "You were about to tell me everything you know about a nightmare creature who looks like a cross between a wolf, anteater, and donkey."

Meier's eyes held Matt's for an instant, then shifted to his feet. "I've never heard of such a thing."

"Thank you," Matt said. As he turned and walked toward the door people backed away from him. It looked like the parting of the Red Sea. As soon as he passed, the crowd closed behind him like water.

Matt didn't stop at the lounge door; he didn't look back. He had to get outside, to cool his temper. He walked from the corridor through the anteroom and into the cloakroom, then down the aisle between the racks, trying to find his topcoat. At first he thought someone had stolen it, but a tan coat and scarf suddenly appeared.

As he reached for it someone said, "Excuse me."

Matt turned toward the voice. It was the redheaded woman from the crowd. "Don't worry," he said. "I'm leaving."

She reached out a hand to shake with him; a wafer-thin gold watch dangled from her wrist. "I teach here. My name's Jael Clarke."

"So?"

"I'd like to talk with you," she said, smiling the smile of someone who likes introductions. "We can get some coffee upstairs."

"You think I'd stay in this building?"

"Sorry," she said. She walked down the aisle, stopped, and removed a cream-colored coat and a briefcase instead of a handbag. "There's a bar a block away."

"I wasn't that impressive," Matt said, "so this can't be a come-on."

She looked at him as though he were a child who'd spoken out of turn. "I wasn't turned on by your Clint Eastwood imitation, if that's what you mean." She continued to walk toward him. "You love your son enough to do some stupid things, trying to help him. That's not a turn-on either, but it's impressive in a way."

Matt slipped on his coat and shifted his shoulders until the silk lining settled into place. "Thanks for the thought," he said, turning away from her.

"I may know something about your son's condition."

Matt stopped and turned back to her. "What are you after?"

"A chance to talk," she said. She draped her coat over her shoulder and approached him. She had pale skin, a complexion as milky and flawless as porcelain, and an oval face with bottle-green eyes.

"I missed your name," he said.

"Jael Clarke."

"I'm Matt Griffin." He looked at her quizzically. "You're a psychologist?"

"A cultural anthropologist." She nodded and slowly raised a hand to the back of her head. "And I don't like talking in closets."

It wasn't the type of bar Matt would have expected her to choose. There were dim red lights. Black-velvet paintings. Peanuts on the floor. The tile was so sticky, it was like walking on Scotch tape. She wore a cardigan that buttoned at the neck, a silk blouse, and a skirt that must have had a hundred pleats and clung to her like liquid. Before Matt could offer to take her coat, she took it off and slid into a booth beneath a Hamm's beer sign.

"You come here often?" Matt asked.

"Too often."

Matt slipped his coat off and sat on the bench across from her. A splinter scratched his thigh. "You're an unusual academic."

"How so?"

"You're what, in your late twenties? The clothes and jewelry you're wearing are a year's salary for an average professor."

"I wait for sales," she said. "What do you do?"

"I want to talk about my son."

"So do I," she said. "You were out of control back there. I want to be sure I'm not sitting across from Jack the Ripper."

Matt loosened his tie and rubbed the back of his neck. He exhaled in a whistle. "Sorry. This hasn't been the easiest month of my life. I'm an attorney. Mostly tort law these days."

She put both hands palms down on the table. Her face was perfectly balanced, almost as though she were a drawing. "Can I get you something to drink?"

"I'm already over my limit."

"A Coke, then?"

"With a twist of lemon," Matt said. As she slid from the bench and walked to the bar the aroma she left behind, a cross between vanilla and lemon, eased the stench of sour beer that filled the room. She had a dancer's movements and silhouette in the light of a Pabst sign; when she returned with a drink in each hand, there was a nervousness in her step that wasn't in her voice.

She set the Coke down in front of him, placed a brandy snifter on the table, then slid down the bench across from him. "If you need any help finishing that," she said, "let me know." Her eyelids lifted and she smiled.

Matt smiled back. His depression started to lift. "You sure you're not a psychologist?"

"Why?"

"You have a great couchside manner."

"I'll take that as a compliment," she said. She slowly spun the brandy snifter as though she were trying to melt ice. "I read a lot of articles in psychological journals," she said. "It's important for my studies that I understand how the mind creates symbols."

"What do you teach?"

"Some introductory courses and one seminar, the study of after-death literatures. They call it eschatology in the course catalog."

"I didn't know there was such a thing."

"Almost every religion has an after-death text," she said. "Parts of the Bible certainly qualify." She paused to sip her drink. Judging from the way her nose wrinkled, she didn't drink often. "I'm primarily interested in pre-Christian texts. The older the better."

Matt looked at the Coke, stirred it with a swizzle stick, then said, "My son's name is Dylan."

"As in Bob?"

"Naturally."

"It's a lovely name."

"He'd prefer Luke, as in Skywalker," Matt said. He looked up at her and, without knowing why, said, "Dylan was an attempt to revitalize our marriage. His name was a link with the sixties—all that idealism, all that innocence."

"Did he work?"

"I'm a six-figure ambulance chaser in the middle of a divorce. What does that tell you?" When she started to speak, Matt interrupted her. "And please don't try to tell me that the divorce is causing all his problems."

"I wasn't going to." She paused. "You mentioned an aura and a roar."

"I've seen things that can't be explained away by brain lesions and schizophrenia and hysteria." Matt felt the blood pounding in his temples again, so he paused. *"No* human could make that noise," he said. *"No one.* It was terrifying. And when was the last time you heard of a human radiating enough light to brighten a room? And the escapade at the zoo . . . !"

"It sounded terrible."

"He scarcely sleeps anymore. He's wasting away. Growing paler, more distant. His psychologist hasn't helped."

"Who's that?"

"Ruth Velde."

"They don't come any better."

"But she's not good enough," Matt said. "I was hoping Meier would be." He took another sip of Coke, bit down on the lemon, puckered his lips, and shook his head. "To give you an idea of how helpless I feel, last week I checked Dylan for puncture wounds."

"I don't understand."

"Remember *Dracula?* Dylan's symptoms are like Mina's and Lucy's. Like he was bitten by a vampire." Matt looked down at the table and shook his head. "Know what's even crazier? I don't know if I'm disappointed or relieved that I didn't find any marks. Carving wooden stakes, wearing crucifixes and garlic—shit, anything's better than sitting around waiting for someone else to do something." He leaned toward her. "Can you help him?"

"I don't know," she said. "But I have proof of the glowing and roaring."

"You're joking!" Matt said. Then he paused, took a deep breath, and held it for an instant. "Did you get it from an insane asylum?"

"Tibet."

Matt shook his head and looked up at the ceiling lights.

"I'm serious," she said. "I was on expedition. Officially I was the translator, but I had the opportunity to study burial customs." She took a sip from the snifter and grimaced as it went down. "I witnessed a ceremony by one of the world's oldest religions. The shaman roared and glowed and I took pictures—"

"Did he live?" Matt interrupted.

"He lived," she said. She leaned toward Matt and spoke more softly. "You said Dylan's nightmares have the same creature."

"We call him the Creepster," Matt said. "In Dylan's nightmare it materializes in the house, stalks into Bekki's and my bedroom, and devours us." Matt paused to scratch his nose. "He describes it in incredible detail—the pulsing blood, the way that muscle fibers twitch in the Creepster's jaws . . ."

Jael lifted her hand to her chin and tilted her head. "Is that all?"

"The creature never hurts Dylan. The way he describes it, it's almost as though they're confederates—that in some way Dylan has a closer tie to the Creepster than us. It just makes things worse. It compounds guilt with the horror."

Jael took a deep swallow of the brandy. "You said the creature's a hybrid of some kind?" Her voice quivered, and she trembled as though a chill had shot through her.

"Are you all right?"

"I'm fine," she said. "Can you be more specific about its appearance?"

"It has red hair, yellow eyes." Matt remembered the crayon drawing he had hoped to show Meier. "This is one of a thousand," he said, taking the paper from his pocket and handing it to her.

She unfolded it and held it up to the light. Her hands shook. She carefully set the drawing on the table and, when she reached for the brandy snifter, knocked it over.

"What is it?" Matt asked, picking up the drawing and drying it with a napkin.

She leaned against the table and shook her head. "Can you bring Dylan to my office tomorrow?"

"We'll be there." He stared at the drawing, held it up to the light, and looked at it one way, then another. "Do you know what it is?"

She tried to catch her breath. "It's one of the gods of ancient Egypt," she said. "Set, the god of terror and chaos." When she closed her eyes, the lids continued to quiver. "And I just realized I've been dreaming about the same creature for months."

PART TWO

ELEVEN

Chicago, Illinois—October 12, 1981

Jael walked into Chris's office, cornered him between a weeping fig and a wall of bookshelves, and kissed him good morning. Judging from his spicy smell, he must have shaved his neck that morning. She shushed him before he could speak, took his arm and steered him to the desk, then pointed to his chair. "Sit," she said. The springs squeaked as he plopped into it. She leaned over his shoulder and laid three tracings in pencil on the desk. The first was of a greyhoundlike creature with a long, curved snout, square, erect ears, and a stiff tail. The drawing looked as though it had been done in a single continuous line; there was sophistication in the flowing curves, the menace in the eyes, the way the fangs hung from the mouth like fruit. The second sketch was more primitive, the lines thicker, the hand less sure, but the animal's features remained the same. In the third the creature wore an elaborate feathered robe and headdress, but they didn't hide the unmistakable snout, ears, tail.

"What do you think?" she asked.

Chris studied them for a few moments, then shook his head. "You shouldn't give up anthropology for art, if that's what you mean."

"Compare them. Number one is a replica of the Bon god Htamenma. I traced it from the handle of the *phurba.*" Jael leaned forward, took a deep breath, scratched her temple, then pointed to the second drawing. "This is of the Celtic god Nodeus. I copied it from a photograph of a burial chamber in southern France. Date it about 300 B.C."

"Number three is easy enough," Chris said. " 'Our Lord, the Flayed One' again: Xipe Totec. Judging from the fact he doesn't

123

have human attributes, I'd say this is a Nahua drawing, maybe A.D. 1200, before the Aztecs decided to adopt him."

"You're amazing," Jael said. "Now, what do you see?"

Chris wrinkled his face, then leaned back in his chair. "If you eliminate the cultural and artistic differences, you could easily be looking at the same cross between a Doberman and a crocodile." He paused and looked up at her. "Have you checked their literatures for other similarities?"

"It took all night to find the drawings!"

Chris kissed his fingertip and ran it under Jael's eye. "Which accounts for these bags," he said. "I was afraid that it might have been the nightmares again." He pulled his rolling chair away from the desk and patted his lap. "Have a seat."

"The presentation isn't over yet," Jael said. She took the crayon drawing from her blazer pocket, handed it to him, then walked around his desk to the wooden chair that was normally reserved for students. Its seat was hard, hurt her bottom, and made her shift her weight and lean forward.

"This is Set," Chris said, placing the drawing next to the other three. "You're right. It's the same animal."

"It's also the creature from my nightmare."

Chris frowned. "You've dreamed about the Set creature all these months without realizing it?"

"Dr. Meier said I was repressing the image," Jael said.

"Your subconscious saw similarities that your conscious mind couldn't."

"Up to last night I might have bought that. Not anymore," Jael said. "I didn't make the drawing; a six-year-old boy did. His father told me that the boy's been having nightmares about the Set creature for as long as I have."

"You met him at Meier's lecture?"

"He'll be in my office at ten-thirty to inspect the pictures and tape."

"And the mother?"

"They're getting divorced."

Chris frowned. "You meet a man with a story like this and you instantly trust him?"

"There's something about him that's easy to like."

124

Chris paused. "Here's some unsolicited advice: Stay away from this mumbo-jumbo." Jael tried to speak, but he cut her off. "These drawings are a real breakthrough, the kind they award grants for. Don't blow it chasing after ghosts."

"Thanks," Jael said, "but I came to solicit advice."

"Be my guest."

"What do you know about Set?"

"He was the only deity in the Egyptian pantheon who wasn't represented by an earthly creature. Horus was the falcon, Anubis the jackal . . . well, Set was this *thing*. No one has any idea what it was," Chris said. "You couldn't have picked a more obsolete god."

"What does that mean?"

"The Egyptians did everything they could to stamp out Set worship—and I mean all traces." Chris tapped his forehead lightly, then said, "Wait a minute." He pushed his chair away from the desk, walked across the room, opened a window, then searched through one of the shelves and pulled out a tall blue book. "Let me quote from the Esfu Papyri":

"O Horus, protect me from He whose name is Evil Day, the Roarer, the Devourer of the Living . . . terrible are the days his spawn descend upon our land. They grapple with us and rip our bellies. They feast upon our flesh.

May the name of his followers fall into oblivion, may his sacred boat catch fire, may his statues be pulled down and trampled.

O Horus, stop their night cries. . . ."

Chris carried the book back to the desk and sat down. "Note the care the scribe used not to mention the name Set."

"Why?"

"He didn't want his hand cut off or his tongue pulled out."

"Back up, Chris."

"Set was the supreme god of Egypt during the Nineteenth and Twentieth dynasties," Chris said, opening the book. "Unlike most Egyptian gods, he wasn't loved, only feared. Anyway, his reign only lasted for a century or so. Then he was out."

"Just like that?" Jael asked.

"Just like that."

"Any conjecture as to why?"

"Something ate away at the country during his reign. Maybe it was the plague, maybe prolonged drought. Gods don't last long when they don't work. The masses suddenly turned their favor to Horus, a sun god," Chris said. "To say Set's fall was abrupt is an understatement." He flipped ahead a few pages in the book. "Here are some of his titles when he was number one: 'Set, the All-Powerful'; 'Set, the All-Knowing'; 'Set-who-knows-no-masters.' " Chris turned more pages. "These were his titles a hundred years later: 'He-who-licks-offal'; 'the Son of Evil'; 'the Bringer of Chaos.' "

"If you used his name, your tongue was pulled out?"

"You got it."

"The ancient Egyptians never struck me as a particularly brutal people," Jael said, tapping the back of her neck.

"With a few notable exceptions, they were brutal only when they had to be." Chris tugged at the beard at the corner of his mouth. "Set drew an unusually powerful response. All of his temples were torn down and their grounds sowed with salt so nothing would grow. His priesthood was hunted down and killed. His statues were destroyed; Christ, they even chiseled his name from burial chambers and erased it from papyri."

"So how do we know about him?"

"A few remnants survived. Most are in the Egyptian Antiquities Museum."

Jael shivered. The cool wind blowing in through the window cut through her blouse and blazer. "It's amazing that Set should be called the Roarer," she said. "If I had to describe him from the features in my dream, it's the name I would have settled on."

"Here's another interesting tidbit: The Egyptians considered Set the originator of nightmares." Chris turned back to the book. "In fact, the term *night cry,* a hieroglyph found only in Set worship, has a root word almost identical to *nightmare,* 'the filthy, evil things which Set has made.' "

Jael leaned back against the hard chair and glanced around the room. Procrastinating wasn't going to help her present the next piece of information. "The boy with the nightmare made the same roaring sound I heard in Tibet," she said, almost in a whisper. "The roaring from my nightmare."

"No, Jael."

"Yes, Chris," she said. "And he glowed! That's what attracted me to his father in the first place. He told about his son's symptoms and I—"

"I thought we were done with that," Chris said. "It's a dead end."

"You should have seen his relief when I said I believed him." She leaned over the desk and said softly, "I didn't tell him how grateful *I* was to find someone who believed *me*."

Chris continued to shake his head. "Drop the parapsychology," he said. "Drop the glowing and the roaring and rediscover the *One* Cult with plain, boring, day-by-day research. Otherwise you'll get laughed right out of the academic community."

Jael locked her hands behind her neck and shook her head. Talking to Chris was like trying to converse with a television. She began to stand and move toward the door. "I'll think about it," she said.

Chris took her hand. "There's another option," he said. "You feel like taking a vacation?"

"Where?"

"Egypt."

She leaned over the desk until her face was a foot from his. "How?" she asked.

"I have an open invitation to conduct some seminars at Cairo University." He traced the outline of her hand with a finger. "Decent money and all expenses paid."

"How would we get the time off?"

"You have an in with the department chairman. We skip Thursday classes, then next week we'd have what, eleven days?"

"Let me guess," Jael said sardonically. "I'd be the translator."

"You'd be my assistant in charge of something," Chris said, shaking his head. "I'd have to stay in Cairo for four or five days, but you could shuttle down to Luxor. I'd meet you when I finished."

Jael gently eased her hand from his. "Thanks."

"You'll learn more in a week at the museum than a year by correspondence," Chris said.

"Let me think about it."

"Think fast," Chris said. "This is my last opening for six months."

Jael glanced down at her wristwatch: nine twenty-five. "Look, they'll be here in an hour, and I still have some reading to do." She took a step away from the desk. "Any last words on Set?"

"Only that he grew to represent everything that was wrong with Egyptian culture . . . that he became a demon worshiped only by black magicians under penalty of death." He picked up the book on Set, flipped through some pages, then cleared his throat. "I'll leave you with one final quote: 'Ombos is pulled down. His temples are destroyed. All who belonged to Him are not. He is no longer.'" Chris placed the book facedown on the desk. "Whatever happened during the hundred years of Set's reign, Egypt was never the same. The dynasties lasted a few more centuries, but Set began the end of the empire: First Asia was lost, then the Assyrian invasions began, then . . ." He touched her hand. "Don't let the same thing happen to your career."

Jael leaned over the desk and kissed his cheek. "I'll get back to you."

"You'd better listen," he said, "or even I won't be able to save you."

Jael closed her eyes, set the pictures of the *chöd* on her desk, and waited for the strange tingling to go away. The feeling wasn't really *strange—vague* was a better description, an awareness she knew but couldn't place, as though her entire body were falling asleep. She shook her head, shivered, then walked across her office to a square of sunlight that fell on the Oriental carpet. She stared out the window first at the sky, then at the line of cars, which looked like a centipede, mindless segments crawling along a strip of concrete. She shivered again and the sensation returned, grew even stronger, and the room started to spin. She rested her head against the cold windowpane; the frame was mildewed, sour-smelling.

Then the thousands of invisible threads began to stir, and she understood. At first she thought of Julie, but no, the impulses, the signals of self were different, as different as tragedies from cartoons or concerti from lullabies. Jael closed her eyes and concentrated until a personality came into focus: a young, frightened boy.

Dylan.

His presence glided into her, tentacles of thought that wove through her mind, her memories. In turn Jael sensed his confusion: He wasn't sure whether to surrender to the incredible intimacy or fight it as he would the nightmare.

So Jael reached out further to him to let Dylan know what was strongest and best in her, to try to assure him, to comfort him so he would know her when they met—not her name, perhaps, but the deep rhythms of personality that revealed so much more. She sensed the guilt he felt over his parents' separation, the nightmare fears he could never express in words. She closed her eyes as the energy poured between them, pulled them closer and closer until they locked, blended into one another: She couldn't tell where her perceptions ended and where Dylan's began. She began to prod him, to call to him with feelings instead of words, to tell him not to be afraid, to come up the stairs. At first the anxiety was too great, so she helped him; he hesitated, weakened, then pulled away from a hand. His shoes slid on the lobby's tile, and his thighs strained on the stairs, ached by the time he reached the second floor. Her strength was his and there were more stairs, still more, and soon his shoes sank into the carpet of her hallway. She smelled the cleaning solvent from the walls, tasted the building's stale air, and the closer he came, the stronger the sensations grew, and she reached up with him to turn the doorknob and pushed with him against the heavy wood.

He stood in the doorway. "Who are you?" he asked in a quivering voice.

Jael ran to him, picked him up, and cradled him in her arms. He buried his face in her hair, and she whispered, "Don't be afraid, Dylan. Don't be afraid," and he put his arms around her neck and hugged her.

Jael heard footsteps and looked up. Matt stood in the doorway.

He took a step, tried to speak, but stuttered, then took another step.

"Please," Jael said, motioning with her head for him to enter.

Matt closed the door behind him. "As soon as we came in the building," he said, "Dylan started to tremble."

"I know," Jael said, but Matt didn't seem to hear. She carried Dylan to the chair behind her desk, sat down, and rocked him back and forth.

Matt approached them. "All of a sudden he started to relax. So did I. Then he yanked away and took off for the stairs. He always stops when I call. I called and called, but he was on the second floor before I started after him."

"I was there, Matt."

Matt stopped, tilted his head, and gave her a look that questioned her sanity. He glanced at her, then Dylan, then shook his head and sat down.

Jael let Dylan's exhaustion and fear melt into her. He settled into sleep, and she rocked him more gently, and his breathing evened, then slowed. The communion stopped when his eyelids closed; his head nodded, then settled on her breast.

"He's normally afraid of strangers."

"I'm not a stranger."

Matt stood and reached for the boy.

"Let me hold him," Jael said. "Right now he needs his sleep more than his father."

Matt plopped back into his chair, leaned forward, and rested an arm on her desk. "Ever since I met you," he said, "what was unusual has become bizarre."

How could she convince him of the impossible? She tried to speak, stammered slightly and stopped, then started again. "I have an unusual power," she said. "Let's call it a gift. I thought I was the only one left who had it. I was wrong."

"What?"

"The gift. Dylan has it too."

"You're making no sense at all."

"You're right," she said. She took another deep breath. "Dylan and I can communicate telepathically." Matt tried to interrupt, but Jael raised her hand to quiet him. "It's been so long since I

130

felt the sensation, I almost forgot what it was. He must have sensed my power and reached out for me. I led him here." She kissed Dylan's hair. "At this instant he's closer to me than he's been to anyone in his life."

"I don't know whether to be grateful or jealous or call for help."

"I'm sorry I'm not making more sense," Jael said. "As well as I know the experience, I still can't explain it."

"Try."

Jael stared at the Chinese landscapes on the wall as she tried to organize her thoughts. "It's like injecting a drop of your essence into someone." She looked at him hopefully.

"Keep trying," he said.

"Imagine that each thought and feeling beams an impulse like a TV station. Most people only transmit signals; they don't receive them. Julie and I, and now Dylan, translate the impulses from one another into sounds and pictures, sensations beyond either. We can *share*."

"Why doesn't he share with his parents?"

"Who knows?" Jael said. "Before today I thought I shared, but now that there's Dylan . . ." Jael started to giggle as though she were seventeen again. "Sorry," she said, trying to regain her composure. "I spent the first eighteen years of my life feeling like this every day, and I thought I'd lost it forever."

Matt cleared his throat. When Jael looked up, she saw more fear on his face than relief.

"I had an identical twin," Jael said. "We had . . ." She paused, knowing the right words wouldn't come. She kissed Dylan's hair and smelled bubble bath; the aroma took her back two decades. ". . . we had *this!* It's like being different moods in the same personality, different expressions on the same face."

"I've heard that identical twins are more in tune than other people. If you and Dylan were even related, it might make some sense. . . ." Then Matt sighed and leaned back in his chair. Silence. He smiled, shrugged hopelessly, and said, "Who cares what I do and don't understand? Can you help him?"

Dylan stirred and nuzzled Jael; his heart beat against hers. "We're helping each other already," she said.

131

Jael watched Matt pace across the room, sort through the pictures of the *chöd* for perhaps the hundredth time, then stare down at the couch where Dylan lay. The boy hadn't stirred in an hour. Matt dropped the pictures on Jael's desk, then walked across the office and stood in the sunlight. "The shaman's glow is identical to Dylan's; so was the roar," he said, tapping his fingers on the window. "At least Dylan hasn't sacrificed any humans."

"Do you have any pets?"

"Goldfish, hamsters, the usual." Matt paused and started to shake his head. "Believe me, Dylan isn't the type."

"He's not the type to glow, either."

Matt nodded his head despondently. "Yeah. I'll check with Bekki."

Jael picked up the pictures and flipped through them: the procession, the climb up the pyramid, the dance. She looked up. "He built an altar?"

"I didn't say altar."

"You said *shrine;* that's close enough."

"His drawings were piled onto a chair. . . . All of his stuffed dogs were arranged in a circle around the base."

"An altar," Jael said, plugging the electric teapot on her desk into an outlet. "There's no way he could have learned about primitive ceremonies?"

"Dr. Velde has already been through all that and decided that there was no way he could have known."

"I'm not surprised," Jael said.

Matt paced across the room to the shelf where Jael kept some small statues. He picked up a jade dragon and turned it in his hands. "Now all we have to do is figure out what the Creepster has to do with ancient gods, human sacrifices, and telepathic communication."

"Don't forget roaring and glowing."

"I wouldn't dream of it," Matt said.

Jael's leg started to fall asleep, so she uncrossed it, stood, and walked toward the couch. She sat on the arm by Dylan's head and looked down at the boy, then back at Matt. Matt covered his face with his hands and rubbed his eyes; Dylan had done the

132

same thing in his sleep, the same movement inward from the ears to the nose, the same circular motion with the balls of his hands.

"It's been months since he slept without tossing," Matt said.

Jael smiled. "I know."

"Yeah. I keep forgetting how *much* you know."

Jael didn't see much of Matt in Dylan—which wasn't too surprising, since they weren't male in the same way yet: Dylan had none of the sharp, aggressive adult features, the high forehead with deep lines. The biggest difference was in the eyes, though. Dylan's eyes were abnormally large with full lashes—no doubt his mother's. Matt's were deep-set and dark, unpredictable in a way that was both frightening and attractive. Matt started to pace again, moving around the hanging spider plant, to the bookshelves, and back to the window again. "Can you share with him while he's asleep?"

"I could with Julie, but Julie and I spent eighteen years on the same wavelength."

"Sharing takes practice?"

"Like any other skill. And age is important. It seems as though the more the intellect develops, the weaker the telepathy becomes." Her teapot started to boil. "Teatime," she said, pouring hot water into a cup. "First cut Darjeeling or Earl Grey?"

"Neither, thanks," Matt said.

Jael took a spoonful of Darjeeling, placed it in her tea ball, set the ball in the water, and watched it swirl, then slowly sink. She bent over and inhaled; it was acidic and sweet and worked up through her sinuses. Jael nodded to Dylan as he rolled over. "He searched me out. If he hadn't, we never would have shared."

Matt wouldn't quit pacing; he was starting to make her nervous. Although she didn't want to compare him to Chris, Chris was the standard these days. They were both like runners, but Chris had the patience and grace of a jogger, while Matt possessed the power and restlessness of a sprinter.

And the suddenness.

He turned toward her and asked, "What's it like being inside the mind of a six-year-old?"

"Crisp and clear as spring," Jael said. She removed the tea ball from the water, added a squeeze of lemon, and approached Matt.

Her eyes were level with his chin. "The sensations were happy or sad, painful or pleasurable, with no shadings." She touched her lips to the tea; it was much too hot to drink. "If either of us perceived the world as he does, they'd call us manic-depressives."

"What sort of things does he take from you?" Matt asked hesitantly. "Any . . . any adult sensations?"

Jael smiled. It was a question that could be asking for a number of different kinds of information. "I doubt he'd register world-weariness, sexual awareness, things like that." She rested the cup on the windowsill to cool. "Since they'd be so alien, he'd let them slip by like shadows. He could understand most of the simple thoughts and most feelings . . . love, uncertainty, certainly loneliness."

Matt smiled and huge dimples appeared on either side of his mouth; they undercut the somberness of the square chin and brooding eyes and made them seem childlike, almost innocent.

"So what do we do next?" Matt asked.

Jael tilted her head and smiled: He had lingered on *we* long enough to imply that he might be referring to something beyond a professional relationship. She stared at him and began to nod. The idea of getting to know a man who used *we* instead of *I* seemed to grow more attractive with each passing minute.

TWELVE

Chicago, Illinois—October 12, 1981

"So what *do* we do next?" Matt asked, watching Jael turn from the window. Sunlight silhouetted her and seemed to make her glow and appear even more mysterious and magnetic than she was. How he wished he could share her feelings instead of trying to gauge the spark in her eyes, what she meant with her smile, in the normal, human way. Maybe that's all sharing was. An extra sensitivity to moods. To gestures. But that wouldn't explain Dylan's sprint up the stairs, or his finding Jael's office, or a thousand other coincidences. Matt shook his head, drummed his fingers, and stared up at the ceiling, the fluorescent lights, and the tiles. "I've always been a rational man," he said. "Maybe that's what makes this so unbelievable."

"If you accepted everything I've said, I'd question your sanity," Jael said.

Matt lifted a small stone sculpture from her desk and tried to judge its weight. "Whether or not I believe in telepathy isn't the problem. What are we going to do to help him?"

"Can I keep seeing him?"

"I couldn't keep him from you if I wanted to."

"Then we can start by getting to know each other." A smile turned the corner of her mouth. "Can you come to dinner a week from this Saturday?"

Matt smiled. "Maybe he'll eat vegetables for you." He walked past her, leaned against the window frame, and stared down into the street. The noon sirens had blown and people packed the sidewalks, mulling around and bumping into one another. If anyone had tripped, he would have been trampled. Like a cattle stampede. "Ever find the city too damn smothering?" Matt asked.

"That's a pretty strange question from an urban lawyer."

Matt turned toward her. "Every time I ask you a question about anthropology, you're a human encyclopedia. Whenever I ask you a personal question, you turn it around and shoot it back at me."

"I'm that transparent?"

"Who knows more about evasion than a lawyer?" Matt asked.

Her eyes glinted in the sunshine. She nodded and, after a short silence, walked to the window and looked out. "I work in Chicago, take in the arts here." She paused. "The best moments of my life were on or in Lake Michigan."

"Do you sail?" Matt asked hopefully.

Jael smiled and took a step closer to him. "Every time I get the chance," she said.

Dylan slept.

And Matt watched Jael. Watched her sit by the boy and stroke his forehead when he whimpered in a dream, place a hand on his shoulder when he stirred. Twice when she was talking to Matt she stopped in mid-sentence and went to Dylan just before he groaned. The connection between them was too real to ignore. The boy reacted to Jael's touch in a way he had never responded to Matt's.

Matt was about to join them on the couch when he heard a quick knock. The door swung open and a face with a blond beard popped through the opening. "Sorry to interrupt," the man said, "but it's past time for lunch." He glanced toward the couch. "That must be the boy," he said.

Jael nodded.

"Then you're the man from the Meier lecture," he said to Matt. He stepped into the office and closed the door behind him. His high cheekbones, delicate nose, and calculated movements radiated privilege, prep schools. His Irish sweater and faded jeans were casual chic. His eyes stayed locked with Matt's.

"You're *the* Professor Shaw?" Matt asked.

"Since Jael mentioned our discussion this morning, she must also have mentioned my skepticism," he said. When Dylan sat up and rubbed his eyes, the man knelt. "Looks like you've had a nap."

"Hi," Dylan said dreamily.

"Chris, this is Dylan," Jael said. When Matt approached them, Chris stood and offered his hand. "This is Matt Griffin."

Chris put an arm on Jael's shoulder and brushed a strand of hair from her face. There was no mistaking the familiarity with which he touched her—or that territory was being declared. "I'm starving," he said.

"Lunch is off today," Jael said.

"What's that supposed to mean?" Chris asked.

"I'm in the middle of a conference."

"Fine," Chris said. From his manner he might have been talking to a student. He turned to Matt. "Care to join us?"

"This is a private conference," Jael cut in.

"Sorry," Chris said. "I hoped we could celebrate."

"What?"

"Our trip to Egypt."

Jael exhaled loudly, looked up at the ceiling, then looked back at Chris. "I never said I was going to Egypt."

"You implied you were."

"I asked you to let me think about it."

"I spent all morning making arrangements," Chris said, enunciating each word precisely. He started to stroke his beard, to pet himself, one of the reasons Matt never grew a beard. Although neither voice had been raised, the atmosphere sparked. Matt had been through enough arguments to know one was approaching.

"Something's come up," Jael said.

Chris stepped toward her. "I gave the Egyptians my word. We leave on Friday."

"I have a visitor," Jael said, turning away from him. "Can't this wait?"

"It's waited long enough," Chris said, sitting down on the corner of the desk. When he turned to Matt, the corner of his mouth twitched. "Since this 'something' didn't exist three hours ago, it must involve you." He smiled coldly. "Do you know how much this escapade could cost Dr. Clarke?"

"I don't want to 'cost' her anything," Matt said.

"Then explain what this 'something' is."

Matt glanced toward Jael and hoped she'd indicate with a nod, a gesture, how much he should say—if anything. She merely glared at Chris and shook her head. No help at all. Finally Matt said, "Jael and my son can telepathically communicate."

"My God, that's lovely," Chris said flatly.

"Chris . . . !" Jael's voice trembled.

Normally it would have been time for Matt to stand, walk past Chris, deposit Dylan on his shoulder, and leave them to fight it out. Not today. Today he needed to know how the fight ended. There was a finality in Jael's tone—the same tone Bekki had used with him.

"I'm sorry about this, Matt," Jael pleaded, nodding toward the door. "I'll call you this evening."

"I'm not through yet," Chris said. "Professor Clarke could be the next Margaret Mead if she wanted. Instead she prefers to play Madame Blavatsky, mystic."

"Let's continue this later," Jael said, taking Chris by the arm.

Chris ignored her and continued in a voice too calm to be calm, "Tibet. Mexico. Wherever I take her, she insists on looking for ghosts." He pulled away from her, walked up to her desk, and held up the sketches of the wolf-gods. "There's no telling what sort of breakthrough these could lead to. . . ." He shook his head in disgust. "It's getting to the point where I'm not at all sure how many more ghost chases her career can tolerate."

Jael clenched her fists and bit her lip. She breathed so heavily that her nostrils flared.

Now it was time to leave. "Please excuse us," Matt said. "Time to get Dylan back to his mom's."

Jael turned briskly from Chris, walked to Dylan, lifted him, and rested him on her hip; it amazed Matt how perfectly children molded to a woman's curves. "You're having dinner with me on Saturday," she said. "I won't take no for an answer."

"Can Dad come?" Dylan asked.

She smiled and kissed him on the cheek. "I'm in the Wilmette phone book," she said to Matt as she handed him the boy. She led them to the door and opened it. "You know how sorry I am about this." She stepped into the hall.

"But I'm not," Matt said.

She touched his hand. Maybe on another occasion she would have smiled. Instead she set her jaw and, when she walked back into the office, shut the door so firmly, it echoed down the hall.

"Grown-ups sure fight a lot," Dylan said, leaning forward and drawing a large *J* in the steam on the windshield.

"You got me there," Matt said. He drove across the bridge by the yacht club and listened for gulls. It was almost dark and a rain fell, cold, misty, and dull. He glanced first to his right at the grayness of the lake, then to the left at the Baha'i Temple. Even the delicate etchings on its huge dome seemed unimaginative against the flat sky. *Autumn in the Midwest,* Matt thought. *A great time to be somewhere else.* Dylan sneezed and Matt turned toward him. He had finished writing *J-A-E-L.* "What do you think of her?" Matt asked.

"She's not here anymore."

The thought sent shivers down Matt's back. "Was she earlier?"

"When we first got in the car. When I wanted her to be."

Matt leaned back into the bucket seat to let the leather warm him. He touched Dylan's hand. "Hey, Cap'n. Don't tell your mom about what you did with Jael."

"Why?"

"Remember how the man acted? Sharing is easy enough for you and Jael to understand, but it's tough on the rest of us." Matt paused to give the next statement more weight. "I'd hate to see her try to keep you away from Jael."

Dylan's face turned red and his eyes filled with tears.

"Just hold on," Matt said, patting the boy's shoulder. "There are only two people who can tell her, and we're both in this car."

Dylan nodded and turned toward the window; his breath thickened the already thick steam. "I like Jael," he said.

"And I like anyone who makes you feel better," Matt said, ruffling the boy's hair. There was more to it than that, though. Jael made him feel like a teenager. He was already remembering pubescent fantasies. From the instant he crossed the Wilmette border, he tried to guess which house was hers. It was silly, giddy, like meeting a girl in study hall and spending the rest of the day creating a fantasy life for her. Scoring ten touchdowns for her. Moving into the woods to live together, alone. . . . He rolled down the window to let the cool air shock the images from his head.

A few blocks after he crossed the Kenilworth border, Matt turned into the horseshoe driveway and circled beneath the leafless elms. The lake smelled as cold and as antiseptic as steel. He braked the car by the portico, slipped the transmission out of gear, and let the engine idle. Normally, Dylan would kiss Matt as soon as the car stopped, then jump out of the car and sprint to the house before the tears came.

Not today.

Matt leaned over and kissed the boy, then opened the door for him. "Remember I love you," Matt said.

"Can't I stay?"

Matt leaned closer and put a hand on the boy's cheek. "What's the matter, Cap'n?"

"The Creepster's waiting for me."

"And things would be better if I went in and scared him away?"

Dylan patted his hands together in delight.

Matt hadn't been inside the house in a month. Usually when he came for Dylan he stopped out front, honked, and waited for the boy to come running out. But today . . . today the idea of seeing Bekki didn't seem as painful. Matt unbuckled his shoulder harness, hopped from the car, and opened the door for Dylan. The boy took his hand and led him toward the house.

Bekki waited for them in the frame of the open door. She wore a weekend outfit: tight jeans, sandals, and the red T-shirt Matt remembered wrestling off her the previous winter in Bermuda. Delicious.

"The Creepster is making an early appearance," Matt said to her. "Dylan thought some reinforcements would help."

Dylan released Matt's hand, ran up to Bekki, and hugged her leg. She kissed him, then shook her head. "They sure don't make doctors like they used to."

"Don't jump to conclusions. Dr. Clarke got him to sleep soundly."

"Hypnosis?"

"Something like that," Matt said.

Bekki looked Matt up and down and smiled. "You have enough time for some coffee?"

Matt shrugged and immediately wished he hadn't. He hated shrugs; they communicated nothing but the inability to communicate. "Of course I do," he said, stepping toward the door. When Dylan started to back toward the car, Matt tucked the boy under his arm, carried him inside, and eased him down on the rug. "Give me a couple minutes with your mom, then we'll go upstairs."

"But he's there *now!*" Dylan whined.

"Just a few seconds."

"Please!"

"Dylan!" Bekki said.

Suddenly, Dylan's eyes turned cold and flat. "I don't need your help," he snapped. He ran down the hallway and disappeared up the stairs.

Bekki sighed and shook her head. "It's been 'Creepster this,' 'Creepster that' for the last week and a half." She hesitated before she continued. "Dr. Velde thinks it's a ploy to force us back together."

"The more I find out, the less I believe that."

"He got you inside, didn't he?" Bekki said. She took his arm and led him toward the kitchen. She hadn't touched him in more than a month; it was all the more pleasant because it was so unexpected. He sat at the kitchen table while she went through the familiar coffee-making ritual. "You look good," she said.

"I've been working hard," Matt said. "It helped keep me sane." Before Bekki could interrupt him, he added, "That will be my only shot for the day."

"You were entitled to one," she said, taking his cup from a shelf and washing it. "I'm glad you're here. Some new things have popped up. Dylan's started sleepwalking."

"How often?"

"Too often," Bekki said. "I put a gate at the top of the stairs to keep him from breaking his neck."

Matt reached for a chocolate mint, removed the green foil

141

wrapper, and placed the candy on his tongue; immediately it started to melt. "What does Dr. Velde say?"

"Less and less. She's decided to call in some medical doctors. Maybe a linguist too."

"A linguist?"

"Dylan talks in his sleep," Bekki said, leaning toward him. "I recorded him three nights ago and gave the tape to her. She speaks fifteen different languages and had no idea what it was."

"He's not just mumbling?"

"There are consistent pauses, inflections. It's not like any language I've ever heard. Dr. Velde was sure it made sense. At least to Dylan."

The Mr. Coffee started to gurgle, spout, make its familiar rumbling noises; coffee dripped into the pot. Matt shifted his weight and rubbed his nose. "Make me a copy."

"Why?"

"Dr. Clarke is an expert in obscure languages. Aztec. Tibetan." He paused. "If anyone can decipher it, she can."

"She's a psychiatrist?"

"A cultural anthropologist."

Bekki frowned.

"A friend told me about her," Matt lied. "That she's special." It was time to change subjects. "Has Velde tried anything new?"

"When's your next appointment?"

It was no use trying to wait Bekki out. None. "Saturday," Matt said.

"Weekend hours?"

"This includes dinner."

"Oh," Bekki said. She gave him a quick, hard glance. "Would she mind if I came along?"

"I would." When Bekki tried to speak, he cut her off. "Dylan's yours during the week, mine on the weekends. That's a five-to-two disadvantage no matter how you look at it." Bekki rolled her eyes and looked toward the ceiling. "Maybe I should just go," Matt said, his voice softening.

She put a finger to his lips for silence. "Drink your coffee and have dinner with your goddamn anthropologist." She walked to the counter, poured the coffee, and brought the steaming cups back to the table. "What else did she tell you?"

"To check for missing pets."

Bekki made a sour face, looked away, and shook her head.

"What's wrong?" Matt asked.

"That's a pretty good guess for an anthropologist." A pause. "The hamster's gone." A longer pause. "Now that you mention it, the aquarium seems emptier than it did two weeks ago."

"We've got to be sure." Matt pushed his chair away from the table and walked to the kitchen door. They hurried down the hallway, past the pantry, the library. The smell of cleaning solvent from the gun cabinet filled the air. At least part of him, his smells, remained in the house even though he was gone. They turned into the game room and approached the twenty-gallon fish tank. Fish glided past the glass, their blank eyes staring past him; others huddled in groups, hid behind weeds, or wiggled under rocks and gravel. "There are only two Jack Dempseys," he said. "There used to be eight."

"The cat?" Bekki asked.

"It's time we talk with Dylan," Matt said. He waited for Bekki at the door, then walked to the stairs and hurried to the top. He opened the accordionlike gate, the one they had bought when Dylan first learned to walk. A half-dozen steps down the corridor and he turned toward Dylan's door.

Closed.

Like the night of the roaring.

Matt's throat went dry; his pulse throbbed in his throat, his temples. He grabbed the doorknob. Thank God, it twisted effortlessly. He pushed the door open and glanced inside.

No Dylan.

The pictures were still on the wall, the chair still under the desk, the toys still harmlessly tucked away in their box—just no boy. Matt walked into the room and checked the closet, under the bed. "Where else does he play?" Matt asked as Bekki entered the room.

"Either here or outside."

"Then we search." Matt took one side of the hallway, Bekki the other, and they moved from room to room, bedrooms, bathrooms, linen closets. Vacant, vacant, vacant. They met at the end of the hall.

"Maybe he's outside," Bekki suggested.

"After dark?" There was a scratching from the ceiling. No, the attic. It sounded as though a trunk were being dragged across the floor. Matt looked at the ceiling and then Bekki.

"As far as I know, he's terrified of the attic," she said.

"Then there are some damn big rats." He held a finger to his lips for silence, then gently opened the door and, without turning on the light, knelt and took the stairs one at a time. There was a glow on the ceiling. A reddish glow and noise. The steady scraping turned to a tapping. The screech of metal against wood. Then a laugh. A laugh like gurgling liquid. A cold breeze moved down the stairs like a shudder. There were fingers of ice at his neck. The attic wasn't heated, but this was more than an autumn cold: This cold was alive. It was a presence; it had being. It squirmed through his clothing and gnawed at his heart. Like a scalpel on his vein. Like splinters of glass in his scalp. The thin giggle again. Was it merely cold or fear? He realized he was terrified. Another step. Another. The red glow brightened the ceiling. Matt held his breath and glanced over the final stair. A swirling mist filled the room, a seething fog that expanded and contracted as if it were breathing. Dylan sat in its heart, his back toward the stairway.

There were tools. And wood. Thin strips of wood. He was assembling something, working with motions so mechanical that Matt couldn't believe a human being could make them. What was it? A playhouse? A chair? No, a frame of some kind. The strips of wood had been joined into triangles, the triangles into pyramids. There must have been three pyramids and another six triangles. It might have been a day's work for a man, but at the rate Dylan was moving . . .

Matt moved closer to the boy, and as he knelt down he began to understand. The pyramids were sections, sections of a star, a replica of the frame he had seen in the pictures at Jael's office. His hand touched something soft, furry. The hamster. It had been disemboweled, partially eaten. And the fish. And two robins. Disemboweled and rotting.

Bekki's thigh brushed his shoulder. Matt tried to hold her

back, but she pushed past him, kept pushing, pushing, until her head was even with his own.

She froze, then started to back away. *Stay quiet,* he thought, *no screaming.* He could almost feel the cry build in her before she started to shriek. When she moved toward Dylan, the room grew even colder. The mist swirled, seemed to move with intent toward the corners and leaked out the cracks in the roof. Dylan's head turned toward them slowly, ever so slowly. Of all the things Matt had seen, the glowing, the roaring, the striking of the snake, nothing—nothing—had been as frightening as Dylan's eyes were now.

They were blank.

As blank as a robot's. Blank as a dead man's. As blank as the fish that had stared past Matt from the aquarium.

THIRTEEN

Wilmette, Illinois—October 24, 1981

A pigeon whirled past Jael's kitchen window and caught her eye. Out in the lake, a half mile away, maybe more, whitecaps rose and grew as they raced toward shore. Although it was almost sunset, the sky was more gray than red; the thin mist stripped the horizon of boats and color. She looked back at the salad bowl and continued to tear the chilled lettuce into strips and add it to the tomatoes, sprouts, and sunflower seeds. How to react to Matt's call about Dylan? Tell him that there was nothing to worry about? That the attack was a once-in-a-lifetime thing? Not mention it at all? There should have been thunder and lightning outside. It only seemed fitting that the weather should mimic her tension.

She heard the grandfather clock chime five P.M. She'd forgotten to feed Osiris. She walked to the cabinets by the chopping block, dried her hands, and reached for the fruit.

Dylan was nearby.

She saw her apartment building as he would see it—the wonder at its height, the expectation and awe. Then other sensations. The smell of oil and gas. He was in the basement garage. A car door opened, then slammed. Rubber soles touched concrete. He was walking toward the parking attendant's office.

Amazing.

Thirteen floors of steel and concrete separated them, yet his sensations were more intense than her own. She hurried through the dining room, through the anteroom, and into the hallway. Her stomach dropped as the elevator lights flashed one through twelve. A bell rang, the down arrow flashed red, and the doors cracked open. Dylan ran from the elevator and hugged her leg; a bright red lunch box smacked the back of her thigh. She knelt

146

down and kissed him, then tapped a finger on its lid. "Hey," she said, "I'm supposed to furnish the food."

He opened the lid slightly and let her peek inside: paper, pencils, watercolors, and more crayons than she'd seen since first grade.

"He insisted," Matt said, walking from the elevator. "He wants to draw you a picture." He offered a hand and pulled her to her feet, then smiled somewhat sheepishly. "Dylan said you'd be here waiting for us." A pause. "Strange. I would have been disappointed if you hadn't."

Jael took one of Matt's huge hands and one of Dylan's tiny ones, then led them into the condominium. She kicked the door shut behind them, and after a few steps they stepped down into the living room.

"Wow!" Dylan said, walking up to the floor-to-ceiling cage. He looked up at the cockatoo and his mouth opened wide. "It's as big as an eagle!" When the bird looked down at him, ruffled its feathers, and squawked, Dylan backed away.

Jael placed three fingers through the wire mesh and let the bird nuzzle her first with its beak, then its crest. "His name is Osiris," Jael said. "He's as friendly as a dog."

"Does he talk?" Matt asked.

"Sometimes. Mostly he screeches."

"Can I pet him?" Dylan asked.

Jael took his hand, led him to the cage, and eased his fingers through the mesh. When the bird nudged him, he squealed with delight. When the bird turned away, Dylan ran to his lunch box, spread some paper on the brown and white rug, and started to draw the cage.

When Jael turned to Matt, he was examining one of the sketches on the wall. "Goya?" he asked.

"I didn't know you were an expert in art."

"It belongs in a museum," he said. Then he spread his arms and gestured toward the other paintings and sculptures. "I suppose you bought all these at the same sale you bought your clothing."

"Ever hear of Powder River Oil?"

"Ma and Pa own it?" Matt asked.

"Pa, actually," Jael said. "Mother's investments are more diverse."

"So what are you doing teaching college?"

"I love it," Jael said. "The research and writing if not the politics. There's a stability and truth in it that most things lack." She led him up the two stairs to the dining room, then toward the kitchen. "It's traditional to offer before-dinner drinks."

"I'm still on the wagon."

"I stocked up on lemon and Coke." She raised her voice and said, "Can I bring you anything, Dylan?" The boy was engrossed with his picture, staring first at the bird, then the paper, then drawing with excruciating effort. He didn't lift his head. Jael took Matt's arm and steered him into the kitchen, pointed to the table, and sat down next to him. "What did Dr. Velde say about Dylan's attack?" she asked in a hushed voice.

"Exactly what you'd expect: that his listening to Bekki and me squabble triggered an adverse reaction." A lengthy pause. "She ignored the glowing, naturally. She suggested that we were hysterical." He shrugged. "Bekki believed her."

Jael leaned against the chair and stared out the window. The sky had darkened; it would be dark in a half hour. Less. *What was Dylan's attack like?* she wondered. *What did he see? Hear? How alone he must have been!* "Why didn't you call me?" she asked.

"I was rushing him to the hospital." Matt slouched and looked past her. "Besides, I thought you had an open line to one another."

"It's one-way. Dylan turns it off and on like a spigot." Jael leaned across the table and took his hand. "Does he remember anything?"

"A complete blank," Matt said. He sighed, then opened his hands in a hopeless gesture. "It was a blank the first time too."

"Call me if it happens again."

"Sure."

"I'm serious."

"And I'm a twentieth-century man," Matt said. "When things go wrong, I think of test tubes and drugs." When Jael tried to speak, he held up a hand to stop her. "I'm trying—believe me, I am. But it's like asking me to practice voodoo or witchcraft."

"If I'm near him, I might be able to initiate the sharing. At the very least I'll be able to experience what he does. And there's a good chance I'll remember."

The timer on the oven buzzed, so Jael started to ease away from the table. Matt grabbed her wrist and slipped a cassette into her hand. "Would you listen to this?"

"What is it?"

"Dylan's been talking in his sleep. Some bizarre language." He forced a smile. "You know more bizarre things than anyone I've ever met."

"Thanks. I guess," Jael said. She set the tape on top of the refrigerator, then walked to the broiler to remove the chateaubriand and put it on a serving dish. After she removed the asparagus from the stove, she drained it and smothered it in hollandaise sauce. "There's French onion soup and wild rice in the microwave," she told Matt as she carried the dishes into the dining room. "Dylan," she said, "chowtime!"

No answer.

Matt walked into the room and set the dishes by the flower arrangement. "I'd check the bathroom before I got excited," he said.

Jael walked to the corridor by the bedrooms. Dylan walked from the bathroom, carrying his lunch box. "You okay?" she asked.

He nodded, took a piece of folded paper from his pocket, and handed it to her. It was a drawing of Osiris. It lacked the sophistication of the pictures of Set, but at least the bird's pinks, reds, and whites were in the correct places. She knelt by him to tuck in his shirt. "It's beautiful," she said, and kissed him on the cheek.

Jael watched Dylan throughout dinner—for lack of appetite, twinges of fear, sullenness. There weren't any. He was even more settled, more at ease, than the first time they met.

Matt took a cut of meat, put it on Dylan's plate, and sliced it into bite-size pieces. "I've been wondering what an academic does after she's learned everything there is to know about after-death states," he said, taking a bite of his salad.

"She writes a book."

"Which I can find in my public library?"

"Maybe someday," she said. "I have to finish it first."

Matt reached past the flower arrangement for another helping of wild rice. "I never asked you why," he said.

"Why what?"

"Why a nice girl like you would get into anything as depressing as after-death literature."

Jael shrugged and sipped her water before she answered. "I was with Julie when she died. I saw, felt, all sorts of things. If I find out what they were, it could answer some pretty big mysteries."

"Like what exists after life?"

"Like what exists after life."

Matt took a bite of asparagus, chewed, and swallowed before he said, "Was she like you?"

"We looked alike, but she was more energetic, more aggressive than I."

"I find that hard to believe," Matt said.

"You change a lot in a decade, particularly when you find yourself alone for the first time."

Dylan tried to gulp a spoonful of soup, but strings of cheese ran from the spoon to the bowl. Matt had to cut them with a knife. "Did kids at school used to make fun of you?" Dylan asked.

"Of course."

"I'm surprised you attended schools," Matt said.

"We didn't at first. Mother insisted we have a governess straight from England. Nose in the air. Class consciousness. By fourth grade Dad decided we . . . I, actually, was becoming too withdrawn, and he's not the type to do things halfway. 'If public schools were good enough for me . . .' That sort of thing. Anyway, the Clarke twins were thrown into the same schools as everyone else, sink or swim."

"You swam well."

"A lot of that was Julie too. Anyone who gave me grief had to deal with her, one way or another." When Jael noticed a look of alarm spread over Matt's face, she smiled and said, "She didn't use any special power except charm. She attracted jocks. Whoever hassled us dealt with them."

Matt took a bite of wild rice and washed it down with water. "Where did you learn to sail?"

"The Cape. You?"

"Bekki."

"Which reminds me," Jael said. "You've been careful to avoid saying anything about your past."

"I'm not that interesting."

"I'll decide that," Jael said.

Matt speared a bite of chateaubriand, then a mushroom, then a piece of carrot, like a shish kebab. "I'm from a long line of potato farmers. The family spread is in northern Wisconsin."

"You've polished your rough edges."

"A lot of sophisticated people knocked 'em off me," Matt said. He lifted his eyebrows to express disbelief. "Our Fourth of July picnic looks like an episode of *Little House on the Prairie.*"

"So what brought you to the city?"

"Bekki," Matt said flatly. He shrugged and shifted his eyes to Dylan, then pointed at the asparagus on Dylan's plate. "Will you finish your veggies if I beg?" he asked. "You don't want to hurt Jael's feelings."

"She doesn't care," Dylan said.

Matt turned back to Jael and made an I-tried-my-best gesture. "Your studies must have taken you everywhere."

"Sorry, Matt," Jael said. "Back to Bekki."

Matt smiled and nodded his head. "You'd love cross-examination." He leaned toward her, rested his arms on the table, and smelled a rose. "I'd never met anyone like her. Slick. Suburban. Cultured. She had done all the things I'd only dreamed about." He rubbed the bridge of his nose. "Her dad's a senior partner in a big downtown firm. I transferred from biology to pre-law the semester after I met her." He stopped to drain his water. "I really would like to hear about those trips."

"I collected a royal tomb in Egypt, was one of the first westerners to visit the Tibetan lamaseries after the invasion, was in on the Tolpectuan dig in the Yucatán—"

"And you're twenty-seven?" Matt interrupted.

"Chris's name opens doors."

"There is something . . . sudden about him," Matt said.

Jael smiled. "He's arrogant enough for five men. If anyone has justification, though, it's him."

"If," Matt said. He turned from her and pointed toward the piano in the living room. "I don't imagine that's for decoration."

"It has been lately."

"I like music," Dylan said, bouncing up and down on his seat.

She turned to him and placed a hand on his head. "I'd been playing for more than two years when I was your age." She looked back at Matt. "My mother traded a career as a concert pianist for housewifing. She didn't want her girls to follow in her footsteps."

"But you stopped."

"Once Julie was gone, what was magic became work." She paused. "I discovered I lacked the energy to excel at both academics and music. My decision was easier than you might imagine."

When Dylan stopped squirming, Jael looked at him. He turned his eyes to the floor. "Teach me how to play."

"As soon as I get back in practice."

"Please."

"I planned to make the offer." She reached over and cupped a hand behind his head. "It's my way of making sure you'll come back to see me every week."

Jael couldn't sleep.

It was as though Dylan had activated a current when he arrived and forgot to turn it off when he left. Sparks continued to pour through her. The grandfather clock chimed four A.M. She pushed away from the desk, walked to the book shelves, and searched for her translation of the *Táin Bó Cúailigne,* but it wasn't there. Fine. It wasn't really necessary. A cross-reference for the few lines she had translated from the tape would be useful, but she knew Cuchulainn's transformation scene well enough to recite it. She sat on the corner of the desk and pushed the play button on the cassette recorder:

> "Is ann sin ro cestriastradh im Coin Culainn co
> nderna uathbhasch iolrechtach iongantach aandrenta
> anaithnidh dhe. . . ."

She pushed the stop button, the fast forward for an instant, then the play button again:

> "Ro-clos bloisgbeimnecha croide ina cliab mar
> glain n-arcon i fothach no mar leoman as tocht fo
> matgamhnaibh. Do-chithi na citnella nime na haoible
> tenedh trichemruaidhe i nallaibh i n-aeraibh osa ccion
> re fiuchadh na fercce fiorgaurbe atract uasa. . . ."

She turned it off.

If it weren't Dylan's voice, so obviously his pitch and tone, Jael would have called Matt up and asked him why the hoax. A six-year-old memorize part of an obscure text? And in ancient Irish? His pronunciation was better than her own.

Osiris screeched, a sound more like a crumbling mountain than a bird's call. No wonder. She hadn't fed him since noon. If he wasn't completely stuffed, there'd be no sleeping for either of them. She rewound the tape, slipped it into her pocket, and walked from the study to the hallway.

A tingling, a deadness, swept over her face. The sleepless hours were starting to add up. She stopped at the bathroom, opened the medicine cabinet, and used some eyedrops, then blinked the sting away. She splashed some cold water on her face, used a Q-Tip to clean her ear, and, as she left, dropped the cotton swab into the wastebasket.

And stopped.

An orange and green box lay partially hidden by a layer of facial tissue. She leaned over and picked it up. Dylan's crayon box. She moved more tissue. Dylan's paints, his paper. More crayons.

Strange.

She had seen the lunch box under his arm when he left. Maybe he'd been disappointed with his drawing and decided to punish the offending tools. He'd probably want them back by morning. She collected them and placed them in a Kleenex box, then walked into the kitchen. An apple and orange from the fruit bowl, a knife from the dishwasher, and she continued into the living room and pulled a chair up to the cage. She pressed down on the orange's navel until her finger sank into the pulp. The acrid smell wrinkled her nose. She removed the peel in a long, circular strip.

The events of the week were too coincidental to be coincidental: the various wolf-gods; the similarities between Dylan's attack and the shaman's possession; a boy reciting an ancient passage about a man who transforms into a wolflike creature.

She licked the sweet juice from her finger and shook her head. It had to make sense. Somehow. There was plenty of information, but the key was missing. She needed help, someone to bounce ideas off of. A key could turn reams of data into a theory. It was time to visit Dr. King, but not until after a week of research so she wouldn't embarrass herself in front of him.

Jael pulled the orange apart and slipped a wedge into her mouth. Normally she didn't eat oranges; but then, she wasn't normally up working at four in the morning. When she poked an orange section into the cage, Osiris glanced down from his high perch and winked.

Then turned away.

Peculiar: He should have been starving. Maybe the company upset him. Well, he never turned down an apple. Jael picked up the Winesap and started to slice. Pain shot through her thumb and she dropped the knife. She held the cut closed, then sucked on it. When the bleeding stopped, she held some apple between the bars. Osiris attacked her hand in a rush of feathers and screeching.

He had nipped the cut, torn it farther open; blood trickled down her thumb and followed the lines in her palm. *"What's with you?"* she shouted. Cold water would ease the pain and slow the bleeding. Jael walked back to the kitchen as the cockatoo shrieked and flapped around the cage. She turned on the faucet.

A note from the piano.

Impossible; it had to be Osiris pecking on the bars of his cage.

Another note, clearly a C-sharp.

Jael wrinkled her face and tried to peer around the corner into the living room. Maybe Osiris had escaped the cage and had landed on the keyboard. She stepped into the dining room to scold him, but he wasn't on the piano. There was nothing on the piano but sheet music.

Four more notes, C-G-A-C played staccato, like a jackhammer.

Suddenly it was cold, terribly cold. Strength drained from her arms, legs. She took two staggering steps, fell against the dining-room table, and dropped to her knees. The room took on a new precision, a new clarity. Dust from the heating ducts bounced off the walls like tennis balls. The trickle of blood smelled like a butcher shop. The walls were a shifting fog.

Her first thought: *So this is what insanity feels like.* Her second: *I am more afraid of going insane than dying.*

Control. She had to get control. There was a logical explanation for the hallucinations, the frozen stilettos that jabbed into her. She had to isolate the components, analyze the sense impressions. They were data like any other.

But first the phone. The phone meant doctor and antidotes for whatever was happening.

An ocean of cold surged over her, and her head bounced on the carpet. A howl rose in her throat. *Control,* she thought. *Fight it off. I am not a child. I have reason.*

Her head snapped back. She stared up at the ceiling and opened her mouth. But she would not let the roar escape, *she would not!* Her eyelids opened till they ached; a red glow lighted the ceiling, a red aura, a luminous mist. A tingling shot through her hand and she looked down. Fingers elongated into paws, nails into claws. Then her nose started to stretch and red hair . . . But it had to be a hallucination. There was no snapping of joints, no stretching of ligaments, no pain.

Data. Just more data. She had to sort through the illusion to find the reality. Create proof that would exist after the attack. She extended one of the long claws and dragged it along the surface of the table. If she had claws, the finish would be scratched.

Routine, she thought. *Multiplication tables. Two times four is eight.* Water lapped at her feet. No, at Dylan's. A deep breath. *Three times five* . . . Headlights streaked past . . . strips of wood . . . a blue glow . . . a pier . . . scattered garbage. . . .

"Eight times five is forty!" she shouted. A deep breath. She stood. "Nine times seven . . ." Another deep breath. She needed to make beds. Clean the bird cage. Another deep breath. The hair was gone from her hands. Another. Her nose was merely a nose. Another. She was Jael, just Jael. "Sixty-three," she sighed.

She yanked the flowers from the vase and used the water to splash her face. She leaned against the table and checked for scratches. None. She leaned over and kissed the dark wood.

Three more breaths and she walked into the kitchen, ran a sink full of hot water, took the dishes from the dishwasher, and started to rewash them by hand. Routine. Suddenly there was incredible comfort in the familiarity of water, of suds, of the artificial lemon aroma of the soap.

Dylan.

Had the water, the dome, actually been Dylan's sensations, or part of the attack? Only one way to find out. She dried her hands, walked to the phone in the dining room, looked up Matt's number, and dialed it. It rang six times before he answered it. "It's Jael," she said before he could respond. "Check Dylan."

"What?" The voice was thick, heavy with sleep.

"Please, just check Dylan's room."

The phone clicked against a hard surface. Then silence. More silence. Jael concentrated, organized her thoughts, focused on the vague perceptions of the lake, the harbor. They were too precise. She'd been there although she hadn't left the apartment.

Clatter in the background. A scratching. Matt picked up the phone. "Is he with you?" The voice was breathless, crisp with fear.

"No, but I know where he is." She paused. "Don't worry, Matt, I know he's all right."

FOURTEEN

Wilmette, Illinois—October 25, 1981

The tires squealed as Matt turned between the rows of parked cars, so he eased up on the gas pedal. Another fifty feet and he skidded to a stop and glanced at the parking attendant's office: Jael's face stared out at him. When he reached across the seat and opened the door on the passenger's side, she ran the ten feet to the car, jumped inside, and locked the door behind her.

"Where is he?" Matt asked.

"The lake. Somewhere by the temple," she said breathlessly.

"Either Gillson Park or the yacht club."

Jael reached out and touched his hand. "Hey, he's all right. I know he is."

Matt didn't have to ask how.

He pulled up the incline to Sheridan Road, pressed down on the accelerator, and turned left; she was trembling, and for the first time since she called, Matt felt protective instead of helpless. "What happened?" he asked.

"The world turned inside out."

He touched her cheek. She was as cold as the night air, perhaps the first sign of shock. "As soon as we find Dylan, you're both going to the hospital."

"Forget the hospital." She shivered when she exhaled. "I had an attack like Dylan's." Another deep breath. "A doozy."

Some approaching headlights glared off chrome, so Matt turned his eyes toward the side of the road; tree trunks shone white in the artificial light. "What's it like?" he asked.

She paused. "The roar? It isn't really a roar. More a cry for help." She took his arm. "But there's ecstasy in it, as much pleasure as horror."

Matt pulled over to the side of the road and turned on the

157

interior light. Jael's eyes were dilated, her eyelids twitched, her breath came in gasps: Dylan's symptoms after an attack. He cupped her cheek in his hand. "Slow down. If I'm going to understand any of this, you'll have to remember this is all new to me."

Silence for an instant. "Ever see a werewolf movie?"

Matt slipped the transmission into first and pulled back onto the road. "I never missed *Shock Theater*."

"Remember the transformation scenes? The snouts and fangs?" She shuddered. "It's like that, only you see things from the wolf man's point of view."

"But Dylan didn't turn into a werewolf."

"Neither did I," Jael said. "Neither did the Bon, though I bet they *thought* they did." She stared out into the night. "Remember the pictures of the ceremony? The wolf masks? The gnawing at bones?"

Matt remembered the feral look on Dylan's face when he had carried the boy out of the attic. If that hatred, that ferocity, was a by-product of the attacks, then thank God Dylan didn't remember anything.

He turned onto Michigan Avenue, followed the brick-paved street for a few blocks, then pulled alongside the curb and shut off the ignition. He turned to ask Jael another question, but she was gone, running across the open park grounds toward the beach. He climbed from the car and followed her. Although the moon was full and stars reached from the rooftops behind him to the lake horizon, all Matt could see was the emptiness in Dylan's eyes, the way his lips rippled on his teeth. He yelled for Jael to stop, but could scarcely hear himself above the waves. She turned south when she reached the sand and ran for the jetty at the mouth of the harbor. There was the smell of seaweed, the chill of wind-borne spray. Matt caught her when she reached the concrete, took her hand, and walked the hundred yards to the boulders that formed the breakwater.

She stared out into the lake as black water oozed over the concrete and lapped at their feet. Was she using reason to locate Dylan or trying to share with him, use his personality like a beacon? She shook her head as if clearing it of something, then turned slowly back toward the yacht club. She walked briskly down the jetty, broke into a run, and headed toward some garbage cans by the coast guard station.

Let him be all right! Matt thought. *God, no sacrifices, no chopping, no bits of muscle and entrails scattered among the paper plates and Pepsi cans.*

Dylan lay in the moonlight, curled between the building and a fifty-gallon drum, as sheltered from the wind and cold as a snail. He was fully dressed; even his shoes were tied. As Matt knelt by the boy Jael dropped to both knees. She touched Dylan as if to awaken him.

"Forget it," Matt said. "He slept for hours after the other attacks." But Jael was already removing her coat. He touched her arm and shook his head. "You need it as much as he does."

She lifted Dylan and held him as Matt covered the boy with his jacket. Not only wasn't Matt sure how to act, he wasn't even sure how to feel. No matter how closely he held Dylan, no matter how much Matt kissed him or played with him, he would always be closer to Jael. Matt didn't even know if he had the right to ask to carry Dylan back to the car. As soon as he placed his coat around the boy, Jael placed him in Matt's arms.

She leaned against Matt and took his arm as they walked back through the trees and bushes and across the sand path to the car. Her shivers were so deep, they shook Matt's arm. "Now the emergency room," he said.

"What happened tonight is over," Jael said. "At least for tonight." Then she rubbed her face and added matter-of-factly, "But that doesn't mean I want to be alone while it's dark."

Matt removed the filter thick with grounds from the Melitta coffee maker and dropped it into the garbage disposal. He popped the lid on the pot, then poured Jael a cup. "Pure Jamaican Blue Mountain," Matt said, handing it to her. "I bought it before I ran out of things to celebrate."

The dawn light reflected off the apartments across the courtyard; it coated the table and floor with a red film. Jael warmed her hands with the cup before she took a sip. "I was terrified when I thought the trances and drawings were random. Now that

159

there seems to be a design behind everything, I'm even more afraid."

"How much haven't you told me?" Matt asked.

She leaned back and stared at the ceiling as though she hadn't heard him. "Something is missing!"

"But the Creepster is still at the heart of the problem."

"Or Set or Nodeus or a thousand others." She shook her head, made a fist, and tapped it on the table.

"Maybe some food will help you sort things out," Matt said. "Any preferences?"

"What's the house special?"

"Sourdough pancakes; the starter's been in the family for years." Matt walked to the counter, then turned back to her and tried to smile. "I like to cook when I'm expecting bad news." He removed the eggs, starter, and milk from the refrigerator, took the flour and baking powder from a shelf, and began to measure them.

"You're about to hear some strange things," Jael said. "Remember, I'm not crazy." She mouthed the words as if trying to convince herself. "For the first time since Tibet, I'm sure I'm not."

Matt raised his eyebrows. "My son disappears. I pick you up and you lead me straight to him. What could be crazier than that?"

She forced a smile. "Imagine waking up in the morning. You're still dreaming, but the thinking part of your mind has started to work. You're able to make rational observations about the dream images."

"It's like having two brains that can act independently of one another," he said, adding some melted butter to the batter.

"The impulses, the snout, the desire to howl, all that, seemed to be coming from my dreams, only I was awake . . . and they were a hundred times as strong as my dreams." She took a sip of coffee and leaned back. "I was able to fight them off with my intellect, but just barely." She took another sip and looked away before she said, "The images seemed to come from outside of me."

"It sounds like you were possessed," Matt said.

160

"In theory, possession is the mind deluding itself."

"But you can share. Doesn't that rewrite the rules?"

"Don't confuse me with the facts." She slumped down into the seat. "The puzzle is all here except for a few key pieces. I know just the man to solve it for me."

"Dr. Shaw?"

"Not this time," she said. "I have another wizard: my undergraduate adviser." She scratched her temple, then rubbed her knuckles on the edge of the table. "But I have a week's research to do before I'll feel comfortable talking to him."

Matt folded the eggs into the batter, put some Crisco in the skillet, and waited for it to sizzle. "You were able to fight off the attack. Could you teach Dylan?"

"If I were six, I'd still be out there, howling at the moon." She shrugged and opened her arms imploringly. "Even an adult in a primitive culture like the Bon wouldn't stand a chance. They give in to the hallucinations and turn the experience into a religion."

Matt turned back to the stove and dropped two dollops of batter into the sizzling pan. "Did the hallucinations start when you were asleep?"

"I was translating your tape."

"At four in the morning?"

"After what I heard, I could hardly go to sleep. It's Old Irish," she said. "It hasn't been used for over a thousand years."

Matt was too surprised to speak. He leaned against the counter and set the spatula down. "Hit me again; I can take it."

"Ever hear of Cuchulainn?"

"What's that?"

"A he," Jael said, brushing a strand of wet hair from her face. "A mythological hero. He was to the Celts what Hercules was to the ancient Greeks."

"Everything I know about the Celts comes from B movies about druids sacrificing virgins," Matt said.

"That's more than most people," Jael said. "Anyway, the voice on that tape recited some passages from the *Táin Bó Cúailigne,* the basic saga of Celtic mythology."

"Dylan knows this thing?"

"It was repeated word for word . . . and my pronunciation

doesn't approach what was on that tape. It could have been a druid speaking."

Matt closed his eyes and wearily shook his head. "What does that mean?"

"I have no idea. At first I thought it was a hoax."

"Never," Matt said, flipping a pancake. "Bekki has her faults, but she'd never try to keep us from curing Dylan. Never."

"It was definitely Dylan's voice. A tad thick with trance, perhaps." She took a deep breath and laid her hands flat on the tabletop. "Here's the most bizarre part of all: Dylan recited the passage describing Cuchulainn's warp spasm."

"His what?"

"I have the translation in my coat."

Matt removed the pancakes from the skillet, placed them on a plate, and set it inside the warm oven. He walked to the closet for her coat and, when he returned, handed it to her.

She searched through the top pocket and removed a piece of folded paper. She unfolded it, set it down on the table, and started to read:

> "The first warp spasm seized Cuchulainn, and made him into a horrible thing, hideous, unheard of . . . his heart boomed loud in his chest like the baying of a wolf at its feed or the sound of a lion among bears. . . ."

"That sounds like Dylan's roaring," Matt interrupted.

"*Our* roaring," Jael said, then continued:

> "Malignant mists and bursts of fire—the torches of Babd—flickered red in vaporous clouds that rose boiling above his head, so fierce was his fury. The hair of his head twisted like the tangle of a red thornbush . . . the hero-halo rose out of his brow, long and broad as a warrior's whetstone, long as a snout. . . ."

"Everything from the glowing and roaring to the snout and the red hair." He scooped out several more spoonfuls of batter, dropped them into the skillet, and watched them sizzle. "Does it make it more believable because it's been recorded in an old manuscript?"

"It reads like a pedigree. There's scarcely an ancient culture that doesn't have the myth of a man turning into a wolf." She turned away as though she were unwilling to continue.

Matt turned back to the stove to flip the pancakes; after he finished he looked at her. "What happened to this Cuchulainn after his warp spasm?"

"He went out into battle and fought off an army by himself."

"Charming," Matt said. He scratched the back of his neck, rubbed his nose, and said, "Why is it called a warp spasm?"

"In the magic cultures there's a very thin line between the real world and a parallel magic world. The Celts called theirs the *sidh.*"

"You haven't answered my question," Matt said.

"Give the witness a chance to respond," Jael said, sipping from her cup. She paused as if to organize her thoughts. "Shamans and others, people who were initiated into the mysteries of the otherworld—people like Cuchulainn—could warp the dimensions, make them overlap, draw power from them."

Matt rolled his eyes in disbelief.

"You're being judgmental," Jael said. "We still have variations of the same concept. Is a priest asking for blessing at a wedding so different from Cuchulainn asking a blessing of power from the *sidh?*"

"Only priests don't conquer armies," Matt said as he took the plate from the oven, added the second batch of pancakes, and brought them to the table.

"Maybe they lack Cuchulainn's skill."

"Or something."

"Precisely," Jael said. "Or *something.* The texts for the ancient rituals were all destroyed. That removed the opportunity to learn what that something was." She chewed on her lip for a moment. "I bet the Bon's attempt to reach Htamenma was a warp spasm of sorts."

"A rather hysterical speculation for an academic," Matt said before she could go on.

Jael shrugged. "It's been a long night."

Matt slid two pancakes onto her plate. He took two for himself, sat down, and placed a large slice of butter on each. Matt watched it seep into the spongy cake instead of spreading it with his knife. "Here's something you may find interesting," he finally said. "The Creepster inhabits a different dimension too."

Jael wrinkled her brow and drew her head back. "I thought he lived at your house."

"Dylan says he wants to escape from where he lives." Matt reached for the jar of huckleberry jam and spread some on his pancakes. "Do these warp spasms go by any rules?" he asked.

"Pardon?"

"Are there limitations as to when they can take place? Where? How often?"

"The *sidh* overlapped our dimension at places where transitions took place. Like twilight, the transition between day and night. Or the mist between the air and the sea. The most powerful points were at temples, dolmens, burial grounds, the places where life and death met."

"My attic doesn't seem to fit."

"Nor my dining room," Jael said. "But that's the nature of research. Find the missing part and the whole puzzle fits together." Jael began to scratch her head, then stood, walked to the window, and stared out. She was silent before turning back to Matt. "Do you think you could get Dylan for a long weekend?"

"That depends on Bekki."

"I'd like both of you to meet my parents."

"Then it's settled," Matt said.

"Except for Bekki."

"If she thinks you can help Dylan, she'll agree to anything." Matt reached across the table and tapped Jael's translation of the tape. "And this should be more than convincing."

Matt noticed the third plate on the dining-room table as soon as Bekki led him inside. Was it for him or her lover?

"I've seen Dylan with more spunk," Bekki said as she turned on the evening news and sat down on the arm of his chair.

"He had a rough night," Matt said.

Bekki was silent as an editorial comment came on, then

frowned, reached over, and turned the set off. "He's been great since you dismantled that thing he built."

"No more disappearing pets?"

"He's even started to catch up on his schoolwork."

Matt reached into his shirt pocket, found a Xerox copy of Jael's translation, and handed it to Bekki. "You might find this interesting."

Bekki unfolded it, read it, then looked down at him and frowned. "What is it?"

"A translation of the tape you gave me."

"Be serious."

"It's from a Celtic epic," Matt said. "Dr. Clarke said you can find the complete translation at any decent library."

"She speaks Celtic?"

"Among other things."

Bekki moved closer to him. A soft arm brushed against his. Her silk blouse was sleeveless and her perfume was sweet, more of a flower scent than Jael's. "Dylan can't stop talking about this Dr. Clarke. Only he calls her Jael."

"She was a hypersensitive child too. Some of her insights into his behavior are amazing."

"Maybe she should get together with Dr. Velde."

"Not yet," Matt said, pulling away from her touch. "Some of her ideas are rather unorthodox. But I'll tell her that you mentioned it."

Bekki made a sour face. "You do that." Then she stood, took his hand, and pulled him to his feet. "How about a game of pool?"

Why not? It would help fill up the time until he thought the time was right to ask about the weekend. She led him into the game room. "Eight ball?" Matt asked.

Bekki pulled the triangular rack from beneath the table, arranged the balls in the proper order, and offered to let him break. "You first," he said. She chose a cue and leaned over the table. She no longer rested the cue on her thumb, but looped her index finger around it and used her other fingers for stability. Her stroke was smooth, and she hit the cue ball with top spin. The balls clicked loudly and the three and five balls rolled into pockets. "Someone's been giving you lessons," Matt said.

"I've had a lot of time to practice. Don't forget, I've been home every day."

Matt glanced around the room as Bekki lined up the next shot. The family pictures were still hanging, and they'd been dusted recently. The awards were still there: trophies for sailing, trophies for riding, the miniature Louisville Slugger he'd received for winning a Little League batting title. It was a good thing they didn't award prizes for marriages that went kaput. There wasn't room for a horse's ass or a stuffed cuckoo.

Bekki miscued on the one-seven combination, and Matt chalked his cue, leaned over the table, and smoothly stroked in the one and two balls.

"A drink?" Bekki asked after he missed a straight-in shot on the four.

"I've given it up."

"Well, I could use one," she said. She rested her cue on the table and walked to the Port-A-Bar in the corner. Somehow her sparkle had diminished. Even her hair lacked luster. Maybe she was just tired. When she returned to the table, she rested the drink on the rail and sank the four, then the seven in combination with the six. She missed a bank shot on the six, and the cue ball rolled and rolled and settled directly behind the eight.

Which was exactly where she'd had him for years.

"Dr. Clarke would like to have Dylan from Thursday through Sunday," Matt said. "There are some tests she thinks might help him."

Bekki leaned toward him and smiled. "Let's talk it over at dinner," she said. "Nothing fancy. Some roast beef. Strawberry pie for dessert."

"What do you think?" Matt asked. "I've been eating TV dinners for a month and you offer me a banquet." He leaned over the table, lined up a bank shot on the seven, but miscued; the cue ball brushed the eight and rolled into a side pocket. "End of game," he said. He stopped to take a deep breath as he returned the cue to the rack. The guns had been moved into a different room. So had his magazines. His smell had gone with the things that had been his. Just a week and he no longer felt a part of the place.

"Dylan seems pretty upset," Bekki said. "Maybe it would help him if you stayed the night."

Matt shook his head. "It's a great idea," he said. "As long as I sleep downstairs in the study."

FIFTEEN

Chicago, Illinois—October 26, 1981

Jael waited for the mob of chattering grade schoolers to surge by, then walked up the foot-worn granite stairs, past the columns and revolving glass doors, and into the museum. Each breath of the musty air held some memory: the mummy exhibition that had given her nightmares in the second grade; the dinosaur skeletons that Julie and she had tried to reconstruct in toothpicks; the Tibetan exhibit she and Chris had helped plan six months before. She paused beneath the stuffed bull elephant, switched the portfolio to her left hand so she could hold the railing, and descended into the basement. It was like entering a catacomb. She made only one stop, the model of the Egyptian tomb with its bright paintings of bare-breasted women, boys singing songs, sunlight and reeds and flowers—a longing for rebirth—then hurried into the corridor that held the administrative offices. She stopped at the third on the right, the one with NATHAN J. KING, ACQUISITIONS in gilt letters on the window, and knocked on the glass.

"Jael?" a muffled voice asked. She waited for Dr. King instead of walking in; he said that at sixty-four, holding doors for young women was one of the few pleasures he had left.

The door opened inward; he had a crew cut and his face, as brown and weathered as elm bark, brightened when he saw her. The pleasure and wonder he expressed with his eyes hadn't diminished since she had met him a decade before. She bent to kiss him, then raised an index finger. "You were going to retire in August. Doctor's orders. Remember?"

He didn't reply; it hadn't been a question. He steered her toward a display case filled with artifacts. He unlocked the glass door, removed a human skull inlaid with turquoise and semiprecious gems, and handed it to her. It was exquisite and gruesome,

168

the trademarks of Aztec art. "A pole ornament from a skull rack?" she asked.

"Always the right answer," he said in his level voice. He took it from her and returned it to the case. "Only one skull in fifty thousand received such decorations."

Jael peered into the case at the golden gods and goddesses, the jeweled serpents and calendar stones. She reached for an obsidian knife; its etching showed a chest ripped open for the heart. Jael whistled.

"From a private collection," Dr. King said. "Now you see why I couldn't retire." He began to smile and added as an afterthought, "To think they pay me to hoard beautiful things. If I had only found this job at thirty instead of sixty!"

"Then you wouldn't have met me."

"You're right. That would be sad." He returned the knife to the case and locked the door, then led her to a leather couch that seemed to fill half the wall. "How is your Chris?"

Jael shrugged. "I haven't seen him in a while."

He gently touched her hand. "Good." He straightened his bow tie as he always did before a lecture. "He is much too pompous for you, you know." He slapped both hands on his knees. "But this can't be the problem you mentioned on the phone."

Jael carried the portfolio toward the bulletin board on the far side of the office, then removed the posters that were pinned there and tacked up the color photos she'd brought. "This is the problem," she said.

Dr. King squinted as he approached them. "I don't remember seeing these," he said, readjusting his horn-rimmed glasses.

"You saw the originals—the Bon shrine. These are blowups of its etchings."

He stared at the pictures, and his finger moved from the etchings of the men dressed in wolf heads to one of Htamenma sitting on a pile of bodies to a replica of a sacrifice.

"What do you think of this one?" Jael asked, pointing to an alignment of ten circles. A large circle, four small circles, two more large ones, then three mid-size ones were arranged in an almost straight line. Despite the graininess caused by the enlarging, the individual chisel marks, the smooth finish of the polished granite, were clearly visible. "It's the central image of all the etchings," she said. "In some of them even Htamenma pays homage to it." She took a black and white photo from the portfolio. "Here's one from the *phurba*'s handle. The same circles in the same order."

He turned toward her and stared down the bridge of his nose. "A method of counting, perhaps?" he said. "The Aztecs counted with dots and lines."

"It's not used in manuscripts or scrolls, only on items used in sacrificial ceremonies," Jael said, shaking her head. "Perhaps it's a map of surrounding peaks? The locations of other shrines?"

Dr. King made a sour face. "The Red Bon haven't kept their ceremonies secret for a thousand years by advertising the sites."

"That bothered me too."

He moved closer to the photo. The collar of his shirt was starched but slightly yellow. On him it seemed just right, the proper combination of attention to tradition and disregard of appearance. "If a god as powerful as Htamenma pays homage to it, it must be a truly great entity, perhaps the soul force of their universe." When he wrinkled his face, the already deep lines around his eyes and mouth grew even deeper. He tapped the photo with a fingertip. "You have others?"

"In my office."

"I'll keep this one, then." He pointed at Jael's still-bulging portfolio. "All your questions are not about the etching?"

Jael leaned against the wall and rested her head on the soft corkboard. She exhaled so deeply, she shook. "A lot of this is so bizarre, I'm embarrassed to mention it." She chewed her lip, trying to think of a place to start.

"Your telepathy?" he asked.

Jael's mouth opened involuntarily. "Do you know about *everything?*"

He laughed gently and placed a hand on her shoulder. "Years ago I had lunch with a favorite student's mother. It was immediately after I recommended that the student continue to graduate school. The mother disagreed. She tried to convince me that my favorite student should return to the piano." He blinked and shook his head. "A very persuasive woman, that mother."

"Evidently not persuasive enough."

"Then I am a stubborn old man," he said, his eyes twinkling. "Part of her argument was that this student would be in danger if she continued to study the dead. The mother mentioned a sister. A special power."

"Why didn't you tell me about this visit?" Jael asked.

"What was the point?"

"And you believed her?"

"She brought articles from scientific journals and newspapers." He reached for Jael's hand and patted it. "Besides, I have spent most of my days immersed in the ancient worlds—a whole lifetime of antiquity. All cultures have legends about such things. Why shouldn't I believe?" Dr. King placed an arm around her shoulder and led her back to the couch. "Now," he said, "what are these bizarre things?"

Jael told him. Everything. Of the dreams and attacks. Of the sickness in Tibet. Of Dylan, his speaking in Old Irish, his horror at the zoo. All of it. Dr. King remained silent, his eyes closed, his chin resting on his chest as always when he concentrated. He didn't open his eyes until she finished.

"You have seen this glowing and roaring?" he asked, opening his eyes.

"First in Tibet. Then during my own attack. I would have roared like a wolf if I hadn't fought it."

His eyes turned back to the portfolio. "There is more?"

Jael reached down and removed a handful of typing paper covered with script. "This is just part of what I found." She chose one at random and started to read, "From the Nagada Papyri, number thirty-five . . .

"His priests receive visions and talk with beasts of burden, with snakes and birds. When we come to them for succor, they answer us like the sun, like the lion. Then the children of Set come in the night and eat our flesh and crack our bones for the marrow. . . .

"Notice how the poet uses the terms 'answer us like the sun, like the lion.' That's a metaphor for the glowing and roaring, or

171

I'm not standing here," Jael said. She could feel her pulse rise just thinking about it. "I know what the poet must have felt like when he witnessed an attack. The disbelief. The horror."

"Mostly awe," Dr. King said. "I note very little disbelief. He had seen something he couldn't explain, so he attributed it to the gods. It was a blessing for him, despite the terror. Think of how absolute faith provides order." He paused and nodded toward the Aztec pole ornament. "Think of the Aztecs who waited in line to be sacrificed. Think of their faith in the otherworld."

"Since you mentioned the Aztecs," Jael said, "here's one from the *Cuauhcalli Codex* . . .

> "Praise the Star-Lord who creates the strong by devouring the weak. His Chosen receive His ecstasy and knowledge . . . they shine in His blessing and roar out His name. Kneel to Him, offer sacrifice, so He does not take you in the night. . . ."

Dr. King raised a hand to stop her. "Note the changed point of view in this reading," he said. "What was terrifying to the poet, a commoner, becomes ecstatic to the priest." He tilted his head and looked at her wryly. "Would you call the sensation ecstatic?"

"Hardly. Then I was fighting the impulse instead of welcoming it. If I thought I was welcoming a god, I suppose animal responses would be tremendously liberating. No intellect. No worry. But that's not me. I thought I was going insane." She picked up another piece of paper. "There are others, but this should suffice: a Red Bon *pho-wa* scroll . . .

> "Why do the Initiated glow with His Being while we do not? Why can they call to Him while we cannot?
>
> We lift up our eyes to the stars but find no relief. We cry in the night, but He does not hear. Teach us your ways, Htamenma, hear us so that our wives and our children will be spared too. . . .

"Time and time again," Jael continued, "references to glowing, to roaring, to a power which priests have that others lack."

Dr. King didn't respond immediately but sat in silence, his eyes closed, his face creased in thought. It was as though Jael had left the room. She had begun to feel nervous by the time he finally spoke. "We are part of these readings." He opened his eyes and stared at her. "In our own ways, you and I are mentioned."

"You've lost me."

"You are, to quote the scroll, one of the 'Initiated,' and I am one of the rest, the commoners, the followers who call out in the night but are never heard. The priests of Set, of Xipe Totec and Htamenma . . . you are all telepathists."

Jael covered her face in her hands, then leaned back and let the fluorescent light in the ceiling illuminate her fingers. Of course! Why did she always miss the most obvious things? She hadn't been sick in Tibet; she had shared, shared with the Bon shaman, probably shared with Yum Gyeba. But if he had known all about her, why had he brought her to the shrine?

"I've seen that look before," Dr. King said. "You're on to something."

Jael had to concentrate to return to the conversation. "Maybe. Things seem fairly vague." She shook her head and frowned. "How is it passed on?"

"Genes."

"Doesn't *initiated* imply going through training, learning esoteric rites?"

"There may have been exercises for increasing the power, but it had to be present." He glanced up at her and smiled. "Doesn't it suddenly seem obvious why these priesthoods were hereditary?"

"But my father and mother are normal."

He nodded at her as though he were using a pointer on the blackboard. "Define *atavistic* for me."

"The appearance of a trait of ancient ancestors in an organism that its more recent ancestors lack."

"And we all have them," Dr. King said. "Example: Say a person with a recessive gene mates, at great odds, with a person who carries the same gene. At tremendous odds the fertilized egg splits to become identical twins—two beautiful girls with a rare gift."

173

Jael stared at him. "Can you think of a way to check this?"

"Why don't you talk to that persuasive mother of yours. Ask her about the skeletons in the family closet. Find out if there was a maiden aunt who read tea leaves, a black-sheep cousin who was more comfortable talking to animals than people—"

"One major drawback," Jael cut in. "The priesthoods in the magic cultures were always large, sometimes a tenth of the population. Why would so few of us be left?"

"A trait that is useful in one historical epoch may be detrimental in another. . . ."

"Still . . ." Jael said.

Dr. King closed his eyes again, began to nod, then, after a minute or so, picked up the translations, reread them, and said, without looking up, "All these texts indicate opposition between the priesthood and the populace. The priests seem immune to a scourge that affects everyone else." He placed the papers down on the couch. "Perhaps the gene for telepathy also carries immunity to illness."

"I was constantly sick as a child."

"Perhaps a specific disease, then." He picked up the translations again. "Since these are from such distant time periods and locations, the plague must have reoccurred with some regularity."

"Great," Jael said, "but why do they all share the same wolf-god?"

Dr. King shook his head and began to laugh. "You've never learned to answer one question before moving on to the next."

Jael smiled apologetically. "Okay, back to question one: Why are there so few members of the gene pool left?"

"How would you guess the average man viewed these priests, these men who didn't have to work, who experienced the ecstasy of direct communication with the gods?"

Jael rocked slowly as she thought. "With envy, I guess."

"What does envy lead to?"

"Hatred."

"And hatred?" Dr. King asked.

"To revenge."

"And revenge leads to violence, and if the target group is small

174

enough—say, a tenth of the population or less—to destruction."
Then Dr. King leaned back and wrinkled his forehead. He
frowned. "But to kill priests would enrage the gods." He
scratched his chin, then rubbed the back of his neck. "What
terrible secret did your ancestors possess? The masses were normally docile. What could have provoked them to such a rage?"

Jael remained silent as she mentally traced the histories of the
magic cultures, their rise to greatness, and their sudden decline
after the appearance of the wolf-god. "It all fits," she said. "These
cults were all exterminated by the religions that followed them."
She removed Dylan's drawing from the portfolio. "What do you
think of the Creepster?" she asked, handing it to him.

"An excellent reproduction of Set."

"This couldn't be a real animal?"

"Not unless you began by breeding an anteater with a dog."
Dr. King pursed his lips, leaned one way, then another, then
shook his head. "That would merely start the process. That erect
tail? There's no purpose for it." He paused to outline the torso
with a finger. "The torso is like a whippet. The snout could be for
sucking as well as ripping. Square ears don't exist in nature.
Now, if they were clipped or broken like a Doberman's . . ."

"Three thousand years ago?"

"You see my point."

"Could the glowing and roaring be passed on genetically?"

"They would have to be," Dr. King said. "Even a normal voice
has great range during times of stress. What of a gifted voice?"

"But a body emanating light?"

"Our nervous system runs on electrical charges," he said.
"What if the special gene allowed it to be channeled in a different
manner. What of the medieval paintings of saints? Don't their
halos indicate the release of some type of energy?" The excitement in his voice faded slightly. "Of course, this is merely a
hypothesis."

"Your ratio of turning hypothesis into fact must approach one
hundred percent."

Dr. King looked at her askance, then peeked into the portfolio.
"Any more of this for me?"

"The rest is lunch. I'll be spending most of the day here."

He took her hand and patted it. "Why not let me help. I'll work on your symbol with the circles."

Jael held up her hand to stop him. "You've already done too much."

"No, you've piqued my interest." He paused. "What day is it?"

"Monday."

"Excellent," he said. "I'll spend some time in the private collections, then get back to you early next week." Then he stood and helped Jael to her feet. "Any more questions?"

"Just one," Jael said. She leaned her head back and stared up at the fluorescent lamp. Suddenly her heart was racing, she could almost feel the beads of sweat pop out on her forehead. "What if the reason the priests were hated was because they did horrible things during the trance? What if they didn't restrict their cannibalism to the sacrifices and ceremonies?" When she felt her hand begin to tremble, she reached for Dr. King's arm so he could reassure her with his confidence and strength. "What I'm trying to ask," she said, "is whether it's safe to sit in the same room with me?"

SIXTEEN

Kenilworth, Illinois—October 31, 1981

Sparrows chirped, then scattered like blowing snow as Matt stepped onto the front porch and rang the doorbell. He paused for a moment, then, when no one answered, rang again. The doorknob started to twist, slid back, then moved again. Dylan. The knob was too heavy for his boy-size hands. Matt turned it and pushed the door; as soon as it opened, Dylan hugged his legs and crawled into his arms. "Hey, Cap'n," Matt said, kissing the boy's hair, "think I was a trick-or-treater?" He carried Dylan into the foyer and peeked into the living room. The blinds were drawn and the gray light that filtered through the curtains scarcely illuminated the rug by the windows. Bekki must have been trying to make it look as though no one were home so no ghouls or gremlins would add more terror to Dylan's dreams. "Where's Mom?" Matt asked.

"Upstairs."

"Your week okay?"

Dylan pursed his lips and wrinkled his face, obviously making a difficult decision. "Now the Creepster makes me feel good. He comes when I call him."

"How often have you called him?"

"Every night," Bekki's voice said from the stairway.

Matt looked up. She must have been going on a date: Her hair had been recently coiffed, her eyes exquisitely accented; her silk blouse was so delicate that her nipples gathered the material in peaks. Her bare feet were silent as she walked down the stairs. "Dylan's things packed?" he asked.

"All but his Halloween costume. For some reason he wasn't interested in scaring people this year."

"I saw your precautions," Matt said, nodding toward the

177

drawn curtains. "Dr. Clarke says no one trick-or-treats at her parents'."

"Thank God for small favors." Bekki walked up and smiled. "Time to chat?"

Matt shrugged. "I told her I'd pick her up at ten."

"Family first," Bekki said, locking her arm in his. She touched Dylan on the tip of the nose. "Grown-up talk."

Matt knelt down, pulled the boy's head next to his, and whispered, "Jael said there are all sorts of things to draw, so don't forget your crayons." He pointed Dylan in the direction of the stairs, patted him on the butt, and watched him sprint up the stairs to the second floor.

Bekki led Matt to the kitchen, to the table; she had goosebumps and her chill transferred to him. "I've only got a few seconds," Matt said.

She spread her fingers over his hand. The gesture seemed forced, awkward. "You sure you have to go?" she asked.

"What's that supposed to mean?"

Bekki's smile lacked its normal glow; perhaps it was the flat light. "Dr. Velde's worried about Dylan's sudden attraction to the Creepster. It started with his meeting your Dr. Clarke."

"This is the best he's looked in months."

"Just because he can sleep at night doesn't mean he's better." She shivered and a look of revulsion spread over her face. "You should see him when he's sleeping. He smiles like the cat that ate the canary."

"Any rest seems like a blessing to me."

"Dr. Velde says—"

"Dr. Velde has seen him for months, nothing. Jael sees him for two weeks—"

"You mean *Dr. Clarke*, don't you?" Bekki asked.

"As soon as she starts to see him, there's instant improvement. It couldn't be professional jealousy?"

"Improvement?" Bekki's look went right through him. "Wait till you spend tonight with him," she said, her voice scarcely under control. "For hours he speaks in God knows what language for God knows what purpose." She blinked and her mouth twitched.

"If you have tapes, Dr. Clarke will translate them."

"What good will that do?" Slowly, ever so cautiously, the scowl left her face and was replaced by an attractive helplessness. "I want it to stop. The attacks. The chanting. All of it."

"She thinks that with some luck, this weekend—"

"This weekend means nothing," Bekki said. She paused, as though waiting for a response, but Matt said nothing. "The more Dr. Velde sees, the more certain she is of her original diagnosis." Another pause. Her voice was searching for a sincerity that wasn't there. "Dylan's problems began with our breakup and will end when we're back together." Bekki lifted her hand to his cheek. She shrugged, smiled, shrugged again, and gave him a wink that was more uneasy than sexy.

Matt pulled away and glared at her. She wasn't much of an actress, but she'd never had to act before. When her every move was magnetic, it all seemed so natural; but now that she was trying to create a feeling that wasn't there, every motion seemed strained, awkward. "What's the matter?" he asked. "Lover boy take his business elsewhere?"

Muscle by muscle her smile melted. "Can you blame him? Every night at home with a sick boy? Imagine how he felt walking into a relationship straight out of *The Twilight Zone.*" She was almost in tears. "And it's me. Every time Dylan's out of my sight, I'm afraid I'll never see him again."

Matt looked away from her face to the recipes on the bulletin board, the Sierra Club calendar by the refrigerator, *anything* but her eyes.

When he stood, she jerked on his arm. "You're not listening!" She worked her mouth so tightly that her teeth ground. "Dylan created the Creepster from his guilt, a way to punish himself because he believes he broke us up. If he starts enjoying the Creepster's visits, he's also enjoying the punishment. Do you know what happens to people who like to torture themselves?"

Matt pulled away from her and walked toward the kitchen door. "I have to go."

Bekki took his hand. The fine bones of her finger pressed into his palm. "We were just getting bored. We could make it if we started over."

Matt spun back toward her. "Great!" he said. "Absolutely wonderful! No sooner do I dislodge your claws from my guts than you dig them back in and start to twist." When he stepped toward her, she backed away from him. "Don't make me feel special or loved—I'm just some slob you dragged off the street to keep the game going." He bit his lip till he tasted blood, then curled his fist and slammed it down once on the table. "Too long. You waited too fucking long." He paused, then said in a whisper so harsh it was almost a grimace, "I found out I could fall out of love with you." He turned, walked from the kitchen, and, when he reached the bottom of the stairs, shouted, "Hurry, Dylan, we're going to be late!" Bekki walked after him, nodding her head as though everything were going to return to normal. "Enough," Matt said before she could speak. "Dylan's yours during the week, mine on weekends."

Bekki's breathing was short, uneven. She rubbed her eyes until red blotches appeared. "Then I want him home on Sunday."

"You said Tuesday."

"He's mine during the week," she said. "Monday and Tuesday *do* qualify as weekdays."

Dylan hurried down the stairs, took Matt's hand, and led him toward the door. "Couldn't find my crayons."

"Don't worry," Matt said mechanically. "We'll buy some more." He let the boy lead him. He was more exhausted than he could imagine.

"His suitcase is in the closet," Bekki said. She kissed Dylan good-bye, told him to behave, and walked him to the door. As Dylan ran to the car Bekki placed a hand around Matt's neck and pulled him down as if to kiss him. "Sunday night," she whispered, "or you can expect a visit from the police."

"Turn at the stone gatehouse," Jael said.

Matt slowed, leaned into the turn, and entered the thick stand of trees; he tried to think of something witty to say. It would have been the first intelligent comment of the morning, but no luck. The situation demanded that he be witty, *alive,* but the sadness clung to him like decay. He was so boring, he bored himself.

The woods opened onto a panorama of the estate: a neoclassical manor house, manicured lawn, marble columns; it looked like a snapshot from the royal family's picture album. "When I was a child," Matt said, "I dreamed that one day I'd be walking through the woods, stumble through a hole by an ancient oak, and fall into a magic castle with dragons to slay and a princess to win . . . and no one would ever grow old or fall out of love."

"Those last two seem like recent additions," Jael said.

"You really should be a lawyer," Matt said with a sad smile. "Anyway, this estate is grander than my imaginary castle."

Jael shifted Dylan higher onto her lap so he could see above the dashboard. "You live here?" Dylan asked.

"I used to. There's a cave in the ravines, a rock that looks like a bear, and the gazebo. You can see as far into the lake from the gazebo as your imagination allows."

A long expanse of terraced slopes, arbors, gardens. And chrysanthemums. Bursts of creams and yellows. Rusts and maroons. Beyond the gardens was a pond with sculpted pines, then, as a background for the entire picture, more forest that was yellow and red with changing leaves.

"I want to draw the trees," Dylan said.

"I have your supplies in my suitcase," Jael said.

Dylan wrinkled his face and peered up at her. "I left them at your house?"

"It wasn't on purpose?"

"I thought I lost them."

The driveway curved past the house, then under a huge oak. Matt slowed, stopped, then set the parking brake. Dylan reached for the door handle, but Jael stopped him.

"This is for *both* Griffins," she said. "I want no talk about nightmares or Creepsters. Get my folks started and they won't stop." She held Dylan until he nodded, then kissed him on the cheek and opened the door. He ran toward the tree.

Matt took Jael's hand before she could unbuckle the seat belt. He wanted to tell her not to expect too much, that both Griffins needed attention—but the words wouldn't come.

No matter.

She winked at him and squeezed his hand.

They stepped onto the grounds through the patio. Jael's mother held on to Matt's arm while her father stayed at his side. The mother's hands weren't as long as Jael's but were even stronger, and it was simple to see where Jael inherited her elegant facial lines. She told him to call her Miriam, but she was the type of person he'd call Missus when he was eighty. The father was like most professionals: quiet for the first hour, sizing Matt up before he revealed too much of himself. The faster Jael and Dylan ran toward the bluffs, the slower the parents walked. *Fine,* Matt thought, *there are some things I'd like to discuss in private.*

"Jael mentioned you practice tort law," Mr. Clarke said. "For companies or private individuals?"

Matt took a breath of the rich lake odor before he spoke. "When I finished law school, I viewed the world in terms of us and them, the injured worker versus the uncaring state, the small landowner versus the corporate entity." He listened to the wind rustle dry leaves. "Somehow the distinction has blurred over the years."

"Dylan's a charmer," Mrs. Clarke said, changing subjects. The polish in her voice made the simplest observations sound like dogma.

"Whatever was best with Bekki and me, he inherited."

"You're divorced?"

"As soon as possible," Matt said, glancing up the path. Jael and Dylan had stopped by a flower bed; she knelt by him and separated the petals of a chrysanthemum, no doubt explaining the different parts of the blossom. Dylan tugged on her hand until she stood and followed him toward some stairs that descended to the beach. They communicated in ways beyond telepathy. "What was Jael like as a child?"

"In what ways?" Mrs. Clarke asked.

"How sensitive was she?"

"Do you mean how intensely could she share?"

"I still have a hard time with that word."

Mrs. Clarke bent to move a white pebble from the red gravel path. "We noticed that the twins were different almost immediately. It was more than a matter of their crying at the same time,

182

their constant desire to be close to each other. . . . There was always something different about them."

"We tried to ignore it," Mr. Clarke added. "Finally we took them to psychologists, then psychiatrists. They sent us to the Duke department of parapsychology."

"I prayed for a cure," Mrs. Clarke said. "Something that would turn them into average girls with average problems."

"And there is no cure?"

"At first I thought sharing was a curse," Mr. Clarke said, making a face as though he'd tasted bitters. He paused when they reached the stairs and pointed down toward the beach. "I used to watch them from here, running through the sand, their eyes on fire. It was as though they'd tapped into the very essence of the air and the sun and the water." Another pause as he stared off toward the lake. "One day I realized that I would give my whole life to spend a single day the way that Jael and Julie spent every day." He shook his head and started down the spray-slick stairs.

Gulls squawked and whirled around them. The sand by the bluffs was soft and dusty, but as they approached the water it became so hard that Matt's shoes scarcely left an imprint. There were no waves, but the lake roiled with an inner turbulence and belched seaweed and dead fish and an odor as bitter as stomach acid. Jael and Dylan ran a hundred feet up the sand, poking through the line of seaweed and flotsam. Dylan had never searched for lake treasures with anyone but Matt. Each time the boy would bring something to Jael, she would bend to his level, examine it, and start an explanation. And he would smile and brush against her leg. Matt clenched his hands together. They were so cumbersome, so awkward—a lumberjack's hands instead of a lawyer's. He expelled a breath with a pop, took both parents' arms, and pulled them toward him.

"How did you handle it?" he asked.

"What?"

"The jealousy, the sudden distance. The not knowing for sure whether your child needs you anymore."

"We didn't have six years to develop a normal relationship, so perhaps we didn't know what we missed," Mr. Clarke said.

"They don't seem to need anyone else."

"Not all times are as harmonious as this," Mr. Clarke said. "The twins had learned to hide the power by the time they reached school, but still, the other children were hostile. Even in high school they only had each other. . . ." Mrs. Clarke started to interrupt, but he held up his hand to stop her. "Granted, there were boys all around, but that was unavoidable, considering the way the girls looked."

Matt picked up a handful of sand and sifted it through his fingers. "Jealous or not, I don't know where Dylan would be if he hadn't found her. For a while I thought I was going to lose him."

Dylan scurried toward them and, when he opened his cupped hands, dropped a small pile of shells, trinkets, and fishbones at his feet. He began to sort through them and hand them to Matt. "Jael said that this is from an alewife, this from a trout, and this —" He spoke so rapidly Matt could scarcely understand him.

"Slow down, Cap'n," Matt said. Dylan dropped a snail into Matt's hand and it began to crawl over the mound of his thumb. The slime and movement made him shiver. When Matt looked up, Jael was within five feet of him, brushing the sand from her knees. She went to her tiptoes to kiss him on the cheek. "That's for teaching your son so much about the lake," she said.

They stayed together as they walked up the beach; only Dylan sprinted from the bluffs to the water in search of treasure. Gulls and the cold northern wind provided most of the sound. Occasionally someone would bend to examine a rock or pluck a partially buried can from the sand. When Jael knelt to pick up a rusted fishing lure, her father placed a hand on her shoulder and said, "We haven't heard much about *The* One *Cult* lately."

"There hasn't been much time to write." As she stood she took a hand from each parent. "Something new's come up. I discovered that members of the *One* Cult were like Dylan and me: telepathic."

Her mother cleared her throat. "And how does one prove such an unusual hypothesis?"

"By looking back through the ancient writings. The descriptions left by priests of certain symptoms and perceptions could only be known to someone who could share." Her mother tried to interrupt, but Jael continued, "Finding Dylan was another

184

key. If sharing can exist outside identical twins, it could once have been fairly common."

"Why is it so rare today?"

"Something turned the masses against it. The rest was a matter of numbers." She smiled mischievously. "As a matter of fact, the three of you could help me prove it."

"How?" Mrs. Clarke asked.

"If I can't find some additional genetic link, some proof of unusual power in other relatives, the theory remains hypothesis."

"We have the most stable relatives in the world," her mother said. She turned to her husband and smiled. "At least my side of the family."

"I didn't expect much, and I'll take anything." She paused. "Try to imagine how sharing would appear if there was no one to share with."

"There are always rumors," Mrs. Clarke said.

"That's just what I'm after."

Even Matt noticed that Jael's mother seemed uneasy.

"It's okay, Mom," Jael said. "If Matt's not family, who is?"

"If it will make things easier, I'll go first," Matt said. He picked up a flat rock and skipped it across the water. "People believed my great-grandmother was a witch. A white one. Herbs. Fortune-telling. The whole works. People stayed away from her . . . unless they needed something done." He shook his head as he searched for another stone. "All this time I assumed she was crazy."

Jael turned toward her father. "As you know," he said, "I don't have many relatives. I never met my grandparents on either side." A pause. "All my dad ever talked about was oil."

"Mother?" Jael asked.

"I don't know," she said, wrinkling her brow. "I used to play with the Ouija board when I was a child. Sometimes I scared myself." She looked away from them toward the lake. "I used to have dreams . . . nothing like you and Julie, but I had feelings and sometimes they'd come true. . . ." Her voice trailed off.

"Was that why you were such a bear about Julie and me staying on the grounds for the graduation party?"

"It was just a feeling," her mother said. "I trained myself to ignore them." Suddenly she turned back to Jael. "I know I never shared anything with you and Julie."

"Your 'gift' may have been slightly different. Not as strong." Jael took her mother's hand as they walked.

What if a degree of the power were in both Bekki and me, Matt thought. *That could explain why we sought each other despite the differences. That something, a link on a level we didn't understand, kept us together for so long despite ourselves.* He stared out at the lake: There was no horizon line. The gray of the sky was the gray of the lake.

"Does this mean both your father and I are carriers?" Mrs. Clarke asked.

"You make it sound like typhoid or the plague," Jael said. "The existence of Dylan, Julie, and me indicates everyone here is a carrier."

"Then you can pass it on too?"

Jael stopped, cocked her head quizzically, and looked toward Dylan. A grin spread across her face. "Only if I mate with someone who carries it."

SEVENTEEN

Glencoe, Illinois—October 31, 1981

Jael rolled over in the bed where she had slept as a child and stared at the outline of the canopy: The lace fringes were still there, as hard to part with as the past. She pulled her cold feet into the legs of her flannel pajamas, tossed for a while, rolled over and tossed some more, then sat up. Moonlight stripped the furniture and the stuffed giraffes of color, gave them the pallor of a disembodied soul. The poster and mobiles, the piano at which she had spent so many hours, were suddenly everyday objects, not the magic carpets they had been when Julie was there to share them.

A shiver.

It was not a night to spend alone.

Perhaps the open window was partially responsible for her goosebumps. She climbed from the bed, hurried across the rug, and took a single deep breath of the night chill; it smelled of moist earth and burials. She closed the window, ran back across the room, jumped into bed, and huddled under the covers until the warmth began to tingle.

There was an advantage to sleeping with Chris. Anytime she grew cold, all she had to do was wrap herself around him, fit all her curves to his angles, and drift immediately back to sleep. The thought made her huddle even tighter, grab her toes and try to rub some life back into them. When she was finally warm enough to stick her head out of the covers, she rolled onto her side and curled up in a prenatal position, a duplicate of Dylan's sleeping pose. Had he inherited that from Matt too?

Matt.

After twelve years of marriage, sleeping alone must not have been much of a treat for him either. But who was to say with whom he spent his time during the week. Jael had a weekend relationship with him, if that.

Matt.

He had his own way of communicating with her. It wasn't like sharing, but there was the same sense of certainty, an intimacy that went as far beyond words as words went beyond smoke signals. His glance left her breathless and confused and *alive* all at once.

Matt.

It was ridiculous that each of them should be lying alone in a cold bed in the middle of a huge room. Was he awake, too, listening for the opening of her door, the almost silent footsteps in the hall?

Her move.

It was her parents' house, essentially their invitation, and Matt was far too proper to violate convention, much less their daughter, while he was a guest. There was the same shyness in him that made Dylan irresistible. How much more of him was in Dylan? At least she wouldn't have to worry about the boy sensing their pleasure: Julie and she had experimented enough to learn that was the one thing they could keep private. If they wished.

She wished.

A half-dozen steps to the closet and she took a terry-cloth bathrobe to cover the pajamas, then she walked to the door, checked the corridor to be sure no one else was up, then tiptoed to Matt's room. She stopped three doors from his to be sure Dylan wasn't awake, then another ten steps and she reached for the doorknob, took a deep breath, grabbed it firmly, and eased it open.

"Dylan?" Matt asked, as soon as the door opened a crack.

It hadn't reached the point where she would be irrevocably embarrassed yet. He hadn't seen her, hadn't heard her voice. If she were to hurry back to her room before he got up, the rejection, the hurt, would be no more than a bee sting. Then she shook her head. If she had spent her life fearing rejection, she never would have climbed out of the playpen. A deep breath for courage. "Sorry," she said. "Just me."

"Is something wrong?" he asked.

How should she answer? That sleeping alone was wrong? That a grown woman having to wear flannel pajamas to keep warm was wrong? Instead she said, "Not with Dylan."

He must have taken the hint. There was a loud rustling, the *thonk* of a knee against wood, then rapid footsteps across the floor. Matt pulled the door open and stood half in the light, half in darkness, his trousers half zipped.

She wanted to say something intimate, profound. "Hi" was all that came out. She felt herself blushing and wanted to push him into the darkness where he couldn't see her.

"Jael," he said, "there are a few things I want you to know."

"No declarations are necessary."

"I'm possessive, old-fashioned."

"There are worse things."

"If this is going to be onetime, I'd rather we didn't."

"Well, we have to *start* at one, don't we," she said, taking his hand. When he closed the door behind them, it was completely dark, so they had to feel across the rug with their toes and, when the bed seemed near, reach out for it with their fingers. When Jael touched the blanket, she moved her shins up to it, then turned around and sat down. Matt turned on the bed lamp, but she reached across him to turn it off. "Not the first time," she said. "Sight is too easy. Let's just touch."

When she drew her arm back, she ran it across the hard muscle of his thigh. He ran his hand over her hair, helped her off with her bathrobe, kissed an earlobe, then reached a hand behind her back.

"The last time I encountered this much flannel, I was hanging my grandmother's laundry on a clothesline."

"It's obvious you've never been cold at night."

"Cold is forbidden in my bed."

"Then move over," Jael said.

When she started to unbutton her pajama top, his hand stopped her. "That's my job," he said, "but not yet." He put an arm around her and pulled her under the covers.

She found the impediment of trousers and pajamas added to the excitement, the challenge. His hands caressed her in long, gentle sweeps, stopping to stroke here, fondle there; he rubbed

189

circles at the base of her spine, touched her nipples to hardness through the soft cloth. There was less hair on his back than she expected to find, and his muscles were smooth and hard and dipped in at the spine just the way she liked, and he shivered when she ran one finger, then two, from his ears to his neck to his bottom, and his hand was soft between her legs, softer with the thick flannel, and she really couldn't help herself, she moved against his hand and unbuttoned the only snap on his trousers, and he arched his back as she slid the pants from his waist to his thighs, down past his knees. She felt him kick them off, then stroked his hardness, rubbed with her thumb, her palm, and she arched so he would remove the pajamas, but he wouldn't, he kept stroking and rubbing and the pleasure became so intense it hurt, so she swung a leg over him, moved against him and felt his hardness through the flannel, and he nibbled on her lips, her ear, and unbuttoned the front of her top so her breasts could be stroked by the hair on his chest, and she moaned and slipped her tongue into his mouth, and he ran a hand down her spine, slid under the elastic of her bottoms, paused just for an instant, then touched her inner thigh, and she spread her legs wider, opened for him, and somehow the bottoms were down past her knees, so she kicked them off, sat up, and settled down on him, and moved and moved and moved, and the chill started at the base of her spine, grew and started to explode, and she grabbed the taut muscles in his hips, closed her eyes and leaned back and moaned as the chill shot through her.

His motions slowed with hers, and when she stopped, he stopped. "You're about the shiveriest person I ever met," he said.

Jael didn't feel like talking. She felt like enjoying his warmth, his gentleness, the way he eased his stroking as her contractions eased. When the tingling had stopped, after she spent a few minutes listening to his heartbeat, feeling the pulse in his arm, she kissed his lips, rose above him, and whispered, "And now it's your turn."

"You get those digging potatoes?" she asked, brushing her fingertips along the muscles in his shoulders.

He moved the matted hair from her temple and kissed her

above the ear before he spoke. "The machines took care of most of that. We weren't rich. I earned spending cash from seventh grade on cutting trees for a pulper. We loaded them by hand."

She wanted to tell him that no matter how strong he was, he didn't have to worry about breaking her, that a touch of roughness was nice once in a while; but then she remembered how nice the gentleness had been, so she kept her mouth shut.

"I haven't felt like this since high school," he said.

"Only you could get away with a line like that."

He paused. She could feel his breath slow, deepen, his muscles tense, then relax. "How does this affect you and Professor Shaw?"

Jael waited for just an instant to let him worry. "Who?" she finally asked.

She wanted to see him, to stare at him so, as Julie once said, his face would be the last thing she saw before she went to sleep. She waited until his breathing evened, till his movements became slow and dull and had long since ceased, then reached past him to turn on the bed lamp. He was facing her, lying on his side so the light hit his back, and he didn't stir. His hair was matted from the weight of his head on the pillow, and the folds left wrinkles on his face. He looked, in other words, beautiful.

Ah, the fickleness of perception, she thought.

There was nothing to do but enjoy it. She reached past him to turn off the light. Before she settled into sleep—before the warmth, the tingle of him, was transformed into dreams—he draped an arm over her and pulled her tight against him so they could lie together as one, nestled like spoons.

Claws sink into the ground, gritty and giving. The sand smells come to life: thousands of humans who sat, ate, played on the grass. Even months old the scents are alive. Mist scatters and a negative world opens: white trees spread into a whiter sky; the sand a black ooze, the water purest white.

A pause to sniff a hollow metal cylinder, white on black. The sugar smell is nauseating, nothing like the sweetness of blood.

Another odor. No, two. Alike in many ways but as different as

191

faces. Seductive odors. Irresistible odors. A howl rises in the throat. No. The prey would panic, flee.

The smell of salt on skin. Of breath warm against the chill. Sight has none of smell's richness. Smell is life. Smell lights beacons of more than prey: warmth filling cold veins; form where there is no form.

A deep breath brings back the thought of prey. A noiseless sprint to a bush. Closer. Silent step after silent step. An ear cocks toward the scents. Murmurs. One male. One female. Consumed with each other. Blind in their rutting, their scents glow with youth.

And warmth.

The prey-drive rises, the craving stronger than sex. Lips ripple on fangs. Creep to a bush. Slide to a tree. The prey-drive is too strong; a howl escapes.

The male looks up. He makes no sound but the liquid gurgling of horror. The female's murmurs build toward a scream; before it escapes a claw finds her throat. White blood pulses from the black skin. No time to feast. The male runs, runs toward a line of twin dots of light in the distance. A shudder. The ecstasy of the chase.

The male runs past the building to the grass. Past a strip of smooth rock. Behind him trails the most glorious smell: terror. The terror in his face is sweet enough to swallow. A final sprint. Fangs rip through sweet skin. Blood pulses warm down the gullet. Then organs. Crack the skull for brains, the bones for marrow. The warmth is sweet. It soars and sings. Sings above the cold night, the cold stars.

Another feast waits.

Back through the white grass, past the black sand before the aura of warmth fades. Teeth pause gently on sweet skin before they pop. . . .

"Hey, it's only a dream," Matt was whispering. His fingers spread across Jael's shoulders, kneading tight muscles. "Just a dream."

He pulled her tight against his chest, rocked her back and

forth, and talked in nonsense words, sharp bits of reality that would lead her from the subconscious back to the conscious.

At first she couldn't speak. Parts of the nightmare lingered. "It wasn't a dream."

"All you did was whimper," Matt said. "No howling."

"I was in a dreamscape, only it wasn't my dream. It wasn't the way I perceive the world." She paused and tried to forget the sensation of sinews ripping between her teeth, of muscle gliding down her throat. "I mostly remember hunger. Hunger like a lion or bear. There was the lake, only it was white instead of blue. And somehow the sand was black. And odors. I could visualize people, their moods and age, through smells that were months old." A pause to shudder. "And the kids. Oh, my God, the kids!" She buried her face in her hands. Another thought. "Let's check on Dylan," she said.

She slipped on her bathrobe and followed Matt into the hall. Dylan's door was unlocked. The boy was awake, sitting on the bed as though he were waiting for them. Crying. "I was scared," he said. "A dream. This boy and girl were on the beach and I snuck up on them and—"

"I know," Jael said, sitting on the bed and holding him. "I know."

Matt's voice broke. *"What's going on?"* he shouted.

Dylan looked up, made a horrible face, and repeated "It's started" over and over and over.

PART THREE

EIGHTEEN

Glencoe, Illinois—November 1, 1981

Each time Dylan closed his eyes the whimpering began, so Matt stayed by his bed. Jael was there too. Close by. Within an arm's reach. Her presence helped Matt as much as it helped Dylan.

They sat on either side of the bed past two, past three, past four o'clock, when the room seemed as cold and dark as a lifeless planet. All the sounds, the creaking of bedsprings, even Dylan's breathing, were unreal, heavy with a cold presence.

"Do you feel it?" Jael finally asked.

"What?"

"It almost feels like the air's coagulating. Like something that's built up is ready to break loose." A moment's pause. The silence was magnified by the room, the mood. "Something has happened. I don't know what it is, but I'm as sure of it as Dylan was."

Matt closed his eyes and tried to concentrate, to project himself inward, to escape his intellect and senses and search for the latent power he *had* to have to be Dylan's father. Nothing. Nothing at all. When he opened his eyes, he saw Jael's outline in the gray light. "What do we do now?"

"Set the alarm for twelve, get up and socialize with the folks, take the obligatory tour of the grounds, then sit down with a good book and try to relax for a change."

"What will your parents think?"

"Nothing, I hope."

"Won't they notice that we missed breakfast? That we spent the night in Dylan's room?"

Jael rested an arm on his shoulder and traced the curve of his ear. "All problems," she said. "But they've had more time to grow accustomed to the bizarre than most."

197

Mr. and Mrs. Clarke led them through the gardens, through the arbors and past the pond, into the forest that fringed the estate. Matt turned into the breeze, which smelled of wet leaves and mushrooms and apples fermenting on the trees: all things that reminded him of pressing cider. He turned to his right and saw Dylan sprint across a bridge that traversed a thirty-foot-deep ravine. He was about to call the boy back, to tell Dylan to stay close until they moved past the sudden drops, when Mrs. Clarke took his hand to stop him. "What happened last night?" she asked.

Jael tugged on his hand and led him to the center of the bridge. Mrs. Clarke walked up to them, leaned against the railing, and said to Jael, "Your father and I have reached that unfortunate stage of life where we don't sleep all night. It hasn't affected our hearing, however."

More silence. Finally Jael said, "Dylan and I shared a dream."

"You didn't share dreams with Julie."

"But we only had each other," Jael said. "This is different, like some outside force is breaking down barriers."

For long minutes the only sounds were the rustle of blowing leaves and the grating call of a blue jay.

"Was it like the recurring nightmare?" Mr. Clarke finally asked.

"The main character is the same."

"And you still experience the 'orgasm of the soul'?" her mother asked, tapping the railing.

Jael leaned against the railing and stared at the tops of the trees that rose from the ravines. "The image isn't as farfetched as you might think. The more I experience it, the more precise it seems."

"You mentioned vampires last time."

"Last night I was the victimizer." A pause. "Ever notice the voluptuous smiles vampires always seem to have? Last night's dream convinced me that other animals have urges as strong as sex." She straightened her back and began to gesture with an index finger, no doubt a mannerism developed in the classroom. "Take predators—a wolf, for example. The desire for the chase, the desire to kill, may be the primary urge. Last night I realized that a vampire is more predator than human."

Mrs. Clarke was shaking her head. There was a touch of pleading in her voice. "Werewolves? Vampires? Will you have to start dreaming about Frankenstein monsters before you go for help?"

"Frankenstein is a literary invention, Mother, a symbol consciously created to represent the dangers of science, of the too-rational mind. That's not true of werewolves and vampires. They existed before the first written story. They're not conscious anything, and they appear in every culture."

"I really don't need a lecture," her mother said. "Dylan was shouting last night, shouting that something had started. What?"

"I honestly don't know," Jael said. "He's a child. He can't make sense of all the things that happen to him."

"But you're a doctor and you shared his dream."

"I'm too close."

"Why not talk to Chris?" her father asked.

"Because he'd laugh it off." She paused. "Besides, he's been in Egypt."

"Your Dr. King?" her mother asked.

"I already saw him. Even he needs time."

A squirrel jumped from limb to limb, scolded them, then disappeared into a hole in a hickory tree. The chatter broke the tension. Jael tugged on Matt's hand and led him back onto a leaf-covered path that was as bright as an Indian blanket. They walked four across toward the break in the forest where the gazebo stood. "Don't worry," Jael said as she leaned over and kissed her mother. "If I find out anything, you'll be the first to know."

While Mrs. Clarke took Dylan upstairs to give him a lesson on the harpsichord, Jael led Matt to an enormous library with mahogany paneling and row after row of leather-bound books. She pointed first to a couch, then to an afternoon newspaper that lay on an end table, then left the room to make some hot chocolate. Matt pulled up a hassock, stretched out his legs, inhaled a deep breath of the wood-rich air, then snapped open the paper. The top half of the page was normal November fare: a feature about some children who had received razor blades or LSD in their Halloween candy; a list of the atrocities committed in the Middle East. In the lower right-hand column Matt noticed an unusual headline:

SUBURBAN TEENS DIE
IN LAKEFRONT ATTACK

Matt squinted, blinked his eyes, and started to read:

By Mark Garland

Wilmette—The mutilated bodies of two youths were found this morning by fishermen in Gillson Park, five blocks north of the Evanston border.

The victims were identified as William DeForrest, 18, and Sarah Freeman, 17, both of Northbrook. Police spokesperson Mary Orne said that the couple had driven into Chicago to view a play and must have stopped in the park while returning home. Since the victims' wallets and possessions were not removed, robbery was eliminated as a possible motive.

Investigators combed the beach, park, and adjacent homes Sunday morning, trying to piece together an explanation of the events. Based on interviews with persons who discovered the bodies and evidence at the scene, Orne gave the following account:

Freeman and DeForrest were sitting on a blanket approximately twenty yards from the lake when they were attacked. Freeman was killed before she could move from the blanket, but DeForrest ran a hundred yards toward Sheridan Road before he was caught and murdered.

"We're not speculating on the cause of death or the murder weapon until after the autopsies are completed," Orne said. "Some of the injuries suggest that feral dogs entered the park after the youths died, and these may have eliminated or camouflaged evidence which would otherwise be apparent."

Both victims were juniors at Glenbrook North High School. Freeman was an honor-roll student and class officer, while DeForrest was active in school plays and a member of the debate team.

Matt lay the paper on his lap, stared out the window, and listened to the brittle notes of a baroque adagio until Jael walked back into the library. She placed a cup of steaming chocolate down on the end table. Matt picked it up and took a sip; a scoop of vanilla ice cream swirled in the cup. He handed her the paper and tapped the headline with a finger. "What do you make of this?" he asked.

She was standing when she took the paper from him, but within twenty seconds she was sitting on an arm of the couch. The color drained from her face as she said, "You're not suggesting . . . ?"

"It's a hell of a coincidence."

She stood, walked in front of him, and plopped down on the couch. She took several deep breaths and shook her head. "I'll grant that there are some similarities."

Matt pointed back to the story. "Read it more closely," he said. "Tell me if you notice anything peculiar."

"Obviously the facts—"

"Beyond the facts," Matt said. "Note the style, the way they chose to present the facts."

Jael drummed her fingers on her knee, then picked up the paper and started to read. She began shaking her head almost immediately. "Sorry, it looks like standard news format to me."

"Note the way the writer generalizes about important facts and presents useless specifics. Look," he said, pointing to the column, "the victims' school, their extracurricular activities, but no description of motive, wound, or weapon."

"It says mutilated."

"What does *that* mean? Knifed and sliced? Hacked with an ax? And what about this feral-dog damage? Does that mean poodle and Chihuahua damage? Or was the flesh ripped from the body and the bones cracked to get the marrow?"

"So what are you getting at?"

"They're hiding something."

"Why?"

Matt moved even closer to her. "Perhaps to avoid widespread fear about something."

Matt could see the relief settle over Jael's face; she rolled her eyes and gave a snort of contempt. "My God, how your generation loves conspiracies," she said, then pointed to the paper's masthead. "Look. A big city daily. How long would they survive suppressing stories that big?"

"They can only print what they're told."

"You can bet they'd dig like crazy for a story big enough to evoke 'widespread fear.'"

"I used to handle criminal cases, Jael. The police cover their own asses first."

"The police, maybe; obviously not the press."

Matt took her by the shoulders and sat her up. "How do you think Mr. Garland became a by-line reporter? By relying solely on police sources? Show me one quote from a witness. A neighbor. A park caretaker. This reads more like a personality sketch than a news story."

"It's Sunday. The neighbors are out, the caretaker's off, and the fishermen had left before he arrived."

"I read the fishing reports," Matt said. "The salmon are running close to shore. That means twenty, maybe thirty people would be on that jetty by dawn. If one of them found two murder victims, you think the rest of them wouldn't gawk?"

Jael stared hard at him and remained silent.

Matt tapped the by-line with a knuckle. "How long do you think Mr. Garland would keep his job if he couldn't track down one of thirty fishermen?"

A longer silence. "What are you driving at?" Jael finally asked.

"The fishermen must have been horrified, to start with. Maybe the police suggested their names would be leaked to the press as witnesses if they talked. Then told them stories of what maniacs do to people they think witnessed their crime." Matt leaned closer to her. "Remember the Scott boy, the one who was sliced up at the amusement park? Twenty witnesses, and not one said a thing until the trial."

Jael stood and began pacing the floor in front of him. She occasionally stopped to stare at the ceiling and bounced a fist off her thigh. She spread her arms helplessly, then walked to the window and stared out. "You think my dream really happened."

"It's a possibility."

She drummed her fingers on the windowpane and kept nodding, nodding. Then she turned back toward Matt, shrugged, and asked softly, "Should I call the police and tell them what I know?"

"How would you explain it?"

"I'd start by giving them enough specifics so that they could determine that I'm for real."

"If I thought it were coincidence, I'd dial the damn number for you," Matt said. "If they think you're for real, they'll probably put you in protective custody. They might say they're protecting you from the real murderer, but you can bet they'd try to pin it on you. Imagine the heat that must be coming down from the press, the public."

At first Jael nodded as though she agreed. Suddenly she shook her head and set her jaw. "Matt, this is Illinois; the Bon are in Tibet!"

"What if there are other telepaths? You can bet most of them wouldn't be academics. You said most people wouldn't be able to fight the impulse. What would happen if they didn't? What if they started a religion? Who's to say? What if voodoo, some of the South American religions, are like the Red Bon?"

Jael let her arms droop to her waist. She sat down next to Matt, leaned against him, and closed her eyes. He could feel her trembling. "Then I really don't have much of a choice, do I?"

"You don't go to the police with information they won't know how to handle," Matt said. He began to shake his head. "Imagine trying to explain sharing. Imagine trying it on a detective sergeant who knows he'll be promoted if he finds this killer. They'd want to see proof, and that means Dylan. Then the press would get hold of it. You think he could stand up to that kind of a zoo?"

"So what next?"

"Be patient. I still have some contacts." He paused and stroked Jael's cheek with the back of his hand.

"But what if someone else dies?"

"All I'm suggesting is that we learn as much as we can before we tell the police something they won't be able to understand. I'll contact my source tonight."

"Then drop me off at my place," Jael said. "I have a couple years' work to do before Dr. King calls back. Besides, I'm not sure I want to go to sleep and dream tonight."

NINETEEN

Wilmette, Illinois—November 1, 1981

Jael unlocked her apartment door and opened it. The darkness inside seemed churning, alive. She took a deep breath for courage, then reached in and flicked on the light. She threw her coat and scarf on the chair in the corridor, then went from room to room and turned on all the lights. Even in the brightness, familiar objects were different, as if she had left the apartment as a child and were seeing it for the first time in decades. Even the piano wasn't an old friend anymore but a prop from a haunted house. Each room looked as though it had been built at grotesque angles to unsettle, unnerve.

And Osiris.

He had perched in the same spot since he had bitten her, near the top of the cage, staring down—not looking around vacantly, each eye moving in a different direction as it should, but *staring*. She took a step toward the cage and his glare intensified . . . or seemed to intensify. How much of her fear was caused by reading her motives into his actions? She couldn't stop thinking of Dylan and the zoo. Of animals acting with intent. Maybe it was all foolishness. If she were convinced that snails could do logarithms, she would probably find intent in the movement of their antennae, calligraphy in their slime trails.

Imagination or not, she couldn't sit where the bird's dark eyes could follow her. She walked into the kitchen, leaned against the chopping block, tilted her head, and ran her fingers through her hair. It would be another long night. All her longest hours were spent at three or four in the morning, staring at the black ceiling of her bedroom, knowing she couldn't force herself to sleep but trying it anyway. She wasn't up to that tonight. She measured some Mocha Java beans out of a jar, placed them in the coffee grinder, listened to it whir, then smelled the aroma before she poured the ground beans in the filter.

If she was going to do research, why not start with her sudden fear of Osiris? One of the Nagada Papyri had mentioned priests talking to birds and snakes; maybe it was another facet of sharing. Then why hadn't it happened before? What would Osiris say? Lecture her? Lead prayers? She tried to laugh off the idea, but it wasn't funny. After the deaths of the teenagers, *nothing* was very funny.

Why not give Dr. King a call? Just for the company. Unfortunately it was after seven, and he turned off his phone after dinner so his studies wouldn't be interrupted.

The phone.

She hadn't checked the recording device to see if any messages had been left over the weekend. She walked into the bedroom. She rewound the tape, pushed the play button, then listened to her own voice say:

> "This is Jael Clarke. I'm not at home, but if you'd like to leave a message, wait until you hear the tone, then speak into the receiver. I'll call you back later. Thanks."

The tone sounded and she heard Chris's voice:

> "I have to see you for professional as well as personal reasons. The lectures I gave in Cairo were successful enough, but the real excitement started when I flew to Ombos to do your research on Set. The temple and ruins had information that might win us that Nobel prize after all. Research *does* pay off. I'll be in my office until midnight. I do love you, you know."

His voice had sounded as self-confident and irresistible as only Chris could be. Jael shook her head and glanced from the phone to the full-length mirror to the statuette of Bast, the Egyptian cat-goddess. She started to tremble. As hard as it would be to face Chris, it would be worse to spend the night alone in the apartment.

206

Whoever had killed the teenagers was probably nearby.

So before the piano started playing on its own, before Osiris started lecturing her in Aztec or Tibetan or Old Irish, she hurried into the corridor, picked up her coat, and closed the door behind her.

And made sure not to turn off any of the lights.

She walked up the poorly lighted stairs to Chris's office and, when she saw light leaking through the crack beneath the door, shook her head and leaned against the railing. If he was arrogant, even demanded an apology, he would make all her decisions for her. Just one harsh word, just thirty seconds of belittling or derision, and the severing process that had started two weeks before would be complete.

She walked the final five steps, hesitated, knocked on the door, and stepped back. There were footsteps muted by carpeting; the door swung open, and Chris was silhouetted by the harsh office light. He reached out and pulled her toward him. His body was still lithe, his heartbeat strong, and his angles blended into her curves as though he were the mold and she the casting. He kissed her forehead, her eyes, her lips.

"I was an ass," he said. He paused to give her a chance to respond, but she honestly couldn't think of a thing to say. "The last time I apologized to someone," he continued, "it was to my parents for getting a B-plus in eighth-grade civics."

She squeezed his hand.

He placed an arm around her waist and led her inside. "All our disagreements are past tense," he said. "History to be forgotten." When they were fully in the light, he held her at arm's length and touched beneath her eye with a fingertip. "You're still having problems sleeping."

"A few."

"Nightmares?"

"It's not important," she said. As her eyes grew accustomed to the light his face eased into focus. He was more tan than he would normally be in November—then, it was impossible to spend time in the Sahara and not tan—but something else was different too. Matt. Although Matt wasn't there, he was.

"How are classes?"

"All right," Jael said. "At least I've started to loosen the reins." She smiled and shrugged: There wasn't anything to say, nothing but chatter. "How was your trip?"

"We hit one squall over the Atlantic; otherwise, fine."

If they continued to talk about themselves, about nothing, she'd feel like crying. It would be safer, easier, to talk about work. His work. "You mentioned that the lectures went well."

"They were fine as soon as I convinced them a westerner could know more about Egypt than an Egyptian." He paused. The radiant smile was still there, the timing, the sparkle, everything; yet, everything was missing. His words seemed like bluster instead of self-confidence.

"Thanks for going to Ombos," Jael said.

"It was a way to underline my apology." He took her hand and led her to his table. Even from ten feet she could smell the age and mustiness from the relics.

"They let you take artifacts?" she asked.

"On loan," Chris said. "One of the men I met claimed to be an expert on Set, as if there were such a thing. Ahmed Hasan?"

"I've read some of his articles."

"He's tall, swarthy, charming—all that an Oxford-educated Middle Easterner should be. He insisted on taking me to Ombos, showing me the best digs, the most relevant papyri—"

"How did he know which papyri were most relevant?" Jael interrupted.

"I mentioned the *One* Cult."

"Exactly how much did you mention?" she asked, her voice starting to harden in anger.

"Only enough to wet his whistle," Chris said. "A few dates, a few places, a few deities. And damn good thing I did. His sarcasm turned to interest after what we found at the temple. He wants to start exchanging ideas with you."

"What does he want?"

"To see the proofs of your book. His chance for a headstart on an article." Chris patted her on the shoulder and let his voice grow serious. "He won't steal your ideas. And believe me, he paid a high price. Look what I got for an article or two." He reached toward the desk and handed her a fragment of an amuletic wand. There was a Set animal etched into the stone, lean and ferocious, preparing to attack a man who wore a pharaonic crown. The man held a sacred ankh in one hand, a short sword in the other.

"I've seen drawings similar to this," Jael said.

"I almost missed it too. Look closer, the sword."

She held the fragment close to the light. The sword's hilt was thin by the handle and grew wider as it approached the tip. There were still traces of the ochre coloring although it was 3500 years old. "A *phurba?*"

"Or the Egyptian equivalent of one." Chris took the fragment from her hand and laid it gently back on the desk. "It's from the end of the Twentieth Dynasty or the start of the Twenty-first. One of the pharaoh's titles was Liberator from Set." He reached onto the desk, picked up a manila envelope, removed some pictures, and handed one to her: an excavation. Judging from the late-model Japanese trucks hauling earth, it must be a current dig. "The rest of the pictures and relics are from this site," he said.

"It doesn't look familiar."

"It hasn't been announced," Chris said. "Hasan's first article on it will be out next month."

Judging from the size of the men in the photo, the dig was fairly small, thirty, maybe forty feet across. "Not much of a temple."

Chris laughed gently. He took another picture from the stack and handed it to her. It showed a walled chamber littered with skulls, bones, and weapons. "A native worker found a gap in the masonry of the foundation of the temple at Ombos. There wasn't dirt behind it, but a tunnel. He contacted Hasan. There are seven skeletons in all. Judging from their robes, they were members of the priesthood of Set."

"And they weren't mummified?"

"It wasn't a burial chamber," Chris said. *"Hardly."*

"Then why the skeletons?"

"Each man was armed with a sword and dagger." Chris paused to hand her close-ups of the weapons, then continued, "When the persecutions against the cult of Set began, things must nave come down terribly fast. Hasan thinks that while the lower priests and workers were fighting off the army of the new pharaoh, trying to protect the shrine, these select few ran into the tunnel and tried to hide in this chamber. Maybe they planned on escaping when it was night. For some reason, when the troops found the tunnel, they didn't go down it; with all the drawings and statues of Set around, they probably didn't know what they would meet. Instead they walled up the tunnel. There was one flaw in the architecture: no escape route."

"There don't seem to be any religious articles," Jael said, turning the picture in the light. "Pretty strange for a priesthood."

Chris grinned. "You ain't seen nothing yet." He handed her a piece of legal-size paper with a list written on it. "You'll note that there are no amulets, no shrines, no statuary—no religious artifacts of any kind. . . ."

"Just beds, incense burners, phalli . . ."

"And pictures," Chris said. "Wall paintings everywhere."

He handed her another photo: a wall painting. It was the closest thing to pornography she had seen in ancient art. The figures were detailed, the colors lush, the organs enormous and locked in every possible combination. Men in wolf masks mounted naked girls from the front, the back. The faces weren't the bland representations of many of the tomb paintings, but graphic, filled with ecstasy, pleasure bordering on pain. Her eyes returned to the wolf mask.

"The Bon."

"Amazing, isn't it. I already checked the pictures in your office. The masks are identical. Other paintings showed there were other masks—other stages in the transformation from man to Set creature." He took three more photos from the stack and handed them to her. A priest with a skin mask led a small boy into a room. Removed the boy's robe. Fondled and mounted him.

"This is like a story," Jael said. "An X-rated movie."

"The walls were covered with paintings like these," Chris said. "This priesthood must have had incredible amounts of leisure time to develop these sort of tastes."

"What was the room used for? Surely not worship."

"Take another look at the list: incense burners, beds, an ivory phallus. Another of gold. A third encrusted with precious gems. And these paintings."

"It sounds like a bordello."

"That was our guess. The priests had power, slaves, but no privacy in the temple. This room was privacy."

"Why no women or children?"

"Things must have happened so fast, they didn't have time."

Jael handed the list and pictures back to him, then leaned against the back of a chair. "There's more?"

"You wouldn't believe," Chris said. He started to reach for a stamped manila envelope in the center of the desk, then stopped. "No," he said, "I'll save the best for last." He picked up a large clay tablet instead and carefully handed it to her. "That's a copy," he said, "but a damn good one."

Jael held it up to the light. Plans for a building were etched into it, a pyramid complete with arches, pillars, and doorways. "This looks like a blueprint."

"It's accurate enough to let us rebuild the temple," Chris said. "Now turn it over."

The clay was covered with a smooth protective glaze. There was another etching on the back, this one of a courtyard with what appeared to be a series of monoliths arranged systematically. Jael looked up in amazement. "This looks like Stonehenge!"

"Compared to this, Stonehenge looks like a schoolboy made it from Pick Up Sticks." He paused for effect. "This would have been the most sophisticated astronomical observatory that existed in the ancient world. Nothing, not even the Mayan and Aztec digs, are close. It must have been destroyed with the temples and priesthood."

"Any idea what they used it for?"

"We'd have to erect the same-size monoliths on the same spot to discover that, then wait around till something happened," he said. "The Egyptian government has neither the money nor the inclination for a project that big."

Jael sat back and shook her head.

"There were a few other relics: bones with deep scratches, miniatures of the Set animal," Chris said. "Some of the paintings had a group of Set animals devouring war captives. The line of captives winds right out of the painting."

"Like Aztec sacrifices?"

"There were at least that many captives," he said. Then he picked up another envelope. "I have photos of all of them."

Jael felt like leaning over and kissing him—but she didn't. "Sometimes you're an angel, you know that?" she said, and thought, *Why now?*

"Only sometimes?" Chris asked. He picked up the manila envelope, the one he had reached for earlier. His expression became serious. "I'm tempted not to show you this one. It might feed your fantasies as well as swell your head. This is of the dominant painting in the room, the one that was in the ceiling's center."

Jael unbent the metal clasp on the envelope, opened it, and slowly removed the photo. The colors of the painting were amazingly sharp, amazingly well preserved; of course, it had spent all those centuries in total darkness. She gasped when she saw the picture: She couldn't help herself. One half of the picture was deepest blue, almost black, and speckled with silver dots—the night sky. The artist had conveyed the chilly loneliness, the eternity, of the universe, of existence without light. The stars swirled like those in a painting by van Gogh, and the void seemed to pulse with negative energy. The other half of the painting was filled with sunshine, bursts of green vegetation, miniatures of cities, pyramids, people: a teeming representation of ancient Egypt. The images grew less distinct, more hazy, as they moved toward the center of the picture. The lines of the buildings quivered; the people became dream figures. A replica of the temple at Ombos lay half in the light, half in the darkness. On the bright side were priests wearing wolf masks, howling, dancing, glowing, their eyes focused on the shrine before them, feral looks on their faces. And on the shrine . . . there was a duplicate of the star-shaped frame Dylan and the Bon had made. . . . In its center was the blue translucent star. Passing through it, half in the light, half in the darkness, was a Set creature, the Creepster, its eyes burning yellow with hatred, its snout long and curved, its fur as red as blood. Jael looked up at Chris, her mouth wide open.

"Don't worry," Chris said. "I didn't point out any of the coin-

212

cidences in this painting to Hasan." He reached behind her head and gently stroked her neck, the rim of her ear. "When the book comes out and we have color plates of the Bon ceremony and this painting, we'll be the most famous anthropologists in the world." He kissed her on the lips. "An early Christmas present." He drew back and stared at her face. "You look more horrified than happy," he said.

Jael shook her head, hoping to clear it, then stared back at the painting of the shrine to be sure she had seen what she thought she had. On its base, confronting her across thirty-five centuries of darkness, was the alignment of ten circles, as clear as if they had been painted the day before. The coincidence circled and swirled through her mind—and eased into a manageable order. "What day is the Feast of Set?" she asked.

"November the . . . why, today, now that you mention it."

Jael stood, reached for her coat, and started toward the door. She brushed past Chris when she reached for the photo of the ceiling painting. "Mind if I take this?"

"Where are you off to?" Chris placed an arm around her shoulder. "You're shivering."

"Suddenly the world's a lot colder."

"I'll keep you warm."

"There was something at my apartment. I have to make sure it's still there."

Chris lifted her chin so that she had to look into his face. He smiled his warm, sexy, I'm-available smile. "Want some company?"

He'd certainly make the drive seem shorter, the apartment less threatening. . . . But there'd be a price to pay; always the price. She started to shake her head and moved toward the door. "I'm sorry, Chris," she said. "Not tonight. Not ever again."

TWENTY

Glencoe, Illinois—November 1, 1981

Matt leaned against the country club's bar, started to order another Coke with lemon twist, then changed it to cognac: The alcohol buffer would help him deal with himself as much as Jim Gissing. Matt felt the same whenever he dealt with policemen: aversion to their us/them, right/wrong, black/white philosophy, and attraction to the certainty it gave. They never seemed haunted by doubts, never felt the need to sift through the nuances of a case the way he did. At least Gissing was more likable than most. Matt had handled his two divorces, but not for money. A sergeant of detectives had access to as much sensitive information as anyone on the North Shore, and it never hurt to walk into a courtroom knowing more than the opposition.

Matt had scarcely taken the drink back to the lounge and sat on one of the soft leather couches than Gissing appeared in the archway from the anteroom. No matter how he dressed, he'd never look like he belonged in a country club. He had a laborer's body, a build more suited to overalls than a sports coat; the more elegant the fashion, the worse it looked on him. He walked toward Matt, grinning uneasily. "Hey," he said, extending a hand that looked as large as a skillet, "long time."

"No need to whisper," Matt said. "This isn't a library."

"Yeah, but you know . . ." Gissing gestured at the sleek set with their jewels, dark tans, and evening wear. "There's me and then there's everyone else."

Gissing claimed to dislike the rich, yet he was fascinated by them, as though they were a different species. Since he was a man who talked excessively when he was fascinated, Matt brought him to the club whenever there was a need for information. "What's new in cops and robbers?" Matt asked.

The corner of Gissing's mouth twitched and he shrugged. "Hear you and the wife are on the outs."

It wasn't like him to avoid questions, even discount questions. Something was different. Matt decided to play along with him. "Is there anything on the North Shore you don't know?" he said sharply.

"Hey, no offense meant."

"None taken."

Gissing unbuttoned his jacket and sighed. How he must have longed for the shapeless sports coats and baggy trousers worn by gumshoes in the forties movies. "A guy tries to look the other way," he said, "but when you know someone, and his wife is hitting the bars with some asshole . . ." He leaned toward Matt and spoke in a whisper. "Anything you want, a tail, someone to testify in court, just let me know."

"Three weeks ago I would have jumped at the offer."

Gissing scratched his nose. "You're not taking her back?"

"I've found someone else."

"Damn straight," Gissing said. His voice had the clipped syllables and the hard vowels of an inner-city Chicagoan. "If she was mine, you could be damn sure I'd send her packing."

A cocktail waitress arrived and Matt ordered a Jack Daniel's for Gissing and another cognac for himself. A sipping cognac. There were still social amenities to dispense with, and his head had to be clear when they discussed the murders. So they talked sports; what else did they have in common? The Cubs versus the White Sox. The troubles with the Bulls and Bears. Another whiskey for Gissing. Then some chatter about deer hunting. Then another Jack Daniel's. Then another. After a half hour it was time to eat. It was assumed Matt would extract the information before dinner so they could eat in peace. The rhythm of the conversation was off. Time to make a move. "There must be some real heat coming down about those murders," Matt said. He noticed the twitch at Gissing's eyes. Silence. When Gissing squirmed and looked away, Matt added, "The ones in Gillson Park."

"When you called, I hoped to Christ I'd just have to put a tail on your wife," Gissing said. Then the nervous twitch again.

"Why Gillson Park? Didn't you used to say there wasn't enough money in criminal cases to pay expenses?"

"This is for a friend."

"A reporter?"

"My dealings with the press haven't been any better than yours," Matt said, trying to sound insulted. "You tell me the last time I leaked classified information."

Gissing chewed a fingernail and scratched his receding hairline. "I wish to Christ I knew nothing about it."

"I could tell that from the press release."

Gissing leaned back in the chair and held up his hands. "Hey, let's just drop it."

"You think I'd push this hard if it weren't necessary?" Matt asked. No answer. Time for some direct pressure. "How did you put the gag on thirty fishermen?"

More silence.

"Jim?"

"There were only five," Gissing finally said.

"With the salmon that close to shore?"

"Some buddies got there at three. They figured to get the best spots and hold on to them."

"They saw the bodies in the dark?" Matt asked.

"They didn't need light." Another twitch. "The smell told them everything they had to know."

"What's that supposed to mean?" Matt watched Gissing's eyes shift from his face to the ceiling and back again. Then at a couple who sat on a nearby couch. "I'll tell the maître d' to hold the table," Matt said. "We'll take a walk outside. Just a lawyer and a client discussing the fine points of a case."

"If any of this goes public, I won't be able to find a job washing cars." Gissing shook his head and chewed his lip. "I sure as hell don't have to tell you about alimony and child support."

Matt slipped the cocktail waitress a five-dollar bill, told her to give the message to the maître d', then picked up their coats at the closet and walked through the anteroom, out the entrance, then back around the clubhouse toward the golf course. The pool was drained, the nets down on the tennis courts, but since light and chatter poured from the curling hut, they said nothing.

When they arrived on the soft grass of the putting green by the first tee, the moon was still low in the sky, too low to reflect off the water hazard by the eighteenth green. As they walked down the fairway, noise from the clubhouse started to fade.

Gissing glanced back over his shoulder. When he finally leaned toward Matt, thin puffs of steam rose from his lips. "Shit, I got the creeps even out here," he whispered.

"You're going to have to start at the beginning."

"I never saw anything like it, and that includes two pretty heavy tours in Nam."

"Like what?"

"Like goddamn butchery." Gissing's voice was a low snarl, vague, scarcely audible. "Fifty firefights in the bush, citizens crashing cars into trees, citizens throwing themselves in front of freight trains. I once saw this eight-year-old girl who'd been floating two months in the lake with the fish and eels. . . ." His gulp sounded like a whimper. "I thought I'd seen it all, but I never lost my cookies before." Although the moonlight was scarcely bright enough to outline Gissing's body, Matt could see a quiver of revulsion run through him.

"You're not making sense."

Gissing laughed. "What does sense have to do with this?" A pause. "The station got this call about three. Some hysterical citizen screaming about a murder down at the yacht club. Body parts strewn every goddamn place. Naturally old Howells at the desk thinks it's bullshit, and since I just finished a stakeout, he asked me if I could drop by on the way home. Why not? It's probably some damn wino who fell into a trash can and can't tell sandwich wrappers from livers. . . ." He grunted and coughed into a handkerchief. "I say sure, it's on the way, and there's no need to send someone who should be on patrol. The rookie . . . Crane was there, so I grab him for company." A longer pause. Matt could hear the trembling in Gissing's breath. "From the moment you stepped out of the squad car, you knew something was wrong. I never felt anything like it. Then I hear this citizen shouting, and I follow the voice, and I pull out my flashlight, and . . ."

Matt didn't say a word. No coaxing, no coaching. If Gissing

217

was having a hard time finding the words, Matt wasn't sure he wanted to hear them. He put a hand on Gissing's shoulder.

"First I saw these gulls—"

"Gulls?" Matt interrupted.

Gissing must not have heard him, because he continued without a pause. "I just hope to Christ my crust never gets so thick I don't react to *that!* The gulls' heads were back. . . . They were gulping down meat like minnows . . . and I can tell you this: There was no problem finding pieces small enough."

"The story said feral dogs."

"That was for the citizens—so things don't blow sky-high in case some fisherman decides to blab." A pause, then a snort of disgust. "Dogs? I once saw a guy take a hit straight on from a B-40 rocket. Bingo. He was all over the rice paddy." He laughed a short, bitter laugh. It sounded more like spitting than laughter. "He was Miss America compared to this."

"There was no mention of an explosion," Matt said.

"That's because there was no explosion. No burns. No bone splinters. No reports from the neighbors of loud bangs."

"Maybe an ax?" Matt said. "A chain saw?"

"At first glance I thought it was teeth. There were scratches on the bones for a couple inches, then *snap,* the bone's in two." A pause. Trembling in his breath. "And I'm not talking pinkies and toes: I'm talking big bones, thighbones, ribs."

Matt scratched his head and stared down the narrowing fairway. The trees skirting the fringes were black, almost blue, against the moon-gray sky. There was the moldy smell of heavily watered grass against cold air . . . a smell like funerals and winter. He realized no land animal had that kind of power—a killer whale, maybe. Maybe a shark. "Are there any reports of escaped animals?"

"Like lions and bears?"

"Or anything like them."

"We checked the zoos first thing," Gissing said. "Nothing is gone, much less something that could do that."

"How about private collections?"

"Like some screwball keeping a grizzly?"

Matt nodded. He could hear the whistling as Gissing exhaled.

"Still nothing," Gissing said. "Even those animals have to be registered; that's the law." A snort of contempt. "Not that some wealthy citizen might not keep one and screw the law." A pause. "You're barking up the wrong bush."

"Are there other bushes?"

"I've hunted Alaska. I've seen wolf and bear damage. There's not a wolf been born that can bite a man's leg in two; gnaw, maybe, but there was nothing to indicate gnawing."

Matt shifted his weight from one foot to the other. "Then why do you think it's animals?"

"Who said I did? The skulls were cracked, the bones sucked dry—"

"That's not animal damage?"

"Maybe not," Gissing said, the caginess returning to his voice.

Matt scarcely heard the words; he turned the evidence over and over in his mind, then said out loud, "If it's an animal, it left tracks."

"There were tracks—only one problem."

"Which is?"

"Got some paper?"

Matt searched through his jacket pockets, found a pen and bar napkin, and handed them to the detective. Gissing cupped his hand so there would be a firm base for the paper, held it up to the moonlight, and started to sketch. He drew a few lines, scratched them out, drew several more, twisted the napkin, then more, then handed it back to Matt. It was a drawing of a paw print, but from no animal Matt had ever hunted. It was four, maybe five inches across, almost filled the napkin, with six delicate toes extending from the front and a single talon-like hook from the back. The toes were jointed, padded, and had unusually long claws.

"Not great, but you get the idea," Gissing said.

"Was the print anything like this?"

"I may be no Picasso, but the details are right and so's the size."

"No animal has seven toes," Matt said.

"Creates problems, doesn't it." There was almost a snicker in Gissing's voice. He cleared his throat. "God didn't make the thing that made that track." He leaned toward Matt. "Want to hear a theory?"

"I'll bite."

"An animal didn't make it."

"Then what is it?"

"A trick," Gissing said. "Part of a game being played by some damn sick citizens to jive with Halloween."

Matt shook his head. He didn't want to say too much—nothing that revealed how much he knew. "Want me to start shooting some holes in that idea?"

"Let's put some maybes together and see if we can come up with a probably," Gissing said. He started to walk toward the seventeenth tee and continued to speak in hushed tones. "Say there's this group. Sure, they call themselves a religion, but you or I would call them a cult. Maybe they're spades, maybe they're PRs; God knows, maybe they're even white." He hesitated long enough to let Matt's imagination play with the thought before he continued. "Let's say they have this unusual hang-up. Let's say they need human flesh for something."

"Why *they?*"

"We're talking about seventy pounds taken off the boy, another thirty off the girl. Unless he brought butcher paper and a cooler, it has to be a they."

If Matt mentioned the Bon, Gissing would want to know his source, then demand to meet Jael . . . and there was no doubt Dylan would be next. "Cannibalism on the North Shore?" Matt tried to sound as though he were laughing the idea off. "A new fad to replace key clubs?"

"Some cults make sacrifices, right? Last year the dicks in Chicago had these babies disappearing left and right from maternity wards. After ten, maybe fifteen, they found that voodooists, satanists, some damn thing, were using the blood to try and conjure demons." A pause. "Didn't hear about it, did you? If they'd let the citizens know that people on broomsticks were murdering babies, all hell would have broken loose, right?" Gissing paused to let him respond, but Matt said nothing. "You're still on the tracks, aren't you?" Gissing asked.

"They're hard to ignore."

"Forget them. The imprints were too light. The lab said that whatever made most of them couldn't weigh more than ninety, a hundred pounds." Matt tried to speak, but Gissing cut him off. "And before you start lipping off, take some time to put it all together: a paw print the size of a large wolf; seven claws; kills two kids and eats them. All this from a hundred-pound animal?"

"Weren't the tracks deeper after the kids were eaten?"

"Maybe, but what animal can eat its weight at one sitting?"

"So what are you getting at?"

"Say there's this bunch of citizens walking around with cast-iron claws on the end of sticks. They press down in the sand. Bingo. A print of a creature that can't exist."

"What about the teeth marks?" Matt asked.

"Gnawing is gnawing. Humans gnaw as easily as animals."

"And the snapping of the bones?"

"Why not a sword with a serrated edge?" Gissing asked. "What cult doesn't use a ceremonial sword?"

Matt rubbed his face, rocked back and forth on his heels, and tried to remember if the sword in Jael's photos had a serrated edge. And if an iron claw was part of the shaman's paraphernalia. And about the bodies—he was sure that Jael had said that the Bon devour *all* the flesh. "Only part of the bodies was eaten?" he asked.

"Cripes, isn't a hundred pounds enough for you? Want me to go into details of what a hundred pounds includes?"

Matt caught up with Gissing; they were almost touching when he said, "Maybe some of this should be released—so the people know that they should stay off the beaches for a while."

"These rich folks pay top dollar to make sure that their streets are plowed, each leaf is picked up, and that the criminals and crazies are kept in Chicago, where they belong. Now you just imagine what would happen if I stand up and announce that if their kids go down to the beach for some nookie, they might end up the main course for some barbecue."

Matt wanted to make one last try to steer Gissing toward the animal theory—and away from Dylan and Jael. It couldn't hurt. "What if you find out that some animals escaped?"

"Let me put it this way," Gissing said. "You're a hunter. When

221

was the last time you heard of an animal killing for something other than food? When was the last time you saw a bear or coyote do some eating, then scatter the rest over the goddamn countryside? There was malice, *intent,* in the way those kids were mutilated. Animals don't savage what they kill; they leave that for us."

"Why the mutilations?"

"Part of the ceremony? Maybe just to terrify." A long pause. The tremble returned to Gissing's voice. "If that was their intent, they did a number-ten job. . . . I haven't taken a step all day without looking over my shoulder and jumping at every little noise."

"One final problem," Matt said. "How do you keep the lid on something this big? There have to be rumors starting already."

"We'll trace the rumors down. Then we scare the fuck out of whoever started them—or we lock them up." There was fear coupled with anger in Gissing's voice. He put a hand on Matt's shoulder and tightened the grip. "I'm going to get those crazies before they cost me my job. If I have to lock up half the village as suspects, fine." Gissing's breath was sour, sour from whiskey and fear. "I'll tell you this," he continued. "I'm ready to do *whatever* is necessary to see that what happened this morning doesn't happen again."

TWENTY-ONE

Chicago, Illinois—November 1–2, 1981

The crumbling ghetto buildings were squat, deformed, almost maliciously alive. Jael turned onto Oakwood and prayed there would be no breakdowns, no flat tires. At eleven P.M. the scarcely lighted streets were empty, and only the alleys and shadows showed signs of movement: A bulb dangled from a street lamp; paper and debris scattered in the wind like frightened birds. She stared straight ahead until she pulled onto Lake Shore Drive, then glanced out onto the lake to avoid the glare of oncoming headlights. For the first mile the only lights on the water were from distant buoys and tankers, but soon there were yachts in the harbors. How wonderful it would be to hop onto one and sail away from all the madness.

The blue star was lodged in the heart of every madness, everything that was inexplicable. If it was gone from the wall safe, Dylan must have taken it. It would fit in an empty lunch box, and she could have thought of the combination any of the times they shared.

Nonsense. The thought was more madness, madness from being alone. Maybe the sound of human voices would help. As she reached to turn on the radio, the dials began to spin. As she shook her head a shiver of fear ran through her as if something were in the car with her. She glanced into the rearview mirror: red hair, glaring yellow eyes. She blinked and they were gone. A car horn blared and Jael swerved back into the right hand lane, rolled down the window, and let the cold air pour in. The chill and sharp smell of the water would help ease the hallucinations. It was no time to be driving . . . if she could make it to the Fullerton Street exit, she could park and wait out the attack. As she turned, a police car twisted down the ramp across from her.

223

If she flashed her lights on and off, even swerved erratically, her problems would be over for the night. But the police were the last people she wanted to see, and a night behind bars wasn't the type of security she was after.

She pulled off the ramp, drove a few blocks, eased into a parking spot, and turned off the engine. Two deep breaths. In the rearview mirror, the light of the Sears Tower and the Prudential Building was vivid in a way it had never been before.

A world like a photographic negative.

White trees. The black glow of a light. Aromas so powerful almost the light can be smelled. The grass alive with the aromas of each of the hundreds of humans who walked on it.

Move to a waiting tree. Claws sink into slick bark. Climb. Each bird, each squirrel, for months has left its wild scent on the limbs. Leap to the balcony and inhale the prey-scent. The sweet singing of warm blood.

Claws sink into the wood and lift. New odors. Harsh chemicals from the floor. Saliva and urine on a toy. The sweet warmth of sleep. Nose, paws, stomach hair, and tail glide across the wood. Pause and listen. All tastes are bland without the taste of fear. Savor the heartbeat, the breathing, the pulsing of sweet blood. A sudden clatter. An adult moves beyond the closed door. The noise fades.

A soft head protrudes from the blanket, breathes the shallow breaths of the very young. Three strides on the quiet floor.

Touch the hair with a claw. A glimpse of the predator will sweeten the flesh. Movement. Touch an ear. The eyes flutter open, black with white centers, then close. Brush the lips. Eyes shoot open, wander from point to point without focus. The mouth opens. The teeth grind, soft and dull. The head shakes. The glazed eyes harden and clear. Pupils focus, then dilate in horror. A scream starts in the lungs.

Fangs pop tender skin. Hot blood spurts into the mouth. The cry is swallowed with muscle, tissue, a layer of sweet fat.

224

"Police."

"What?" Jael asked groggily. She tried to see the face beyond the voice, but a flashlight beam blinded her.

"Police."

Jael breathed in the wet air and tried to shake the fading images from her mind, the tastes from her mouth. "Headache," she said.

"Need a lift home?"

Jael paused as the sounds registered as words. "A few more minutes." The beam turned off and left red dots dancing in the darkness.

"A car like this will draw creeps. I wouldn't want to be here when they arrive."

"Thanks," Jael said as she started the engine. The police car waited until she turned around, then escorted her up the entrance ramp. She concentrated on driving, didn't swerve or waver, so the policeman's lights faded, then turned. It would be so easy not to stop at the condominium, just to keep driving north through Wisconsin, the Upper Peninsula, to Canada or Alaska or God knew where. But it didn't matter where she went. She wasn't chasing knowledge.

It wasn't a matter of pursuing anymore; it was a matter of being pursued.

The apartment still blazed with light.

Jael opened the door and took a step inside. Total silence. Osiris was either asleep or indifferent to the fact that she was home. Great. She wouldn't be home for long.

She dropped her coat on the anteroom chair, then hurried down the hallway to her bedroom. She went to the bookcase, removed a handful of books, and the safe appeared. One twenty-one right, 12 left, 144 right, 113, wait for the tumblers to align, then depress the latch and open. Stocks, bonds, some jewelry.

But no star.

Now what? Dylan couldn't reach that high, and the only furniture other than the waterbed was a desk. Which weighed at least two hundred pounds. She removed the paper and jewelry and set them on the shelf. Still no star, but the *phurba* was there. She removed the protective cloth: Even in the fluorescent light the blade had an aura. It might not be much protection, but it was all she had.

She started for the hall, the blade in her hand. And stopped. Better call Matt first. She sat on the bed and looked at the nightstand: The phone recorder held some messages. She rewound the tape, pushed the play button, and listened to her voice repeat the instructions. A gentle voice said:

> "It's Nathan King, Jael. Please come to my place tonight. I can hear you saying, 'What's the old man doing up so late against doctor's orders?' but he has a reason. The ten circles aren't a secret anymore. There's more. You really should spend the night here. I'll be waiting."

Some static. Again Jael's voice repeated the instructions. Matt's voice was excited:

> "Stay put. Don't open any doors or windows. I'll be right over."

The tape recorder turned itself off.

Jael leaned back on the bed and shook her head. What had he thought was so urgent? She dialed the number for his apartment. No answer. Then the club. The maître d' said he had left ten or fifteen minutes before.

Jael carried the *phurba* into the hallway and stopped before entering the living room so she could peer at Osiris's cage. He was still on the top perch, his back toward her. Now, if he just stayed that way . . . She walked into the living room, sat down on the couch, turned on the floor lamp, and drummed her fingers on the end table. Still no movement from Osiris.

Maybe she could stay after all.

After a minute she wasn't so sure. Every clack of the heating pipes made her jump. Each hum of the window in the wind. When she checked the balcony door to be sure it was locked, she fought off terror so strong that she couldn't swallow. Despite her chill, drops of perspiration formed on her forehead.

226

She shivered again.

When she'd been a girl, each time she felt scared or alone, she played the piano to relax. She flipped through the sheet music until she found *The Moonlight Sonata,* then sat down on the piano bench, spread her fingers above the keyboard, and tried to capture the proper mood. No luck. The notes she played were so stiff, they made her grimace. They were just sounds, sounds without magic. *Remember Julie,* she thought, Julie cutting into a minuet with Fats Domino, Julie improvising Brubeck on Mozart. Jael bowed her head and her mind filled with headstones and tears and walks alone on the beach. Her breath slowed. When her eyelids fluttered open, she touched the first key. Suddenly her wrists were pliable and her fingers as free as when she practiced every day. It was somber, desolate music, magical sounds with their roots in the past. She played the first movement by heart, floated round and round with the melody.

A scratching at the balcony window?

She looked up. Nothing. A tingling swept over her, a sensation as sharp as touching bare wires. She shook her head, took a deep breath, and tried to concentrate on the sheet music.

The notes weren't notes anymore: hieroglyphs. She tried to stand, but she couldn't move. The sensations were nothing like a dream, nothing like sharing. It was as if there were two halves to her consciousness: Jael, who performed the actions, and another presence that programmed her thoughts.

Her hands involuntarily extended to the keyboard and she played four notes, C-G-A-C, the nightmare notes. She tried to pull her hands back. Impossible. The pressure of the keys was the same, the air was filled with her aroma, the smells that made her apartment safe, *hers,* as familiar as her face. The rose walls and cream carpeting were the same—everything was the same—but she *could not* pull her hands away.

A flash on the balcony. She turned and saw a silhouette of a familiar shape pulse through the drapes. All her instincts screamed *Run, sprint through the open door to the elevator, hide,* but the presence called her to the balcony. *Reason,* she thought, *fight it with reason,* but this wasn't like the other attacks. The presence gave direction, order where there was only disorder, the

227

promise of all knowledge. . . . Jael tried to think of the mutilated teenagers, the taste of the child, but there was such unity,
such peace—salve for the raw ends of her life.

Jael stood and took a step toward the balcony: a step beyond
time. The perception of things moving forward, always forward,
stopped, and she saw things not chronologically but all at once.
All time as *now*. The emptiness of space, the flood of constellations, weren't vast and terrifying anymore but the basis for unity,
the single blueprint that joined her to the air and water, connected everything with threads of light. Form where there was no
form.

A step toward the balcony. Another. No questions anymore,
just answers. She shuddered ecstatically as her face brushed the
curtains and she reached for the lock.

Something pulled her hand back.

An arm pressed to her back; another locked behind her knees.
She was lifted, carried for a few moments, then eased down. Soft
cushions pressed against her spine. A hand stroked her hair, her
forehead.

Matt.

She looked up at him, tried to see his face, but the light was
directly behind his head. "You look like hell," he said.

It took a conscious effort to speak. "I almost saw a god," she
said.

"Pardon?"

"The magic cultures . . . they tasted heaven." She tried to sit
up. "Flint knives were tickets to eternal pleasure." Her head
started to clear. "Mythology as fact, not metaphor."

"Sure," Matt said, patting her shoulder. "Sure."

"You didn't see it?"

"What?"

"The glowing."

He looked quizzically at her. "When I saw your door open, I
lowered my head and ran like hell." Cold waves ran through Jael
and she snuggled close to him. "Do those shivers mean shock?"
he asked.

"I don't have time to go into shock," she said. "There was
another murder tonight. A small boy."

Matt rubbed an eye, then scratched his head. "They're not just murders, they're savagings. Sergeant Gissing gave me some pretty ghastly details."

"I *lived* them," she said. A pause to let the room harden into focus. "How did you arrive at just the right time?"

"I was watching the good sergeant swill down Jack Daniel's when I was paged to the telephone. Bekki. Dylan had awakened her, said the Creepster was coming after you. She tried to put him to bed, but he screamed until she gave in. She tried the apartment, the office. He kept after her. Finally she thought of the club."

Jael's voice lowered. "It was on the balcony."

"What?"

"The Creepster."

"On the thirteenth floor?"

"There are balconies and a fire escape, and I'm not sure it would have made any difference."

Matt stood. "Fine." He took a step toward the sliding door, then stopped. "Hallucination or not, I'd feel better with a gun."

"There's only this," she said, handing him the *phurba*. "It was too big for Dylan's lunch box."

"What's that supposed to mean?"

"I'll explain later."

Matt rested the sword on his shoulder, walked to the door, slowly opened the drapes, and turned on the outside lights. Silence.

"It *was* there," Jael said.

He unlocked the door, slid it open, and stepped outside. Jael closed her eyes and held her breath. Cast iron furniture scraped as it was moved. It seemed like minutes before he stepped back inside. "Visitors," he said. "Someone crawled over your flower box, uprooted your roses." A pause. "And left seven-toed tracks." Another pause. "And blood." He closed his eyes. "It's time we call Gissing."

"We need to be able to move freely."

Matt sat down and took her by the shoulders. "Look, there are crazies running all over the North Shore. They eat people. They scatter guts all over the goddamn place. That's not happening to anyone I love."

Jael touched his cheek. "Do you trust me?"

"I love you."

"That's no answer."

"How could I love you if I didn't trust you?"

At another time she would have kissed him. "Call your sergeant in the morning. I want you to meet someone first. He knows about gods."

"More people will die."

"Not tonight," Jael said. "Maybe by tomorrow we'll know what to do."

Matt shook his head. "He won't throw us out and call the police?"

"There are some books in the study I want to show him. If you get them, it will give me a chance to test my walking legs."

Matt left and his footsteps faded down the hall. Jael stood, leaned over, and touched her toes. When she rotated her neck, her eyes settled on the cage. On Osiris. Staring at her. She had never seen a look as intelligent or savage. She moved a foot; he turned his head. She lifted an arm; he spread his wings. She took a step toward the hall and he jumped from the perch to the cage door and clawed maniacally at the lock. She didn't have time for another step before the latch snapped.

A bird as large as an eagle burst from the cage. Jael picked up a cushion and braced herself for the impact. The pillow almost flew from her hands as the bird bit and gouged, a frenzy of beak and claws, ripping and tearing as it drew closer to her throat, and she tried to hit it, but it snapped at her arm, and she felt each grasp of each talon, each tear of the beak, and there was less than an inch of padding left, so she pushed, pushed with all her might, then rolled onto her stomach, covered her face with her arms, and curled into a ball.

A thud.

She tensed for the attack, for the incomprehensible pain. Another thud. Another. She slowly uncurled. Matt stood ten feet from her, holding the floor lamp above his head like a club. Osiris, broken feathers and blood, lay on the floor. Matt threw down the lamp then helped Jael to her feet. "I've seen animals act like that before," he said, "at the zoo, with Dylan." He picked up the books he had dropped, took Jael's arm, and led her toward the anteroom. "It's about time we see a man about some gods."

TWENTY-TWO

Riverwoods, Illinois—November 2, 1981

Light from the fireplace threw the shadows of a battle-ax and a mace across the room, distorted them, and made the den look like a chamber of horrors. Dr. King's antique rocker stopped creaking as he leaned forward, closed his eyes, and nodded at Matt's final words. There was something so innately confident about Dr. King that he made Matt's and Jael's stories—two hours of what must have sounded like lunatic ravings—seem almost plausible. "And Sergeant Gissing is sure that these savagings were done by humans?" he asked.

"What are his options?" Matt asked.

Dr. King smiled gently and shrugged, then jotted down notes on his legal pad; most of the pages were already covered with writing and sketches. When he finished, he stood and walked across the room to open a window, then turned toward Jael. "You're positive that the consciousness you entered wasn't human."

She answered slowly, as though she were drifting back from sleep.

"Unquestionably."

"Not even a man who *thought* he was a wolf?"

"Things were too disconnected, too intense. This was a negative world. And I perceived humans . . . like a butcher would view cattle, only with more hatred."

Again Dr. King nodded, then walked to a display case by the couch where Matt sat. With his tufts of white hair, his polka dot bow tie, he reminded Matt of a wizard full of centuries of mischief and magic. He inserted a key into a glass cover, slid the panel open, and removed a foot-high stone statue, a stylized ver-

232

sion of the Creepster: A half-eaten limb protruded from its mouth; its huge claws crushed skulls. It sat on a pile of bones.

"I bought this in the thirties," Dr. King said, holding it out to Jael. "Strange that I didn't realize its value until our last meeting." He wiped a smudge off the case with his handkerchief. "It's called the Monster of Cruachan. I always assumed that it symbolized the death-dealing aspect of some deity."

Jael blinked. "Past tense?"

Dr. King nodded as he turned the statue over and stared at its base. "Let me read you its inscription." He cleared his voice and chanted:

"I have news:
the sun is low; Samain is gone; the stars line up
like geese.
* I have news:*
the Children of Nodeus came like flurries before the storm; now
* they are like a blizzard in winter.*
* I have news:*
cold has seized the heart of the tribes; the Season of Death is
* upon us."*

Again Dr. King cleared his throat. "At first I thought it was merely more proof of your *One* Cult," he said. "Then I saw this." He handed a magazine to Jael. "Turn to page forty-five."

Jael flipped through the pages and stopped. She blinked, shook her head, and handed the magazine to Matt. The title of the story read: "Doomsday Alignment: The End of the World?" Beneath the story was a drawing of the solar system, nine planets, and the sun arranged in an almost straight line. Jael handed Matt the photo of the ceiling painting from the temple of Set: The alignment of planets in the magazine matched the circles in the painting.

"This arrangement of planets was first noticed by the Egyptians more than five thousand years ago; they were the first to call it the Doomsday Alignment," Dr. King said as he walked across the room. "Ever since then it has appeared every seven or eight hundred years—each time the ancients predicted the Apocalypse.

This article suggests that the end will come by earthquakes and tidal waves instead of a sudden influx of demons."

"That's it!" Jael said, tapping her forehead. "Of course! The stars line up like geese. . . ."

"Always you reach my conclusions before I do," Dr. King said softly.

"But I don't," Matt said. "I need explanations."

Jael edged closer to him and put a hand on his knee. "The Doomsday Alignment appears in the Bon etchings, the temple painting, and now a druidic chant." She stared past Matt toward the open window. "To the ancients these planets were just large stars."

"They didn't have telescopes."

"But they were obsessed with astronomy," Jael said. She stood and started to pace, to gesture. "The Celts had Stonehenge, the Aztecs astrolabes atop their pyramids, the Egyptians—"

"Weren't those for predicting crop failures, the changing of the seasons, things like that?" Matt interrupted.

"So we thought." Jael paused and chewed a fingernail. Matt noticed that a nervous tic had developed in the corner of her eye and that her hands trembled. She continued: "But what if all these observatories were built to predict the Doomsday Alignment?"

"Step to the front of the class," Dr. King said as he sat down in the rocker. "As soon as I realized what the circles represented, I decided to go on an intellectual goose chase—to place the arrival of the Doomsday Alignment within the rise and fall of each of these cultures."

Jael stood and walked across the room. Her footsteps echoed on the hardwood floor but quieted when she stepped on the Oriental rug by Dr. King's chair. She looked emaciated in the bulky sweater and gray wool skirt. Matt left the couch, sat on the rug next to her, and took her hand. "Let's go back to the Twentieth Dynasty, about the twelfth century B.C.," Dr. King said. "After thousands of years of stable rule, the Egyptians turn to the worship of Set. Within a few centuries the Assyrian invasions begin, the borders shrink, and soon—"

"Maybe the Egyptians extended their borders too far," Matt said.

"Perhaps," Dr. King said. "Let's move forward eight hundred years. The Celts control most of Europe. They begin to worship our friend Nodeus, Crom Cruach becomes the site of thousands of sacrifices, and the Roman conquests begin."

No interruptions this time. Matt sat back and listened.

"Let's move forward to A.D. 450," Dr. King said as he rocked back and forth. "The Red Bon rule Tibet. The cult of Htamenma suddenly appears, and Tibet becomes a Buddhist country." This time Dr. King continued with scarcely a breath. "Now another eight centuries. Aztec civilization is reaching its zenith. The cult of Xipe Totec appears, wars are fought to capture sacrificial victims instead of territory, and in a very short time the culture is destroyed."

"Didn't the Spaniards have something to do with that?" Matt asked.

"How many conquistadores were there? A few hundred? How did they topple an empire of close to a million Indians?"

"Add eight hundred years and you're in the late twentieth century," Jael said. *"Now."* She stood and started to pace again. She rubbed her hand over her arms as if to warm them.

Matt walked to the window and ran his finger across the sill: dust. He opened the window, took a breath of the cold air, shivered, then closed it and walked toward the fireplace. He picked up the poker and jabbed the glowing wood. "The thing I don't understand is what you're trying to prove," he said.

"Remember when I mentioned that I saw mythology as fact instead of metaphor?" Jael asked.

"I was ready to call a psychiatrist."

"Stretch your imagination," she said. "Imagine that myths aren't stories invented to explain a natural phenomenon or the human psyche . . . that Set doesn't symbolize evil with a capital *E* or the flooding of the Nile . . . that the stories about him aren't myth but journalism, a simple recording of the facts."

"You're saying that the Creepster actually existed," Matt said, "and he exists again."

Jael turned toward him. The flickering red light exaggerated the angles of her face, the shadows around her eyes and mouth. "Precisely," she said.

"Lovely," Matt said. "Only where does it come from—and go to?"

"Try to remember what I said about how the magic cultures viewed the otherworld."

"It coexisted with this world," Matt said, poking the fire and watching sparks fly. He turned back to her and made a sour face. "You're not suggesting that the Creepster can leap between dimensions?"

Jael moved a step closer to him. "What is a warp?" she asked.

"A bend in something."

Dr. King walked toward them and said, "Let's change vocabularies; let's enter the world of physics and call these otherworlds parallel dimensions. All types of matter are affected by different forces." A pause. "What if some tremendous force was exerted on the dimensions? What if the force of the planets aligning caused the dimensions to warp?"

"They'd overlap," Jael said. "Once every eight hundred years. Cuchulainn's warp spasm."

Matt looked askance at her. "And werewolves pour in and gobble us up?" He pointed toward his eyes. "I need proof."

"You believe in the existence of atoms," she said. "Ever see one?"

"Too many things don't add up," Matt said. "Your article says that the alignment doesn't take place until March. This is November one."

"But the warping would take place gradually," Jael said. She stared at the ceiling for a moment, then looked back at him. "What were all the kids doing in scary costumes last night?"

"Celebrating Halloween."

"Which was called Allhallows Eve, a night of demons, in the Middle Ages. Know what else? November first is the feast day of Set. It was sacred to the Celts too. They called it Samain."

"The same Samain mentioned on the Monster of Cruachan," Dr. King added. "Stretch your imagination, Matt. Could the chant be saying that the *first* of the creatures arrive at Samain—

236

that slowly, as the planets draw into alignment, more and more appear until they are as numerous as the blizzard?"

"Samain could be the Celts' way of marking the first day when the transformation was possible," Jael said immediately. Matt had seen the same effect when he brainstormed with other members of the firm: The intellects fed off one another, prodded each other, grew sharper and sharper with the competition.

"Even if all this were possible," he asked. "How do you and Dylan fit into it?"

"What if the creatures need help to find their way into this dimension?" Dr. King asked. "Who would be more natural to use than the telepaths? Who would be easier to make build the sign posts, the directional lights?" He pointed to the blue star in the nave painting. "The blue star is mentioned in all the magic literatures . . . here the Set creature passes through it from eternal darkness to light, from one dimension to another." Then he pointed to the priests wearing the wolf masks. "Who do you think made the transformation possible?"

Jael shuddered and she grabbed Matt's hand. "Yum Gyeba knew I was telepathic. He didn't guide me to the shrine: He *lured* me so I would take the star back with me and build another portal."

Dr. King slapped his hands together; the sound echoed through the quiet like a shot. "And that's the crime of your ancestors!" he said. "The creatures needed them, so they were spared from the slaughter . . . for a while the masses worshipped the priests as though they were gods too."

"If you were the creatures' favorites, why would they send nightmares?" Matt asked. "Why the animal attacks?"

"To wear down resistance," Jael said. "The weaker I grow, the more susceptible to their control I become. Tonight I was walking to certain death, and what difference did it make?"

"Good enough," Matt said. "But why would the priests keep helping after they knew how deadly the creatures were?"

"Power," Dr. King said flatly. "Imagine that you've been a freak your entire life. That you're an outcast because you hear voices, see visions. Suddenly you communicate with the gods.

237

Instead of insults, you have riches, women, limitless power. Would you give it up?"

"Of course not," Jael said. "You'd form a priesthood. And your power would be passed on to your children—if you mated with a priestess. You'd be as powerful as a king, and your line would be more stable."

Dr. King's face grew dark. He stroked his chin and walked back and forth in front of the fire. "The killings would seem random at first, but as the number of creatures increased, so would the killings. Soon the king would consult his priests, who would say that the gods accept *chosen* victims. The king decides to cull his flock. The criminals are the first to walk into the temples. Then slaves. Next the poor."

"But the gods are insatiable," Jael said, "and who will work if all the slaves are dead? The king calls in the generals. They decide that other societies must feed their gods. . . ."

"But no matter how many captives are taken, more are needed," Dr. King said. "Soldiers die . . . the treasury is drained . . . but it must go on and on. . . ."

Matt raised his hands. "That tape of Dylan's . . . That man didn't let monsters into the world: He *became* a monster."

"I'm sure he *thought* he did," Jael said. "And put yourself in the place of the masses. A priest named Cuchulainn howls like a wolf, starts to glow, then walks back into a temple where the star frame is hidden. A few moments later the scourge of hell walks out. If you were the storyteller, what conclusions would you draw?"

"Why would the *One* Cult finally fall?"

"Once the creatures enter our dimension, they might become trapped in it," Dr. King said. "Perhaps they become vulnerable to *our* physical laws, *our* mortality. Eventually they could be killed or die off."

"And without the gods to protect them, the priests become expendable," Jael said.

Again Matt held up his hands and shook his head. "You two are jumping from point to point so fast that you're missing the obvious. These kings must have found out some of the secrets. Why wouldn't they leave instructions showing how to destroy the creatures—or how to keep them from making the transformation?"

"Perhaps they concluded that the temptation would be too great," Dr. King said, "that it would be wiser to eliminate the priests, extinguish their seed, and destroy any evidence that the monsters ever existed. Perhaps they didn't believe something this horrific could happen again."

Matt leaned forward and touched the back of his neck. Sopping wet. Although he felt chilled, sweat popped from his forehead. The words shouldn't have scared him. Perhaps his subconscious had accepted what his conscious mind couldn't. He spread his arms hopelessly. "You're telling me that *all* history is a lie?"

Dr. King's voice grew even more distant. He walked away from them toward the couch. His shadow filled the far wall of the den as he paced. "The historian is only a builder, not an architect. He merely arranges the blocks that have been left to him. What sort of structure would he build if the cornerstone of the building is hidden? The building would sit for centuries, wobbling, waiting for an earthquake to arrive and topple it." He paused. His face flickered with the orange light. "Tonight you are hearing the first rumbles."

Suddenly there was total silence in the room, and Matt thought he heard a moth flutter against the window. Jael walked toward an Aztec sundial in the far corner of the room. The vague light accentuated the bags under her eyes, the pallor of her skin.

Matt knew he would do anything to help her, even if it meant trying to believe her. "Just one more thing," he said. "If this creature needs Jael, why the visit? It didn't have blood on its claws for late-night trick-or-treats."

Jael covered her face with her hands and shook her head. She was silent for half a minute before she said, "I honestly don't know."

"You're too close," Dr. King said. "That's the easiest question of all." He walked up to her and put an arm around her shoulder. "If you can enter the creature's mind, what makes you think it can't enter yours? It knows how you've been struggling against it, that you are its only threat in a world that is ignorant of the past."

Dr. King leaned against the fireplace and shook his head. When he looked back at Jael his mouth bent into a grimace and all the luster drained from his eyes. He placed a hand on Matt's shoulder. "With all your questions, Matt, you forgot to ask the most important one."

"Which is?"

Slowly, carefully, Dr. King said, "Now that a creature is here, how do we get rid of it? How do we keep it from getting to Jael?"

TWENTY-THREE

Chicago, Illinois—November 3, 1981

A fly landed on the jade plant near Jael's hand, stroked its eyes with a leg, then slowly spread and settled its wings as though it were gathering strength for some great effort. Chris brushed against the plant as he walked by, and the fly took off toward the office window. Even the buzz sounded slow, numb from the autumn chill. Before it reached the glass, it stopped in midair, then shuddered, dropped, and dangled. Jael moved her head slightly and sunlight caught the web at a different angle; it glistened. She hoped the fly would break free, but each time it moved it sent tremors, a signal, through the silken threads. She turned away when the spider took its first delicate step onto the web.

Enough of that.

She was in plenty of danger as it was, and depression would only make her more vulnerable. Maybe if she concentrated on familiar objects, the remnants of a more secure time, the despair would lighten. She took a breath filled with the smell of dried citrus peelings from the wastebasket, the sugary sweetness of the candy stick in Chris's hand.

They helped.

A little.

When she glanced up, Chris was still pacing the floor, smiling and shaking his head. "Nathan, she hasn't really talked you into believing this?" Chris said.

"We arrived at the theory together," Dr. King said as he picked up one of the Set relics from the table and studied it.

"Werewolves? Parallel dimensions?" Chris dropped the candy into the wastebasket; a hollow gong echoed through the room.

Jael didn't say a word. Of course, Chris was being sarcastic: He always reacted to surprise by pretending to be amused. It was his

241

way of drawing far enough away from a problem to analyze it objectively. He stopped at a bookshelf and turned around. "What about you, Griffin?" he asked. "I've always heard that lawyers are levelheaded types."

"I don't know enough about mythology to have an opinion," Matt said, straightening himself in the couch. "This much I know: People are being torn apart." He picked up the morning paper from a cushion and tapped a headline. "She knew about this boy's murder as it was happening. That's no coincidence. The killer was on her balcony last night. That's no coincidence, either."

"It seems I'm the only one who *wasn't* on her balcony last night," Chris said.

Dr. King walked to the window, stopped to give Jael's hand a reassuring squeeze, then stared out at the sky. "Chris, we need your help. It's already afternoon. Three people have been murdered, and unless we move tonight, Jael will be number four."

Chris selected another candy stick from the jar on his desk, removed the cellophane, and walked toward Jael until they were almost touching. "So far you're the only one who hasn't had anything to say."

Jael took his hand and tried to make him *feel* the exhaustion, the terror and helplessness. Then she said softly, "After what I said last night, do you think I'd be here if it weren't necessary?"

He seemed to blanch through his tan, and his mouth twisted into a grimace. He turned abruptly and walked to a sculpture of Janus, the two-headed god of comings and goings, which sat on a pedestal by the door. Jael didn't say any more. He'd been pushed hard enough; either he'd help them or he wouldn't. He tapped his fingers on one of the stone heads for what seemed like minutes, lost in concentration. Finally he turned toward Dr. King. "How can I help?" he asked.

"Start by assuming everything I've said is the truth."

"Why not call the police?"

"Matt thinks they'd put us in protective custody."

"But Matt's been wrong before," Matt said. "It's gone too far. We need the police."

"Not yet," Dr. King said. "They'd merely get themselves

killed and we'd miss our only chance." He took a pill from his pillbox and swallowed it. "There was only one killing last night; that means only one creature. There could be two, more, by tomorrow morning." He pulled his hands apart and brought them back together. "With their power, their speed . . . how could we fight such creatures if their minds worked as one?" He turned from the window and stared at Chris. "You'll come with us?"

"At worst I'll see a ceremony of the *One* Cult. . . . If your wolf-god makes an appearance, it could mean a ticket to Stockholm at Nobel prize time."

Jael's eyes moved from Dr. King to the windowsill. The spider was gently spinning the fly, sticking its wings tighter and tighter together with silken thread. Matt leaned forward and took her hand. "How do we find it?" he asked.

"There'll be no problem with that," Dr. King said, nodding toward Jael. "It will find us."

"You're suggesting we stake her out like a piece of meat?" Matt asked.

"There's no option. It knows where she is—always. She is the source of everything we know about its habits, its strengths and weaknesses. It has to kill her." Dr. King walked back to the table and began to study the artifacts again.

"What do we know about it?" Chris asked.

"It has an unbelievable sense of smell," Jael said. She paused and tried to reenter the visions, to strip away the revulsion, the glimpses of jagged bone, the taste of blood, and isolate the other perceptions. "It can sort through scents that are months old. Its hearing is good, its eyesight weaker." The nausea of fear shot darts through her stomach. "And it's intelligent in a savage way."

"Which is to our advantage," Dr. King said. "Since it considers us sheep, it won't expect any surprises from us."

"Can we surprise it?" Matt asked.

"We can start by setting our trap in Gillson Park." A pause. "And turn to the folklore of vampires and werewolves for assistance."

"You mean we'll use wolfsbane, garlic, things like that?" Chris asked.

243

Dr. King raised his eyebrows. "Why not?" A pause. "What trait do both plants share?"

"They smell horrible."

"And smell is the creature's most powerful sense," Dr. King said. "These otherwise harmless plants have an honored place in folktales. Why?" He picked up the fragment of an amuletic wand and glanced at it. "Perhaps the ancients used them to cover trails, scents that the monsters could otherwise follow."

"That's no less plausible than everything else you've said," Chris said. "Why not go all the way and throw in some holy wafer?"

"What's that supposed to mean?" Matt asked.

"When a person wants to protect himself in vampire country, he crumbles a holy wafer and spreads it around him in a circle," Chris said. "Vampires can't pass over it."

Dr. King set down the relic and walked toward them. "And remember that when one religion replaces another, it also replaces the symbols. The star is the central symbol of all the magic religions, just as the Body of Christ, holy wafer, is the center of Christianity."

Jael tried to sort through his statements, order them into a single light point in the darkness of her exhaustion. "You're suggesting that the spirit traps have the same function as holy wafer?"

"How did the Bon use them?"

"To limit the creature's movements. Strange—then I thought it was all barometric coincidences. . . . You mean that if we stay inside the spirit traps, we'll be safe?"

"There's no way to be sure."

"That's comforting," Chris said, standing and starting to pace. He stared at the ceiling and scratched the back of his neck. "Who's going to hold it down while we drive a wooden stake into its heart?"

"Matt, you're a farm lad," Dr. King said. "You must have hunted."

"A gun won't work," Jael cut in.

"Don't worry about that," Matt said. "I have a rifle that can drop an elephant with one shot."

"Which is why we must use Gillson Park. It's open. The creature won't be able to sneak up on us, and we won't endanger others when we shoot," Dr. King said.

Jael's eyes strayed back to the web. The spider was gone and all that remained of the fly was a silver ball glistening in the sun. It made her think of her first day at Barnard—sunshine after a semester alone at Juilliard that had become a fog, a blank as vivid as pain.

"There's a huge sunken bowl with row after row of cement seats," Dr. King said abruptly. "The Wallace Bowl. It's like a Greek amphitheater. The park district holds plays, gatherings there, and it's wide open except for some thick bushes at the entrance."

"So when do we leave?" Chris asked.

Matt cleared his throat. He stood, paced across the room, and sat on the corner of the desk. He leaned toward Chris. "When was the last time you shot a gun?"

"A long time ago."

"At something alive?"

"Pheasants . . . maybe it was quail."

"Ever shoot at anything large enough to hurt you if you missed?"

Chris's silence was answer enough.

"And you, Dr. King?" Matt asked.

"I grew up in New York City right after World War One. I've never fired a gun."

Matt shook his head. "I've hunted all my life, except for the past five years. But that hardly makes us a Special Forces team." He exhaled in a sigh. "I hate to be the one to pop the bubble, but what about the legal consequences of all this gunfire? Suppose it's just a cult and we kill some*body* instead of some*thing*. What do we do then?"

"There won't be any people," Jael said.

"Then suppose it *is* a werewolf? A Doberman, for God's sake. How do we explain firing all those rounds to the police? How do we explain knowing what we know?"

"So you insist on calling the police," Dr. King said, shaking his head.

"Just Gissing," Matt said. "He wants this case over so bad, he can taste it—bad enough to keep his mouth shut and do what he's told." He stood and nodded his head. "I'll tell him to meet us alone."

"But—" Jael said.

"No *but's*. Gissing makes his living using guns; we don't. It's either Gissing by himself or I call in the whole force."

Again Jael tried to speak, but Dr. King took her hand and patted it. "We'll do what you think is best," he said.

"One more thing," Matt continued. "I took city friends hunting when I was in college. One almost blew my head off. I watched another empty five unfired rounds from his rifle without ever pulling the trigger. Buck fever."

"You're taking a long time to get to a short point," Chris said.

"Jael has to be there. So do I. So does Gissing."

Chris turned very slowly toward Matt and took a step forward. "I'll try to put it simply: I'm going."

"I wasn't suggesting you stay," Matt said. "We might need an expert in case we have to ad lib."

"It's me you want to stay," Dr. King said.

"You'll only be a liability around guns."

"It *is* my plan, you know."

"Just tell us what to do," Matt said. "We'll follow your instructions to the letter."

Dr. King stared at Matt, his eyes dark. "Can you promise that your Sergeant Gissing will follow them?"

"He'll do what he's told."

Dr. King slowly shook his head. "He won't believe the truth any more than you do."

"He's a realist," Matt said, "just like me. He'll believe whatever he sees."

Jael reached over and put a hand on Dr. King's shoulder. She kissed him on the cheek. "You have a bad heart," she said. "I want you there more than anyone in the world, but if we get killed, there has to be someone alive who knows."

"You're very gentle with an old man's feelings, my dear," Dr. King said. He pointed a finger at Matt. "You *must* use the garlic and wolfsbane. You *must* stay inside the circle of spirit traps."

His voice lightened and he shrugged. "And while the creature is visiting you, I will search for his portal."

Sergeant Gissing wasn't under the street lamp where Matt said he would be. Jael squinted, peered into the darkness, and noticed an orange dot outside the ring of light. As Matt braked and eased the van toward the curb, a dark lump like a boulder sprouted arms and legs and took a step toward the light. Gissing was huge, slouched like a wrestler, and carried a thin aluminum case. He slid open the door of the van, threw away his cigarette, and exhaled the smoke before he stepped inside.

"It's nearly ten," he said. His voice was thick and rusty. "An hour late."

"We had to get some exotic things," Matt said.

Sergeant Gissing took a deep breath and grimaced. "What's the stink?"

"The things."

When the sergeant closed the door behind him, the overhead light went out, but light from the street lamps flooded through the windows. He sat down on the floor and glanced around. "You the girl with the gift?"

"Jael Clarke," she said, shaking hands with him. Her fingers scarcely reached across his palm.

He looked up shyly. "John Clarke's daughter. What's someone like you doing in a cesspool like this?"

"Trying to stay alive."

His broad face spread into a smile. "I'll try to see you get your wish." He turned toward Chris. "Which one are you?"

"Chris Shaw. I chair—"

"I know what you do," Sergeant Gissing said. "Professors on parade." He leaned forward and shook his head. "I should have brought some eight-by-ten glossies to show you what you're getting into."

"I saw the newspapers."

"You didn't see scat," the sergeant snapped. *"Ever see a seven-year-old with his throat gone to his spine, his body parts all over the room?"* He snorted with contempt. "Jesus, you saw the newspapers."

Matt slipped the van into gear and moved away from the curb. Since Jael was sitting on the floor, she felt each crack in the pavement, the tingle of the tires whirring on concrete. The van's interior brightened as they passed under street lamps, then darkened again. Although the sergeant smelled of cigarette smoke, sour sweat, and fear, his presence was comforting. He knew how dangerous the creature was, and he clearly knew how to take care of himself. They passed under a light. The sergeant reached across the van and picked up one of the rifles Matt had brought from his apartment. "This isn't a rifle," Sergeant Gissing said. "It's a cannon."

"A present from Bekki's father. A Holland and Holland .370. To hunt Alaskan brown bear."

"Gentleman's sport," the sergeant said. He tapped the side of his nose. "This tells me tonight is going to be dirty." He pushed his sleeves up to his elbows before he opened the aluminium case, as though he were going to begin manual labor. Two halves of a shotgun lay in molded rubber.

"What's that?" Chris asked.

"A poor man's weapon—a cut-down twelve-gauge pump." He snapped the two halves of the shotgun together, then took some shells from his overcoat and slid them into the chamber. The sound of greased metal slapping together hurt Jael's ears. "The first three are buckshot, the last two lead slugs," he said. "In case the *them* I'm expecting turns out to be the *it* Matt mentioned." He turned toward the front seat. "Where is this Dr. King?"

"He has a bad heart."

"He's a man I want to see."

"You will. Tomorrow morning."

Sergeant Gissing took a flashlight from his pocket and turned it on. Jael could see the exaggerated contours of his face in the white light. He wrinkled his nose and reached for the box. "What's this?"

"Wolfsbane and garlic," Chris said. "Guaranteed antidotes for bogeymen."

"Is this a goddamn geek show?"

Matt glanced over his shoulder. "Jael says that the killer has exceptional smell. This stuff might help disguise our scents. If it doesn't smell the three of us, it might blunder into our range."

Matt turned left, and the tires began the sharp buzz of rubber on bricks; they'd turned onto Michigan Avenue, were almost there. Jael's mouth opened and her breath quickened. It was suddenly colder, and her senses were alive, almost painful. She pulled her knees up to her chin and tried to conserve her warmth. She heard a soft thud and looked up.

Again the sergeant was rummaging through the box. He held up one of the star-shaped wooden-and-yarn spirit traps and dangled it in front of his face. "Christmas ornaments?" he asked.

"More protection," Chris said.

"More Dr. King?"

"Jim, he knows his stuff," Matt said.

Sergeant Gissing dropped the spirit trap back into the box and closed the lid. He drummed his fingers on the floor; they made a hollow, metallic sound. "You never mentioned why you got involved with all these *experts,* Counselor."

Matt twisted his head to the right and said sharply, "Look, we made a deal: Do what you're told and your case gets solved."

"Back off," the sergeant said in a low growl. "You're in this ass-deep. I put you under surveillance last night and you've been under it ever since. We know you were at Miss Clarke's, the good doctor's, the university, then to your place for the guns." A pause. "Even if you hadn't called me, I would have been watching you at the park . . . as protection." His voice softened and he leaned back. "The only reason you're not down at the station is because we're tight."

"What's that supposed to mean?"

"That everyone in this circus is an anthropologist, people who know about cults, might practice strange ceremonies—except you. Why?"

Matt shook his head. "Your men are waiting for us?"

"Three squads are hidden in citizens' garages within five blocks of the park. We closed it at dark. No one's been going to the beach much anymore. The murders were messy enough to keep the gawkers away." The sergeant rested the flashlight on the floor and pulled a walkie-talkie from his coat pocket. "An insurance policy," he said. "I don't push the mike button every five minutes, and my men are on us like stink on shit." He turned toward Jael. "You'll pardon the expression, Miss Clarke."

Matt tapped the steering wheel with his ring; the clicking echoed through the van. "What if I call it off?" he asked.

"Then we take a right on Lake Street and keep going till we hit the station. Then we spend the night there . . . and as many other nights as it takes to find out what's going on."

Matt pulled up to the curb bordering the park, turned off the lights, and set the parking brake. Jael almost hoped he'd say no, that he'd offer his wrists for the handcuffs and let the sergeant take them to where there were thick bars and thicker walls. "I'm glad your men will be here," Matt finally said. "Before the night's over, I may be kissing their feet."

"Here's a better idea," Sergeant Gissing said. "Just buy them dinner."

The night was cold, brittle. Alternating light and moon shadows washed over Jael, and the wind cut through her heavy coat and scraped her skin; at least it was regular cold, the kind that worked from the outside in. When she rubbed her eyes, tears cut down her cheeks, followed the ridge of her nose, and left a salty flavor on her lips.

Ever since the late sixties, the war-on-TV days, Jael had wondered what it would be like to be on a night watch, to be alone and vulnerable and in enemy territory. Now she was there. And it wasn't the night's first fantasy: First she'd been marooned on a desert island with Matt; then she was sitting on the beach with Julie on their twelfth birthday; then she was a high priestess of Isis about to make a sacrifice to the moon. They'd all been pleasant. Imaginary phantoms were always preferable to the real thing. When she leaned against the elm tree, the ridges of bark pushed into her back and made her shift every few seconds. She looked up through the leafless limbs: Spirit traps twisted in the breeze above her, brushed against the trunk, and intertwined with the branches. Wolfsbane and garlic were tied to the branches and the outer fringe of the clumps of juniper.

Not even the breeze could chase away the odor.

Sergeant Gissing cleared his throat, moved from his crouch, and reached into the box for the Thermos. He could shift his weight without seeming to move, one of the advantages of his bulk. He poured himself a cup of coffee, poured another, and handed it to Jael without a word. She slowly stretched her leg to ease the stiffness and tapped Matt's leg with her shoe. Matt lay in a prone position, flat on the ground, his rifle at his side. He'd been that way past eleven, past twelve o'clock. He hadn't made a sound, just stared past the bushes to the open field.

A brushing noise above her: spirit traps.

Jael sipped the coffee and tried to concentrate on its warmth as it flowed down her mouth, down her throat, and into her stomach. The wonderful warmth made her shiver almost as much as the cold. Matt crept back toward the tree.

"Coffee!" he said, shivering. He took the cup from her, sipped, then handed it back.

"I didn't think you were ever cold," Jael whispered.

"A rubdown and sauna tomorrow will be considered payment in full," he said. Then he leaned so close to her that she felt the warmth of his breath on her ear. "How's it going?" he whispered.

"Just standard, everyday frostbite."

Sergeant Gissing must have heard them, because he crawled back from his post, crouched next to them, and warmed his hands on his cup. "To be here," he said, "I have to be as crazy as you."

"Dr. King thinks that whatever's going to happen will take place between midnight and dawn," Matt said.

"Yeah, but he's not out here, freezing his keester."

There was a scraping to Jael's right. Chris backed up against the tree, looked over the amphitheater for a final time, then leaned against her.

"See anything?" Gissing asked.

"A squirrel at eleven-fifteen," Chris said. He glanced at his watch. "Close to an hour ago."

"You're the resident expert," the sergeant said. "How come nothing's happening?"

"We don't know that it's not," Chris said. He reached up with a finger and pushed a spirit trap. "Maybe these things are working *too* well."

"Then maybe we should take them *down,*" Sergeant Gissing said.

"They're up there for a reason," Matt said. "If this doesn't work, you try it your way tomorrow night."

More silence.

Jael took another sip of coffee, passed the cup to Matt and then Chris, then sat back and listened to the waves wash across the sand.

"Nature calls," Chris whispered, nodding toward the bushes.

Matt handed him a pistol. "Take this."

As Chris walked along the bushes toward the Frisbee/golf course, Matt and Sergeant Gissing moved back to back so one could watch the bowl, the other the slope to the beach. Jael turned toward the lake, then back toward them when she heard a soft beep like the alarm on a wristwatch. The sergeant pulled the walkie-talkie from his coat.

And the first terrible chill ran through her, an annihilation of light and warmth.

First Jael tried to move, tried to do something to fight the cold, but it was useless, utterly useless. She felt like an insect trapped in amber, her arms and legs already immobile, afraid to open her mouth for fear of what would pour in. She tried to lift her hand to her face to rub warmth back into her cheeks—her head shot back and a howl started to rise. A deep breath. She'd been through this all before. Maybe she could fight it off.

Again the tension built in her throat, and she glanced around: There was whiteness where there had been black, the whiteness of a tumor. Her hands started to radiate a shuddering redness, an evil glow, and the cold forced her to her hands and knees. Again the urge to howl. Again she fought it off—most of it. A faint sob escaped. Her eyes closed and the cold shook her and shook her and suddenly her head jerked back as though someone were going to slit her throat.

When her eyes shot open, she was staring at the sky. There, above her, she saw the spirit traps through limbs that writhed in a sudden wind. But they no longer moved in harmony with the branches; they no longer swayed with the gusts.

They hung as heavily as butchered beef.

And blue light swept over her with the force of water, a tidal wave of light: Light with mass and power swept her up and out and it was so thick that she tried to swim, to float, but there was too much power. Debris swarmed around her, a portrait of Jesus from a Sunday-school coloring book, Roman legionnaires, a cheerleader's uniform, a stained-glass window, all appearing and disappearing, spinning toward her, then spiraling away before she could reach out to touch them. An Easter basket filled with green paper straw, colored eggs, and chocolate rabbits flew at her, through her, and vanished.

They were all illusions.

Images. She was in a flood of dreams, of memories, a clearinghouse of her past. As the spinning stopped, dark tunnels appeared, endless tunnels that held innumerable creatures, things, some ancient gods, some more like vegetation, some so unnatural that they remained merely outlines of presences, never registering as *things*. There were countless portals, each leading to a different darkness, and the portals opened and closed, breathed as though they were part of some unimaginable organism, a single living entity, and as she was sucked toward a tunnel of light, she fainted, and when she awoke it no longer felt as though she were touching the light, no, it was like being absorbed, digested by the light, and it entered through her eyes, her skin, coursed through every fiber, every nerve cell, and suddenly there wasn't up and down anymore, no beings or objects—no *things*. The laws of her past life were as meaningless to her as the lives of ants or worms had once been. She had become the energy that had once made her talk and laugh and love, moved onto one of the invisible threads and traveled, traveled. The threads were highways that went beyond all separation, beyond otherness to the very source of everything she had looked for—Julie yet more—and as she reached out with her being toward the source, the light began to fade and what had been light took form, mass, and she felt as though she were sinking, falling from unity, and down and down she spun, down through the wave, the portal, and as she fell she became more and more Jael—the utter sadness of being Jael again—and down and down into a world of self and other. But when she settled back into consciousness, she wasn't Jael but the hunter.

It was the negative world, the world white and black, hungry, always hungry, full of hate. The *self* was full of loathing and lust for the kill . . . and the *other* she saw before her was Chris.

TWENTY-FOUR

Wilmette, Illinois—November 3, 1981

Matt watched Chris take a few steps toward the bushes, then turned, backed up against Gissing, and glanced over the rows of concrete seats, past the stark trees at the rim of the bowl, and up at the sky. The moon was brilliant; he could have read a book in its light. The night was a trip back to childhood, up before dawn in the November cold to hunt for ducks or deer. Although the breeze off the lake was hard, it couldn't budge the elm, which cast bars of blue shadow across his legs—a web of moonlight. The effect of the night, coupled with the stakeout, made him as alert, as alive as he'd been in years. A cloud slid toward the moon, rolled silver, then swallowed it like a serpent from one of Jael's myths.

A soft beeping.

Matt turned toward Gissing as the sergeant took the walkie-talkie from his pocket, pulled out the antenna, and pushed a button. "No breaking radio silence!" he whispered into the mouthpiece.

The cheap speaker crackled and hummed. Then a voice: "Jesus! Oh, Jesus!"

"Norris?" Gissing asked. No answer. He pushed the mike button again. "Norris? You all right?"

"Glasgow was just stretching his legs, that's all. He just stepped outside." The voice stopped and was replaced by heavy static. "There are pieces of him all over the yard!"

"You hear anything? See anything?" Gissing asked.

"He couldn't have been more than thirty feet away . . . and his gun's still in his holster!"

"Get yours out," Gissing said. "Put your back to the wall so nothing can sneak up on you, and get your ass back in the ga-

255

rage." He cleared his throat, tilted his head back for an instant, then lowered his face to the mouthpiece. "Wilkens? Hart?"

"Hart here," said a soft voice partially covered by static.

"Wilkens," another voice broke in after the pause.

"Stay in your squads, windows up, doors locked. Don't budge till you hear from me. Don't—I repeat, don't . . ." Gissing stopped in mid-sentence and slowly turned in Jael's direction. As soon as Matt saw the red glow reflecting on Gissing's face, he knew what was happening.

Slowly, ever so slowly, Matt turned toward Jael. A faint red aura pulsed from her head, her shoulders. It grew stronger, weaker, then was almost as bright as the moonlight. Her eyes rolled up in the sockets, then back down again. Suddenly she caught his stare, pleaded for help. Again the sockets filled with white. Her head jerked back so sharply, Matt thought it would come off: a wolf raising its cry to the moon. The ligaments, the muscles, in her throat pulsed and throbbed. Her skin pulled tight against her skull.

A living death mask.

"Sweet Mary, Mother of God," Gissing said.

The aura around Jael brightened again, and when she opened her mouth, her lips rippled over her teeth.

The noise began.

The roaring.

Like Dylan's, but worse. First the deep grating, then an increase in volume as though trees were being ripped apart by huge hands. It tore through Matt's head. He grimaced, squinted, tried to shake the pain from between his ears. Gissing tapped him on the shoulder, and Matt turned. The sergeant's mouth was moving; obviously he was talking, but the roaring smothered all other sound. The glow faded with the screech, and Jael crumpled forward. Her legs twitched. Her fingers. When her head flopped toward Matt, the eyes were still blank.

Before Matt could kneel next to her—before he could take her in his arms, cradle her, and tell her everything was going to be all right—the roaring started again.

Only not from Jael.

At first Matt prayed it was an echo, just the sound rolling back across the park from some buildings, perhaps a thickening of the air at water's edge. No, it was too loud. Louder than Jael had been. It wasn't an echo.

But an answer.

Matt looked up as the moon slid from behind a cloud. Chris was standing by the farthest bush, fumbling with his zipper, staggering backward. Staring at something. Suddenly he raised a hand to his throat as though he were fending off an attack.

Matt's eyes followed the direction of Chris's stare, out past a solitary tree, out toward the row of houses. Movement. A twinkling like bog lights. Like a will-o'-the-wisp. Like a handful of scattered snow glittering in a red light—flakes spinning, gathering in a tighter and tighter whirl. There was no defined form, not yet, but it was the source of the roaring. Suddenly the dust condensed into a vague but familiar outline. Faster the specks swirled, faster and faster; they clustered, surged. It was fascinating, hypnotic. Then the haze hardened into a quivering form, more a specter of the Creepster than real flesh.

Chris took a step backward, then another, then turned and tried to run. In a movement like a snapping spring, the haze was between him and the circle of spirit traps. Matt raised the rifle to his shoulder, tried to find a clear firing line, but there wasn't one. A heavy bullet would tear through the fog and hit Chris. Matt ran from one side of the tree to the other, tried to find an open shot, but there was no open shot, so he sprinted from the elm to the bushes, sighted on the center of the pulsing light, and fired. Pain shot through his shoulder, and the muzzle jerked skyward.

Nothing.

The pulsing light continued its steady movement toward Chris. Matt fired again; again the recoil. Still nothing. The thing wasn't thirty feet away. He was sure he had hit it, but it hadn't moved. It hadn't even twitched.

Matt snapped open the breech, slipped a heavy bullet into each chamber, and snapped the rifle shut. Chris stood perfectly still, as though he were in a trance. In the red glow Matt could see a look of intense pleasure, of expectation, on his face, and Matt remembered the gutted victims in Jael's pictures of the Bon sacrifice. Then the rapture vanished and was replaced by a look of elemental horror. Chris cringed, lifted the pistol, and fired once, twice, three times at point-blank range, but the haze engulfed him, went through his throat as if he were clay. Its strength, its quickness, were like dream movements, like flashes from a nightmare.

Each detail was magnified, the sounds of ripping and chewing, the lapping. All Matt's sensations, all the hideous images, were dulled as though emerging from a mind heavy with sleep. Although he felt no physical change, the moment had a slow-motion quality. The landscape was a midnight horror stripped of reason and previous experience. Matt dropped to one knee and fired. And fired again.

Still the thing savaged.

Matt opened the breech and reloaded.

Then it turned toward him.

It was and it wasn't like Dylan's drawings: a blur, a shade, a shadow. It was there, yet it wasn't. As Matt turned and tried to run back toward the spirit traps, a fearful longing swept over him. A warmth as pleasurable and sure as childhood sleep.

There was no fear anymore. There was nothing to fear. Just a pair of yellow eyes in a red mist, eyes that knew everything, held all answers; eyes that would pull him in and . . . the ecstasy swept from his head to his heart and made his knees buckle.

A sound by his ear, incredibly close yet faint. Gissing's shotgun firing. Loads of buckshot cut through the mist, slid between the swirling specks. The creature didn't even blink.

Now it was less than ten feet away.

Abruptly the rapture fell from Matt's eyes; he could feel the thing reveling in his horror. No mist anymore, no shimmering flakes: Gore dripped from its curved snout; its lips rippled over curved fangs; its smell combined the stenches of sulfur and a gutted animal. And the eyes. Savage. Loathing. More than intelligent. The eyes of a demon blazing with fury.

Matt brought the rifle up and fired both barrels as it crouched and went into its leap. There was a swift-moving shadow, a human silhouette to the left, and the creature tried to correct its leap in midair, tried to turn and face the new danger, but it couldn't and it roared as its momentum carried it into Matt, a sound so loud that it came in solid waves, and the creature flew over the top of him. Something protruded from the creature's side, and it ripped at it with savage teeth, tore at it with four-inch-long claws, but the hilt remained firmly embedded. The creature turned onto its back and the roar became a wail, and soon its struggling eased into shudders that passed through its body and out through its legs in a final spasm.

It lay still and started to disappear.

To vaporize.

To dissolve like the vampires in the grade-B movies. It shriveled and the flakes started to scatter, to shoot off toward the moon. The form held for another instant, a quivering mass, then vanished in a red burst of light.

Gone.

Only the grass smoldered where it had been. And a sword.

Matt rose to one knee and tried to fight off the faintness, the nausea. His shoulder ached and fear shook him. Jael? Where was Jael? One, two deep breaths and the fogginess eased into clarity, and he shook his head, took another breath, and felt a hand settle on his shoulder.

"Please tell your Sergeant Gissing not to shoot me," a voice said.

Matt turned toward the voice. Saw the deep wrinkles. The sparkling eyes. "Jesus, Jim, let him be!" Matt shouted.

Gissing leaned toward them, shotgun to his shoulder. "Who?" he demanded.

"Dr. King," Matt said.

"Like fuck! I had him followed. He went straight to Miss Clarke's after you left Shaw's office. He's been there ever since."

"Please take your finger off the trigger in case you pass out," Dr. King said.

The muzzle lowered.

"Thank you," Dr. King said. "Now, may we go to Jael?"

"She was breathing a minute ago. She can wait." Gissing gasped. "Explain!"

"I had planned to come straight here and hide, but when I noticed your young man following me, I went to Jael's condominium," Dr. King said. "It is only a mile away, you know, and the doorman knows me well enough to let me in. I parked the car, took the elevator up, straightened the mess in the living room, then changed into the black clothing I brought along. I opened a perfectly good bottle of Jael's wine, burned the cork for blackface, then left the lights on and walked down the fire escape to the beach." Another pause. "Don't be too hard on the young man. I would guess he's still watching the front entrance."

Gissing turned toward Matt. "What is this? Some kind of a scam?"

"He told me he was going to look for the portal," Matt said.

"The *what?*"

"You can tell him, Matt. If he's the realist you think he is, he'll have to believe you now."

Instead, Matt turned to Dr. King. "What are you doing here?" Matt asked, wrinkling his eyebrows.

"Waiting. I have been waiting here since right after dark. Granted, I'm cold and stiff and full of branches from the hedge—"

"You were supposed to be looking for the portal."

"That was only the plan I told you. I would never find it. There are too many private cemeteries, too many mausoleums and unmarked graves." He rubbed some of the blackface from his face. "Besides, you needed me here."

"Why?" Gissing growled.

"Bullets wouldn't kill the creature," Dr. King said matter-of-factly. Before Gissing could interrupt, he continued, "If you went to the trouble of having me followed, you must certainly have checked into my past."

"You're an expert in ancient cultures, in folklore."

"And in all my readings, I never once encountered a vampire, a werewolf, or a god who could be destroyed by ordinary weapons."

"They didn't have guns," Matt said.

"Swords, arrows, spears, kill by penetration, just like bullets," Dr. King said. "These ancient soldiers were ferocious men who practiced their art every day. Do you really think we are so superior that we can do easily what they found impossible?"

The authority in his voice shocked Matt. "Why didn't you tell us that before you sent us out here?"

Dr. King stopped to blow his nose. "There was no choice. Whatever Jael knew, the creature knew. Each movement. Each word. How do you think it knew exactly when to attack. How do you think it knew when Chris walked from the circle of protection?"

Matt lifted his eyes to the stars, slowly shook his head, then dropped his face into his hands. "Why didn't you tell Chris . . . or me? We wouldn't have told Jael."

"But you would have. Perhaps not with words, but with the movement of your eyes, the way you refused to look at the bushes. You know how perceptive she is, not to mention the . . . *thing.*"

"So instead of just staking Jael out here, you offered us all. And got Chris killed."

"I would have let you die, too, if it came to that." A pause. His voice faltered slightly. "Even Jael. These creatures destroyed every culture they encountered. What makes you think ours would have been different?"

And suddenly it all fell into place. Matt started to shake his head. "The wolfsbane and garlic—that was to cover your scent, not ours."

"If the thing thought I was on a chase it knew would be useless, it would concentrate on the four of you." He reached a hand up and put it on Matt's shoulder. "I'm glad you decided I couldn't come. If you hadn't, I would have been forced to feign a heart attack or plead cowardice."

"What if it had sensed you?" Matt asked.

Dr. King smiled and shrugged. "Then we would all have been killed."

Gissing took a step forward and patted the barrel of his shotgun. "If *this,* if Matt's goddamn elephant gun, couldn't touch it . . . ?"

"I used a *phurba,* a Tibetan exorcising dagger," Dr. King said. "It's made of unknown metals, tempered in an unknown way. It's even more special than the silver bullets and daggers in the werewolf and vampire tales. Today, in Chris's office, I saw part of an amulet that had pictures of a pharaoh killing a Set monster with a dagger like this. Jael said her monk clutched this when he thought he was in danger. . . ." He slowly picked the dagger up from the ground and handed it to Gissing. "I could have been wrong, but what were my options?"

The sergeant slowly turned the knife in his hand. "This is shit!"

"How many shells did you fire at it?" Dr. King asked. "Could you have missed at that range?" He motioned in the direction of Chris's body. "What killed Professor Shaw? Your imagination?"

"Where did its body go?"

"To whatever hell it came from."

Matt heard the roaring of engines and turned to his right. Two squad cars, lights flashing, bumped over the curb and raced toward them.

"Sergeant," Dr. King said, "a question before your men arrive: What could be worse than a creature like this?"

"More of them."

"Which is exactly what you're going to have unless you free us for the rest of the night."

"You're lucky I haven't blown you away."

"The portal is the point where the creatures enter our dimension. It must be within a few miles of here. If we don't find it before dawn, I give you my word that what happened here tonight is just a start."

Slowly the barrel of the shotgun lowered toward the ground. "How you gonna find it?" Gissing asked.

"Through Jael . . . if you'll let us go to her."

The police cars slowed as they weaved through the trees. Gissing glanced toward Chris's body and grimaced. "What am I gonna tell the chief? The press? Two more torn-to-shreds bodies, one of them a cop, and I got no suspect, no modus operandi. What am I gonna do? Point at a goddamn patch of burned grass?"

"Cover up," Matt said. "Just like the Chicago cops who caught satanists killing those babies." He put a hand on Gissing's shoulder. "No witches, no broomsticks, just one huge lunatic who was wounded but got away. If no one else is killed, you'll be a hero. Everyone will assume he crawled into the lake and died."

The brakes on the police cars squealed. The policemen jumped from the squads, guns drawn, but before they had a chance to approach Gissing, before they could evaluate the scene, the sergeant shouted, "Wilkens! Put out an all-points bulletin. Red Mustang. Mid-seventies. Illinois plates. Suspect wounded and extremely dangerous!" He held the shotgun at his side as he walked toward the blinking lights. "Norris, make sure no one gets near Glasgow's body. Hart, call in all the reserves you can get. Seal off the park and try to get this body in a bag before the goddamn press arrives!" He paused for a breath. "Now *move!*"

After the policemen had gone in the direction of Chris's body, Gissing slowly turned toward Matt and said under his breath, "Get the fuck out of here and take your friends with you." A pause. "If I don't see all of you down at the station by ten tomorrow morning, I'm coming after you myself."

As cold as the air was, Jael's face felt colder. Matt held her head in his hands and tried to rub some warmth back into her cheeks. "Wake up," he whispered. "There's no time to sleep."

"Perhaps we should treat her for shock?" Dr. King asked.

"She's acting the same way Dylan did after his attacks. If we can bring her out of the stupor, she'll be all right."

"Carry her to the van. Once we warm up the engine . . ."

Matt hooked one arm under her back, the other behind her knees, lifted, and felt the muscle tone in her legs, the incredible resilience of her flesh.

As he walked across the grass she stirred and her eyelids fluttered. When they opened, they were blank with horror. She started to scream, then choked and buried her head against Matt's shoulder. "I killed Chris!" she gasped. "Oh, my God, I saw, felt *everything!*"

Dr. King slid open the door of the van, and Matt handed him the keys, then set Jael on the floor and sat next to her. "Follow Sheridan Road until you hit the Kenilworth border," Matt said to Dr. King.

"I was with it when it attacked Chris . . ." Jael sobbed.

"You didn't kill anyone," Matt said, holding her against his chest.

"I couldn't stop it. . . . I saw the look in Chris's eyes and I felt his terror, and no matter how hard I tried, I couldn't make it stop. And when it finished and turned toward you . . ."

"There's nothing you could have done. No one has ever been strong enough to fight it," Matt said. Her sobs were so deep, they shook him as well. He whispered, "We have to find the portal tonight. You have to be strong."

"I never want to think or feel anything again!"

How could he help her? With all that she'd read and felt and experienced, how could he possibly tell her things were going to be all right? How could he think of anything she had not thought a thousand times before? The helplessness! He stared at the front seat and bit his lips until he tasted blood. All he could do was whisper and touch and hold her so close that she could draw from the beating of his heart. Then a thought. He whispered, "Dylan will need you."

She sobbed. "Where is he?"

"With Bekki. We're going to him now," Matt said. "He's the key to finding the portal, and we have only three hours left."

"We'll never find it. The killing will go on and on. . . ."

"If he built it somewhere—very deep, maybe, but *somewhere*—he knows where it is. You have to find it for us."

Jael covered her face with her hands and shook her head. "I can't share with him unless he starts it."

"What makes you think he won't?" Matt asked. "He's been through everything you have. He needs your strength."

"If he shared what I feel right now, it would destroy him: A child's mind couldn't—"

"Then you don't have the luxury to mourn tonight," Matt interrupted.

The shuddering slowed, but a quiver remained in her breath, her voice. She sat up. "When I tried to discover something Julie was hiding, I followed the memories like a trail." She brushed a tear from her eye.

"Here's the place to start: We had just left your place, and he talked about the cockatoo all the way home. I fixed him some hot chocolate before bed and read him *Where the Wild Things Are* right before I turned off the lights."

"That'll help."

"Kenilworth border," Dr. King shouted.

"Take a left on Woodstock," Matt said. He helped Jael to her knees. "Brace yourself. You're about to meet my ex." He touched her cheek. "Think you can handle it?"

Another shudder. "I don't have much of a choice, do I?"

At least they didn't waste time arguing with Bekki.

In fact, she acted as though she were glad to see them. Dylan had been crying since twelve, and even the extra Librium she had given him hadn't helped. But he quieted as soon as Jael entered the house. Dr. King worked his magic on Bekki, gave her his credentials, told her that if she would let them take Dylan for the night, his hallucinations would end. Maybe it was her frustration, maybe just desperation, but she even helped Dylan dress. And Dr. King continued to talk with her while Jael took Dylan into the study and closed the door, told Bekki of his travels and books. A half hour later, when Jael carried Dylan from the study and nodded toward the door, Dr. King and Bekki were discussing mutual acquaintances. When Matt climbed into the van and started the engine, Jael told him to go north on Sheridan Road until she told him to stop. It had been less than a mile when they pulled into a side road, stopped, and left Dylan asleep in the van. The Librium had finally taken effect.

They walked along the fringe of an estate toward the lake, then stopped at the crest of a steep wooded bluff and stared out at the black water. The moon had set, and whatever light remained in the sky came from the sprinkling of stars. "It's somewhere between here and the beach," Jael said.

"There's no cemetery," Matt said.

"There used to be Indian graves all along these bluffs," Dr. King said. "None of them are marked. And that's not to mention pioneers and robbers and God knows who else."

"Now what?" Matt asked.

"Now we search." Dr. King pulled a flashlight from his coat pocket and descended into the slope's thick foliage.

Matt turned toward Jael. "I think you should go back to the van."

"I want to go with you."

265

"You're exhausted." A pause. "And we don't know what effect the portal will have on you when you come close to it. I'd hate to have you fighting for the other side."

"You're going to need more directions."

"We have plenty of time, and the area isn't *that* big. If you fall, you'll only slow me up. The van will be warm and dry."

"Matt," she said, "I've been searching for this my whole life."

"Yeah," he said, taking her hand. "Let's go." They descended the steep slope, kept close to the bluff, and tried to cover as much ground with each sweep of their flashlights as they could. The ground was slick with frost, and Matt slipped several times and scraped his knee. Wild berry bushes tore at their legs, and the low branches of trees slapped their faces. Up and down the slope they went—slide down, crawl up. After forty minutes Jael began to shake with exhaustion and they took a short rest. The white dots of the flashlights were too small and the forest too large. As soon as they started walking again, Jael bent down to go under a limb, stepped on what must have been frozen moss, and slid five feet before Matt caught her.

Enough of that trail.

Instead they started to crisscross the slope and hadn't walked for two minutes when they almost tumbled into a small ravine. It was less than twenty feet across and twelve feet deep—a perfect hiding place. Matt spotted Dr. King's flashlight beam and shouted until the doctor answered. Then he held Jael's hands as she lowered herself down the rocky slope; he held on to some long branches as he went down, and she steadied him when he let go of the branches and fell the last two feet.

After a dozen steps he saw the blue glow. The frame was identical to the one in the temple painting: three, maybe three and a half feet high, a three-dimensional wooden pentagram with a blue crystal star hanging from its apex. It was carefully hidden behind a boulder and camouflaged with wastepaper and beer cans—an incredible mixture of the ancient and sacred with the modern and profane.

"It's hard to believe that a six-year-old could make so perfect a structure," Matt said.

"Only a six-year-old's hands," Jael said. "The mind behind it, the expertise, belonged to something thousands of years old."

And there was something hypnotic in its ever-changing prism. Like staring at a campfire, being drawn further and further into the light, watching the individual patterns of the flames, the way the embers glow and breathe and crumble; only this was infinitely more complex, more beautiful with its blue like a moonlit grotto. . . .

"Turn away from it," Jael said, "or it will possess you."

Matt shook his head and looked at her; she was blue in the aura. "Everything about this is magical," he said.

"It should be," Dr. King said as he approached them. "You're looking at a piece of eternity."

The glow brightened and illuminated the far side of the ravine. "How long before the transformation begins?" Jael asked.

Dr. King pointed his flashlight at his wrist. "It's four. Sunrise isn't until after six. If the folktales are as right about the time of the dimensional shift as they are about everything else, we have at least an hour."

"Let's not cut things too close," Matt said. "Let's just dismantle the damn thing and give it to Gissing."

There was silence for a moment. "What will he do with it?" Dr. King asked.

"Use it to get his promotion. Probably turn it over to the government. Compared to this, splitting the atom seems like small change."

More silence. "And how will *they* use it?" Dr. King finally asked. "As the key to unlock eternity, or as the ultimate weapon?"

It was Matt's turn to be silent.

"The ancients destroyed all traces of the *One* Cult rather than pass on its secrets," Dr. King said. "Now do you see why?"

Matt leaned against the rough bark of a tree and let the thoughts shift and settle into place. Then he touched Jael's arm. "Do you want to do it, or should I?" he asked.

"I don't want to touch it, Matt."

Matt took the penknife from his pocket, sliced the string that held the blue star, and lifted the crystal in front of him. It rested

in his palm as warm, as alive, as a pulsing heart. It was unbeliev-
ably heavy, not so much from the weight of the crystal as the
weight in his mind; he doubted he could hold it up any longer,
much less throw it. Then he glanced at Jael and thought of Dylan
—and the eyes of the Creepster in the most vivid moment of his
life.

He drew back his arm and threw the crystal against the boulder. It shattered when it touched the rock. The flecks flew in all
directions, began to fall, then swirled up like a handful of snow
thrown at the moon and vanished.

EPILOGUE

Glencoe, Illinois—November 26, 1981

Jael's eyes followed the gray sky down past the treeline, down to the pond. Rising steam clouded the willows on the far side, but she could hear their limbs scratch the ice that fringed the shoreline. A few dark leaves still floated on the water, but the brilliant leaves, the golden birch, the red and orange maple, had sunk to the bottom weeks before and turned brown with mud and decay. Her thoughts drifted toward Chris's funeral—all those tears, all that guilt, all the words she *wished* she had to say over again—so she tried to concentrate on Matt's breath, where there was warmth and life.

Dylan slid across the woolen blanket, snuggled against her side, and looked up at her. "Can't I have a drumstick?" he asked.

"Mother bought the turkey with your drumstick in mind," Jael said.

Dylan wrinkled his face. "I won't have to eat any carrots, will I?"

Jael leaned her head back on Matt's shoulder and asked, "What do you think?"

"He's put on six pounds. He deserves a reward," Matt said. "That's more than I can say for you."

"I've been better the last few days."

"You still look like you've been fasting."

She patted his hand to reassure him. "I'm getting better," she said. "I really am."

Dylan rested his cheek against her knee. "I'll eat all my dinner if you will," he said.

They shook on it. Jael heard a snap and glanced up at the oak that towered above them. A leaf wove through the branches; it fell for what seemed like a minute, then spun past her head and settled on the water. She started to take a deep breath, then realized she'd smell only late autumn, so she buried her nose in Dylan's hair and savored the bubble-gum aroma of children's shampoo.

"Let's walk on the beach," Dylan said. He wiggled free, stood, and tried to pull Jael to her feet. Matt helped her shake the blanket free of leaves, then draped it over her shoulders as they walked toward the path. To her right, only the occasional white thread of a birch tree broke the gray and brown monotony of the forest. When they reached the top of the stairs by the gazebo, a frost stiffened spider's web dangled from one railing to the other. Jael shuddered and took a step back, but Dylan melted it with a breath and hurried down the stairs.

Matt took her hand and squeezed it. "More than anything I want to help," he said, "but I don't know how." His face was furrowed with concern. "I haven't mentioned the Creepster or Chris since the funeral because I thought it would help you forget."

She tried to smile. "Hey, I'm gonna be all right." She patted his cheek with a gloved hand. "I promised to eat my carrots, didn't I?"

As they started down the stairs the woods to their left rattled as a squirrel bounced through the leaves. They held hands to steady each other. "I haven't heard from Sergeant Gissing in a week," Jael said.

"The heat's off him, so he's taken it off us."

"That's why he let Dr. King go to Europe?"

"He didn't have any choice," Matt said. "Dr. King has friends in high places. Lots of them. He goes where he wants." A pause. "Will he get anyone to believe what happened?"

"He's a very persuasive man. Eventually he'll convince the ones who *must* believe. . . . Together they'll leave a record of what we've learned for the future."

They walked the final few stairs in silence, then stepped onto the sand and grass at the base of the bluffs. "I'd like to think it's in the past—all the suffering, all the unknown," he said. "Since I know you're going to keep searching, I just hope you'll make some room for me."

"For you," she said, "there's room."

Matt pulled her tight to his side and walked toward the beach. "What if the search for Julie takes you back to the Creepster? What if *the end* is an eternal nightmare instead of paradise? Wouldn't it be better if we didn't know?"

"It's not a nightmare, Matt. What I experienced was as beautiful as it was frightening. It was different, very different. The Creepster just proves there are things that science can't explain. That's a start." She took a breath of the wet air and shivered. "If there's a key to the Creepster's dimension, there must be keys to others." She looked out to the point where the gray water met the gray sky; there was no horizon line, only a vague, uncertain swirl where gray met gray. "I want to reach out to all those who died before I was old enough to understand them." She took another long pause and tried not to think of Chris. "There are so many things I wouldn't have guessed about so many people. Even if I never reach them, maybe, just by reaching out, I'll learn about myself."

Matt shook his head and smiled. "So how do you start?"

"I'm going to finish reading all the after-death literatures. Those ancient priests, the Tibetans, the druids, they were explorers, cartographers—only their continents were otherworlds. When I've read enough, I'll finish *The* One *Cult.*" A breeze raised small waves on the lake and cut through her sweater and blanket. She rested a hand on Matt's hip. "When that's done, I'm going to look for other telepathists. The ones who think they're alone, maybe crazy. Some will be old. Some will be dying. I want to share with them. I want to be an explorer too."

They stepped closer to the water. The lake spray had coated the sand and frozen. The water smell was extra cold, extra strong. Dylan was searching through one of the piles of seaweed that had been left by the night swells. He poked through the green mass, wrinkled his nose, then poked some more. Finally he found something, held it to the sky, and ran toward them. He placed a round, flat object in the palm of Jael's glove. It was a piece of an old beer bottle that had been worn perfectly smooth by the sand and waves and time. After she held it up to the sky, she looked down at Dylan and smiled.

"I couldn't find much today," he said. "Only this."

"It's perfect," she said. Dylan started to run back toward the seaweed when he stopped, turned his head toward the bluff, and cupped a gloved hand by his ear.

"Hear that?" he asked.

Jael tried to sort through the calling gulls, the flow of the waves, and found the soft, distant notes of a Mozart sonata. "Mother must be practicing," she said.

"You promised you'd teach *me* how to play," Dylan said.

"But only after I had a chance to practice."

"No *but's*," Dylan said. He ran past her toward the stairway. Jael tilted her head and looked up the crest of the bluff; the gazebo was clearly visible through the mist and naked branches. Before she had a chance to stare at it too long, before the grayness had a chance to settle in, Dylan ran back to her and grabbed her fingers. "No *but's!*" he said.

She took a few hesitant steps with him; then, when he began to tug on her arm, she ran with him up past the gazebo, up toward the vibrant sounds.